THE OLD CRANBERRY LADIES GARDEN CLUB

THE GHOST AND THE KEY

ISBN: 979-8-9925426-0-8 Trade Paperback
ISBN: 979-8-9925426-1-5 eBook
ISBN: 979-8-9925426-2-2 Audiobook

Library of Congress Data: To come

This novel is inspired by and based on actual historical events. The author has taken the liberty of fictionalizing some of the characters, names, incidents, locations, and events for dramatic effect.

Book design by Glen Edelstein, Hudson Valley Book Design
Cover Illustration by Robert Hunt

Candice O. Abraham
4.0 out of 5 stars This saga covers several centuries, but is truly contemporary.
Reviewed in the United States on January 13, 2025
Verified Purchase

Elcira Cranberry is mysterious! She remains so over several centuries of family history. Perceived as either a villain or a heroine, all the while her family saga is the centerpiece of a contemporary legal battle for a historic estate. Murder and money, the perfect formula to hold my attention.

Terence L.
5.0 out of 5 stars Great Start
Reviewed in the United States on February 15, 2025
Verified Purchase

Great first novel by Bill Cusano. The story has well developed characters that made this an enjoyable read. There were plenty of twists and turns to keep you engaged and trying to figure out what happens next. Looking forward to reading the next book in the series.

THE OLD
CRANBERRY
LADIES
GARDEN CLUB

THE GHOST AND THE KEY

BILL CUSANO

4610
PUBLISHING

Dedicated to my wife, Kathleen, and her extraordinary ensemble of dedicated and loving friends in their book clubs, garden clubs, interfaith committees, altar guilds, women's clubs, and dozens of volunteer activities who were and remain the inspiration for the Old Cranberry Ladies Garden Club Series.

Acknowledgments

I would like to thank my editors, Kathleen Foxx, who assessed my first draft, and Caroline Tolley, who assessed my second draft and line-edited my revised manuscript. I would also like to thank Glen Edelstein who designed the book, along with Robert Hunt who created the original artwork for the cover.

I also owe a debt of gratitude to my readers who helped me see the story through their eyes and bring it to life: Barbara, Carol, Jim, James, Mary, Mary, Jessica, Hal, Kyra, Nancy, and Lynn.

Finally, I would like to acknowledge the many book clubs and reading groups that are keepers of the light that shines in our hearts.

Cast of Characters

The Cranberry family is rich with characters spanning over 200 years and eight generations, taking us from the early 1800s to today.

Mildred Cranberry Smith is the present-day matriarch of the family and owner of the Cranberry property. She prefers to use her maiden name, wanting to hold onto the family heritage.

Maggie Payton is Mildred's granddaughter. She is a Doctor in the children's cancer unit of the local hospital. She will inherit the Cranberry property on her wedding day.

Sylvie Rose is Mildred's Aunt Sylvie. She lives in the carriage house on the estate, the parcel of land that has changed hands over the years.

Jacqueline Hudson is the Old Cranberry town busybody and gossip. She has money and influence in the community. She has a longstanding gripe with Mildred.

Tilly Parker is the only member of the garden club who professes to be able to see and talk to spirits.

David Parker is Tilly's son. He is a lawyer who knew Maggie in high school.

Kendal Lightfoot is a one-time noted journalist and owner of the local newspaper.

Sam Castleby is Maggie's fiancé. He lives at home and works for his father at a property development company.

James Castleby is Sam's father, and the owner of Castleby Development Company, which is sorely in need of funding

Harriet Castleby is Sam's mom. She volunteers at the hospital where Maggie works.

Effie (Ephedra) Devine is the adopted daughter of Tilly who prefers to call Tilly her aunt, a label she used when Tilly was her foster mom, and her own mom was still alive. She feels she has the right to claim the Cranberry property for herself.

Elcira Engels Cranberry is the ghost/spirit who surfaces when a key is found that could prove Elcira killed her husband, Chester, and should not be able to inherit his land.

Deborah Townsend is the daughter of Colonel Townsend's slave, Grace, and she worked for the Cranberry family as a nanny for the children.

Chester Cranberry is dead, murdered in 1832 by person or persons unknown.

A little Cranberry Family History may be helpful here.

Chester married Jessica Hammond, who died in childbirth, leaving a son, Garfield Cranberry.

Chester remarried. He and Elcira had seven children. They are Felix, Susie, Sally, Marty, Tubby, Wally, and Tootsie.

Felix married Lorraine Peters, and they had three children: August "Auggie", C.J., and Julie.

Garfield Cranberry married Penelope Townsend, and they had a daughter, Mildred "Millie."

Auggie married Millie, and their firstborn son was Daniel.

Daniel married Mamie Simmons, and their firstborn son was Joseph.

Joseph married Daniella Hochstedt, and their only child was a daughter, Mildred Cranberry.

Mildred married Alfred Smith and their only child was Audrey Smith.

Audrey Smith married Thomas Payton and their only child was Maggie.

So, here the story begins, or does it? The Cranberry family saga
continues by going back in time to Elcira's day.

Prologue

The Cranberry Farm, Connecticut, 1832

Dressed in her husband's shirt, overalls, and boots, to avoid soiling her fine clothing, Elcira Cranberry takes the long way around from the main house to the potting shed at the edge of the carriage house property. She stops to press her face into the down-soft syringa vulgaris, better known as the lilac. Here, bordering the two parcels of land her husband planted all seven colors of the species, one variety each year for each of their children. What a loving thing to do, she had thought, until they started blooming and it became apparent that their spring-like lily of the valley fragrance was the perfect way to overpower the stench from the nearby outhouse. So much for romance. But she enjoyed them, her other children, as she called them, and each year she clips, grafts and coddles a new generation into life, hoping to extend their lives beyond the one-hundred-years they are expected to live.

"Be careful, dear," he told Elcira when he saw her cradling the flowers to her nose, "some lilacs can be quite toxic."

"I intend to enjoy every moment of my life with them."

She steals away to her favorite place and unlocks the potting shed door with a brass key. It occurs to her that, dressed as she is, a passerby or nosy neighbor, like Colonel Townsend, could mistake her for Chester.

Elcira locks the door from the inside and pockets the key. She unbuttons the overalls and lets them drop to the floor. The work shirt becomes a work dress, and its function is to keep her cool.

The sunlight barely sneaks in—a voyeur, a peep, a trickle of light—enough for her to see her potted friends. The scent of lilacs and fresh soil erases all thoughts from her mind. This is her peaceful place.

While she works at making a V-shaped cut in the stem of the yellow lilac, a sparrow chirps to her chicks in a nest under the eave of the roof. The nest sits precariously between the crossbeam and the top of the wall. The shed doesn't offer much protection from the elements, but it provides shade from the sun and some cover from the rain and snow. Mostly, it provides Elcira with an asylum, a place to go to be alone with her thoughts.

"Elcira!" Chester barks. "Where are you? I need something to drink."

She knows he is in the barn again, moving piles of hay from one place to another, pitchfork in hand. He will be loading the hay onto the wagon to bring to the horses. If only the children were old enough to help him, she would have more time to spend with her horses. Theirs is the life, running within their rounded-fenced paddock on the bottom fifty, beyond the hill, drinking from the pond whenever they need refreshment. Why don't you go down there, stick your head under, and breathe in all you can?

She brushes the dirt from her hands and wipes them on the overalls before stepping back into them. She doesn't have much time to herself, but at least with Deborah watching the young ones and the older ones at the schoolhouse in town, these few hours are her time unless he calls. At least he's not twiddling his fingers beneath some young thing's whalebone corset.

She has thought about hiring one of those newly freed slaves as an all-around domestic as some of Elcira's garden club ladies have done. No doubt Chester would want to choose one whose looks he fancies. It doesn't matter to him what the skin looks like. His eyes roam where only modesty and necessity should venture. Freed slaves, like Deborah, do still turn some heads in town, but here, on the edge of their property, where the Colonel lives, she is safe from wandering eyes and hands. Rumors do make their way from the wagging tongues of the garden club ladies, who are often more reliable than the local newspaper.

Elcira unlocks the potting shed and approaches the well. Deborah is sitting on the ground, her back against the stone well.

"Oh, Mrs. Cranberry. I didn't expect anyone at this time of day." Her nose is running, and her eyes look like ladybugs, red and black.

"You didn't want to be seen. What's wrong?" Elcira is unaccustomed to involving herself in the affairs of others, but Elcira has known Deborah since she was born. Her mom, Grace, was Colonel Townsend's slave and nanny to his daughter, Penelope. Now, she is often alone in the house here on the edge of the Cranberry Farm while the colonel is away with his militia. Chester sold this property from the row of lilacs down to the small house to Colonel Townsend for a mangy mule and some seed. One of those neighborly deeds he is famous for, making him look like a true gentleman among all the other "true" gentlemen of this idyllic New England paradise lost.

Deborah places a hand on her belly and starts to cry. Instantly, Elcira understands.

"Who is the father?" Elcira expects her to say it is the colonel, but Deborah puts her head down and wipes her eyes with the hem of her skirt, revealing her legs. Even with her dark skin, Elcira spots remnants of bruises. If this is the twiddler's work, God help him.

"Elcira! My water!"

"Oh hush, you old hoot!" Elcira reaches for the pail to lower it into the well, but Deborah takes it.

"I'll do it," she says.

Elcira grabs Deborah's hands in hers. Their eyes meet. Neither of them moves. "Did he do this to you?" Elcira asks.

Deborah's lip quivers. "I'm so sorry, Mrs. Cranberry. I couldn't stop hi—"

"Hush now." Elcira reaches for Deborah and hugs her. "I know, I know."

This was not the first time he'd done it. But this isn't one of the women who frequent the tavern looking for some company for a price. This is Deborah, her friend.

Elcira tightens her grip on her hands for a moment, taking a deep breath before letting go.

"I'll take the water to him." Elcira lowers the rope to fill the pail, her lips tight, pressed against each other as if the pail is too heavy. When she pulls it up, Deborah takes it from her.

"This is something I need to do myself," she says.

A chill rushes through Elcira. Should she let Deborah confront the man who violated her? Deborah kisses Elcira on the cheek and says," I'll be fine. Go back to your lilacs. They will miss you."

Elcira leans closer and kisses her on the cheek. "I will be in the shed. We can have privacy there." She hands Deborah the brass key. "Keep it. You can unlock the shed at any time and lock it again from the inside. In case you need to get away by yourself, that is. I do it all the time."

"What about you?"

"There is another key. I keep it on a hook in the shed, in case I get locked in," she says, nodding toward the barn. "He won't miss it."

Elcira walks back to the shed. On the way, she notices that Charley, Colonel Townsend's horse is tied to a post at the house. Good. Deborah doesn't have to be alone. She looks up at the barn. Chester wields the pitchfork like a hammer, stabbing bundles of hay to loosen them. Seeds and dust spray the air, glistening against the sun. He wipes his brow, jabs the pitchfork into a bale beside him, plants himself on a throne of hay, and takes the pail of water from Deborah.

Elcira clips a few branches from the white lilac bush near the door and brings them inside. The intoxicating aroma pulls her toward the porcelain white cups of the flower. Several fall off, a sign that the season is waning. Soon all the buds will be cast to the wind and the bushes will go back to serving as a hedge. When the flowers die, time dies with it.

She reaches for the key near the door's hook. It is missing. It must be in the house.

"Elcira!"

For God's sake. Leave me be. She grabs the door handle and gives it a turn. It won't move. It's locked.

"Deborah!" Elcira calls her name several times, but there is no answer.

Mildred

Cranberry Farm, Old Cranberry, Connecticut, 2024

Thursday

Mildred Cranberry greets the morning not as a queen addresses her subjects but as a faithful guardian accepts her charge with outstretched arms and several deep breaths. Her father would be proud. He had raised her to be a good steward of the land, honoring the generations who had worked this land and sacrificed for it. She soaks in the view to honor them.

From late Spring to late Autumn, Mildred keeps the French doors to the second-floor balcony open day and night. It is a constant reminder of her purpose, to pass along what she inherited so the legacy can continue. The mosquitoes and other flying pests that make their way from the pond are an annoyance, but she copes with a canopy net over her bed and a few well-placed bug-zappers. What must it have been like two hundred years ago when the farmhouse was little more than a shack with no insulation and no plumbing? In her seventy-five years, she has seen many improvements, making this a much more comfortable home than when she was a child. Back then, servants and workers kept the farm, stables, and orchards running. She has seen photos and drawings, but it is still hard to imagine these beautiful gardens and park-like grounds with rows of corn and mounds of hay.

Her husband, Alfred, didn't see what she sees. To him, this much land was a burden, a costly maintenance headache. Yet, he worked by her side to help her raise a child. Had he lived long enough to experience the loss of that child, that would have killed him. If it wasn't for Maggie, Mildred's granddaughter, it might have killed Mildred as well.

Her dream, now, is to accompany her first great-grandchild on a daily stroll from one end of the property to the other, with screams of joy as the stroller bounces along the path to the pond. Bug-eyed and filled with wonder, this future child will strain to look over the hedgerows to the iron gate and garden of the carriage house, where great-great-aunt Sylvie will be setting the table on the patio for tea. When that day comes, Mildred's mission will be complete. She will be able to hand over the reins to a new generation.

The buzz of the landscaper's edger reminds her that there is still much to manage before she can resume her role as doting matriarch of the family estate and hand over the job of running the place to her granddaughter. But Maggie is unmarried. This would be a perfect day for a wedding. The sky is a pale blue, dotted with wisps of clouds, the "happy" kind one paints on the canvas with a fan brush and just a kiss of titanium white. Another electric motor starts up, tackling the wayward branches of the hedges, flipping small clippings and bright green leaves onto the stone path which only gets the sun when it is highest in the sky. The slates will remain cool throughout the day. Someday, Maggie will make her way to the Carriage House along this path and Mildred will escort her. But not now. She needs to find someone else. The next one will be the right one for her.

Mildred adjusts her black and white straw sunhat, its wide brim dark enough to make the few strands of her silver hair that refuse to stay in place look intentional as teased highlights to the age-appropriate waves down her neck. A woman her age needs to train the eyes of onlookers away from the things one cannot change to focus instead on what one can change. So, for Mildred, foundation and a touch of rouge, not too much to make her look like a porcelain doll, are sufficient on most days. One needs to look her best at all times. She inspects her hands for age spots. Soon she will have to start using foundation on them, just to avoid the obvious cover-up of white gloves, like Jacqueline. *Why does that obnoxious woman always have to pollute my thoughts?*

"Can I get you something, Mrs. Cranberry?" Josie calls out from within the bedroom, the vacuum wheels squeaking as she passes. She continues toward the walk-in closet, the only other room in the main house that gets any real use now that Maggie has been working longer shifts at the hospital. Whatever free time she has, she spends with Sam, a post-COVID convenience. As far as Mildred is concerned, Sam will not be the one. *He can't be.* The one she marries will need to agree that this property is too important to be divided up and parceled out the way so many have desecrated the beautiful open spaces throughout New England. This will stay in the hands of the family. It has survived all these generations and is the last remaining peaceful setting in Old Cranberry. Mildred can feel the heat rise in her neck, even though the sun isn't touching it.

"Oh, hello, Josie," says Mildred, but the vacuum drowns out her voice. So much happens here to keep the place worthy of guests, deserving of a garden club luncheon or tea. It's tradition. Perhaps it is time to invite the club back now that membership has fallen and the parish hall is proving too large.

In the distance, Mildred hears a pile driver hammering steel pilings into the ground a mile or so away. A flock of birds fly overhead, seeking refuge in a nearby tree. Mildred watches them disappear into the branches one by one, and then in groups, taking shelter in the thick leaves. The breeze blows the branches, turning the leaves over and over, flashing dark to light in the sun, but the birds remain invisible, holding onto their temporary haven. "I know how you feel, little ones," she says. "I don't like it either. Don't worry. You will always have this place to come home to. That is my promise."

She steps back into the bedroom, closing the French doors behind her. Taking hold of the dresser, she slides her feet into her Ferragamo espadrilles. She would rather wear heels, but at her age, that would be too much of a gamble. These will work well with her floral print, O-neck, two-piece midi dress. She grabs her purse and cautiously navigates the staircase to the entrance hall. Double doors stand open at opposite ends of the corridor, letting the morning air cool the room naturally. Mildred takes a moment to soak in the view from the patio before stepping down onto the stone path that leads to the carriage house.

The three-quarter pink sleeves of her cover-up hide most of the age spots and imperfections although they don't bother her as much as they do the more self-admiring ladies of the club. Aunt Sylvie, on the other hand, will surely fail to notice the new outfit. Lately, her thoughts have been elsewhere, scrambled and forgetful at times. Of course, she could just be preoccupied with her roses. She spends most of her time tending to them in the garden.

The iron gate that marks the old border of the property groans as Mildred pushes it open and steps along the gravel path through the rose garden. The carriage house is Aunt Sylvie's domain now. She pulls at her dress to keep it from snagging on the thorns, but she fails to keep the hem of her cover-up free. The head of the rose slaps against her leg, and she has to stop to unhook herself from its thorny hold, causing her to drop her purse. Her cell phone spills onto the path.

Mildred notices that Maggie has sent her a text. *Grandma, Sam proposed.*

A photo of her with her left hand raised shows off a diamond ring. Mildred's chest tightens, and she takes a moment to breathe. "No, no, no. She can't marry a Castleby."

As she approaches the garden bench, the air grows colder. Mildred pauses, a shiver running down her spine. It was something other than the brisk air. Something she had last felt when her daughter died. Suddenly unsteady, she sits on the bench, waiting for the feeling to pass.

Her heart thumps, the rhythm erratic. Her throat tightens. Arrhythmia. More noticeable than usual.

With a hand on the bench, she takes a deep breath and exhales slowly. On the next inhale, she smells lilacs. There aren't any lilacs on the property. Where could it be coming from? She pushes against the stone bench to stand, and something touches her hand, sending her back onto the bench. There is nothing there.

A flock of birds bursts from the old oak beside her, circling overhead before flying off over the carriage house's roof.

"Millie?" Aunt Sylvie calls from the patio, where she sets the tea table. "Don't think I can't see you sitting there. Come. Keep me company. Unless you're waiting for someone to join you."

Mildred's legs shake as she crosses the lawn to the patio to join her aunt. She holds her arms to her sides as if walking a tightrope. At one point, she looks back at the bench in the shade of the oak. She can't shake the feeling that she isn't alone.

Mildred

THURSDAY

As Mildred steps onto the patio to join her aunt, Sylvie is fishing a biscuit from her tea, scooping up one of the islands of cookie pulp from the Earl Grey sea. Sylvie raises it to her lips, puckering to reach the spoon before the cookie crumbles and falls back into the cup.

"Auntie," asks Mildred, "do you ever get lonely here?"

Mildred pulls the wrought-iron chair directly across from her aunt and lowers herself onto the cushion.

Sylvie continues hunting for errant biscuit pieces floating in her cup, hooting when she manages to snag one, and then fights to steady her hand to bring it to her mouth.

Mildred waits for Sylvie to notice her but then helps herself to a cup of tea, lifting the bone China teapot and pouring the tea into a matching cup.

"I could have done that for you, Millie," says Sylvie.

"Auntie, how often have I told you how much I despise being called that name?"

"But it's your name, dear." Sylvie lifts her cup to her mouth, holding her little finger apart from the rest.

"My name is Mildred."

"Since when do we have to be so formal with each other?" Sylvie returns her cup to its saucer before reaching across the table to retrieve a card, pen, and envelope. She studies the card as if she hadn't seen it before. "What did you ask me?"

Mildred watches Sylvie open the card and read it. From the front, she can see that it is a sympathy card.

"Oh," says Sylvie, making the sign of the cross with her steadier hand. "Someone died?"

Mildred rolls her eyes rather than address the comment. Instead, she holds up her phone. "Look," she says.

"What?" Sylvie answers without lifting her head. Her lips pucker, and her brow wrinkles as if she is trying to remember something. "Oh, Gertrude. That's who this one is for. I should just fill them all out ahead of time and label them."

"Look," says Mildred, leaning forward to push the photo Maggie sent closer to Sylvie's face.

"Oh, it's Margaret. She's so pretty. Looks a lot like her mother, God rest her soul."

"Auntie, she wants to be called Maggie. I know it's challenging, but you always flip it around. I'm Mildred, not Millie, and she's Maggie, not Margaret. Got it?"

"You never used to be this angry, dear," says Sylvie. "Can I call you that, or do you have a problem with that, too?"

Sylvie takes another sip of tea, wrinkles her nose, and puts it down. "Why do I smell lilacs?"

"You, too?" Mildred looks around. "You don't have them in the house, do you?"

"I wish I did," she says. "I love them. I think there used to be lilacs on the property back when I was a young bride. That was before you came along. It was your father who cut them down. He hated them." She places a forefinger on her chin and taps.

"Where were they?" asks Mildred.

Sylvie points past Mildred to the iron gate. "From there to the

7

pond, where my roses are today, on both sides of the old oak. I think they were on our side of the property line, but he told my father they had to go."

"Was that when he bought the property from your father?" Mildred hadn't heard the details of the transaction before.

"Mother was so upset. She loved those lilacs. I can still smell them." Sylvie takes a deep breath and then grabs her side.

"Are you O.K.?" Mildred stands and comes to her aid.

"I'm fine. I just had a pain. They come and go." Sylvie pats Mildred on the arm and smiles. "Would you like me to make some more tea?"

Mildred grabs the teapot. "I'll do it. I need to use the restroom."

"Do it the right way, Millie. No tea bags."

Mildred sighs and enters the house through the open French doors. In the kitchen, she fills an electric kettle with water and plugs it in. She scoops two teaspoons of leaf tea from the tin on the counter, gently lets the tea fall into a mesh infuser and places it in the teapot. When the water heats and starts releasing steam, she adds the water to the pot and visits the restroom.

Before leaving, she checks the medicine cabinet. Nothing unexpected. Creams, deodorant, lotions, cotton swabs. No new medications.

Mildred returns to the kitchen and grabs the pot.

Sylvie is bent forward, her head just inches from her tea cup when Mildred returns. Mildred taps her on the shoulder and Sylvie jerks up, hitting the chair back. "Where did you go?"

"I went to make the tea."

"Oh, I thought you left."

"I'm starting to worry about you, Auntie."

"I worry about you, too, dear."

"You said nothing about Maggie's engagement when I showed you the photo." Mildred reaches for her phone again.

"Oh, well, she sent me a picture, too," says Sylvie. "But I had already seen it on that Face Place."

"She posted it on social media?" Mildred drops into the closest chair. "I thought I could talk some sense into her before she announced it to the world."

"I don't know why you're so upset. She's been seeing Sam for over a year. It has been that long, hasn't it?" Sylvie starts counting on her fingers, stopping at the ring finger on her left hand. She stares at the ring's golden rose. Mildred wonders if Sylvie has lost her train of thought again.

"Yes, it was a year ago that I saw him with his mom. Or was that a different time? I have so much trouble remembering these things. I'm getting to be like you."

"Auntie, why do you know these things and I don't?" says Mildred.

"You used to be the smart one." Sylvie chuckles.

"Very funny." Mildred pours the tea and then leans on the table, facing Sylvie.

"Do I have something in my teeth?" Sylvie asks.

"I need to talk to you about this, Auntie. I'm serious. Maggie cannot marry Sam Castleby." Mildred's heart is pounding again.

"My father worked hard to make sure this property was safe from all those greedy land grabbers who wanted to turn Old Cranberry into a modern suburb, and I'm not going to let it go to the son of a progressive-leaning property developer like James Castleby." She starts hyperventilating.

"Calm down, Millie," says Sylvie. "Mildred. There, I said it. You will give yourself a heart attack. It runs in the family you know."

"Don't remind me. But it's a stroke I'm more worried about, and I will definitely have one if the property winds up in Castleby hands after the wedding."

"I do believe it was you who promised to transfer the title to Margaret, not Maggie, because Margaret is her legal name, and you did this legally in writing, remember?"

"What are you trying to say?" asks Mildred, holding her cup steady as she raises it to her lips without putting her elbows on the table.

"You did this to yourself," says Sylvie. "You can undo it. Oh, but you made it so public. Everyone in the garden club knows, and now they know she's getting married, so that's that."

Mildred watches closely as Sylvie raises her teacup to her lips. She finds herself mimicking Sylvie, puckering her lips to sip her tea.

"Too hot," says Sylvie. She goes to return the cup to the saucer, and the tea spills on her hand. She grabs it with her other hand. "Ow!"

Fumbling with her cup, Sylvie sends hot tea over the edge onto the saucer. She snaps her fingers in the air to shake off the sting. A few drops fall onto the open card and Mildred rushes with a napkin to soak them up.

"Auntie, the card."

"Not are you hurt, Auntie? Or would you like some ice for that terrible burn, Auntie? No, thank you." Sylvie wraps a cloth napkin over her hand. "Who is the card for?"

"It's your card, Auntie," says Mildred, placing the card and pen out of Sylvie's reach. "I assume it is for Gertrude."

"Oh, yes, poor Gertie," she says.

"I can't believe how much time we wasted talking about how sick she had become."

"Dear Gertrude. Such a long, difficult time."

"For all of us, I agree." After placing the tiny apple blossom cup on its matching saucer without letting it rattle the way Sylvie's did, Mildred leans back and crosses her legs. She lets her foot rock in the air.

"Remind me to buy more sympathy cards, Mil." She gives her an evil grin. "I would hate to go to a wake without one." Sylvie's eyes squint, and she leans forward.

"What are you looking at?" asks Mildred. She follows Sylvie's gaze to the old oak shading the garden bench. A cardinal sits on the lowest branch, the one around which Mildred's dear departed Alfred had tied the rope to create a swing for Audrey when she was a child. Audrey would spend most of her free time down here, sitting on the garden bench, playing in the gazebo near the pond, and swinging on the tree swing.

"Life is too short," says Sylvie, continuing to ignore Mildred, looking past her. "You really should stop worrying about your legacy, dear."

Mildred turns back. "What do you mean? I'm only trying to hold onto-"

"The past. You're living in the past, if you call that living." Sylvie's eyes meet Mildred's and she is suddenly more alert. "Your only grandchild has just gotten engaged and all you can think about is your damn property."

"You live on this property too, Auntie," says Mildred, feeling the heat rise in her neck again.

Sylvie pushes against the arms of her chair to lift herself up. "Well, maybe you shouldn't have made that stupid public promise to give Margaret the property on her wedding day."

Mildred feels the pain of that comment and struggles to find words.

Sylvie reaches for her walker and pulls it close. As she struggles to maneuver around her chair, Mildred stands to offer help. "I can do it," says Sylvie.

As she crosses in front of Mildred she passes gas.

"Auntie. Must you? Don't you dare do that at the luncheon."

Sylvie reaches into the pocket of her garden smock and produces a brass skeleton key. "I forgot to mention that I found Elcira's key."

"What?"

Sylvie lets the key fall back into her pocket and walks away.

"Auntie. You can't drop this on me and leave." Mildred starts after her.

"I have to poop. I thought you would have figured that out," she says, passing gas again.

Mildred freezes in place, lost in thought. Could it be the key? Could the stories of Elcira's clever deception be true? Did she lock herself in the potting shed after stabbing her husband with a pitchfork? This is the worst possible time to stir up speculation about a two-hundred-year-old murder. Whether Elcira did it has remained a mystery for two centuries. And if it was discovered that she was indeed guilty, it could change everything. All of Mildred's plans to bequeath the property to Maggie could be in jeopardy, whether the wedding happens or not.

The smell of lilacs returns, and a cold breeze wraps itself around Mildred like a blanket of ice. She can't shake the feeling that someone has just grabbed her. Unlike last time, the grip on her arm is real, as if someone or something wants her attention. *Now.*

Sylvie

Friday

Sylvie loves how all the members don their best outfits and bring something to share at the snack table. Legend and club minutes boast that back in Elcira's day, the garden club meetings were afternoon teas, so some of the women bring more traditional delicacies, petit-fours, scones, and spinach and cream cheese sandwiches with the crust removed, of course.

Today, though, Sylvie is on a mission to corner Tilly and tell her about the key. The Access-A-Ride driver escorts Tilly to the entrance of the parish hall just as Jacqueline Hudson plants her ebony walking stick in the path of Sylvie's walker.

"Sylvia Rose, just the person I want to talk to," she says.

Not wanting to converse with Old Cranberry's Queen of Gossip, Sylvie reluctantly looks up at the woman who towers over most of the members by at least a head, due mostly to their osteoporosis and scoliosis, not to mention gravity.

"Oh, Jac-lene, I was just on my way to talk with Tilly. We have a bit of business to attend to."

Jacqueline Hudson places her white-gloved hands on the handle of the walking stick and bends at the waist, presumably to show off her diamond necklace, draped across a deep blue satin blouse. She never dressed so well when her Preston was alive. He kept her in her place, along with all the other skirts he managed to find in all his secret places.

Sylvie focuses her gaze on Jacqueline's right eye, avoiding the one that tends to travel on its own. God knows what it has in its sight, if anything.

"Tilly can wait, my dear. I noticed the lovely photo of Maggie on social media. Are you worried about where you will live when she gets married?"

"Why would I worry about that? You know where I live. You've often commented how you would love to scoop it up when I pass on. You'll just have to wait in line."

Sylvie shifts her weight on her walker to free herself from Jacqueline's prison, but Jacqueline replants her stick.

"No one really believes she'll go through with it. It was just guilt talking when Millie made that very public promise to transfer the property to Maggie on her wedding day. After all, her only child had just died and Maggie is all she has left. Oh, and you, of course. Did she consult you about it?"

Sylvie chuckles. "I know what you're trying to do, Jac-lene. And you can just forget it."

Tilly motors her way from the far wall avoiding the rows of folding chairs and the snack table. Sylvie spots her and waves. "Tilly!"

Jacqueline places a hand on Sylvie's walker. "Before you run off and talk with that crazy lady, I want you to know, when I do take ownership of that property of yours, you can always visit your precious rose garden."

"Don't you get tired of hearing yourself? Unless you are planning on marrying our Doctor Margaret Payton, you can kiss your hopes of stealing away Elcira's property goodbye."

Sylvie presses her lips together to form a fake smile and snaps her walker away, sending Jacqueline's walking stick to the floor. The sudden movement sends a lightning bolt of pain from her hip, reminding Sylvie that the clock is always ticking. She slips her hand in her pocket to palm the key. Could it be that Jacqueline knows she found the key? Is that why she thinks she can steal the property away from Elcira? How would she know?

Jacqueline fetches her stick and resumes her stance. "Where is that Gertrude? You know she's always late, due to her condition. I hope she's all right."

Tilly motors by in her wheelchair. She is so short and round, she almost disappears in the seat, with only her stubby arms and feet popping out like a Chatty Cathy doll. "I guess you didn't hear, Jac-lene. Gertie has left the nest, gone home, she's taken the midnight train to Pottersville, or wherever that train goes these days."

"What are you babbling about, you crazy woman?" says Jacqueline.

"Gertie is dead, Jac-lene," says Sylvie.

Sylvie bends and gives Tilly a hug. "Come. We can talk over by the window." She drags her walker across the hall followed by Tilly. As she approaches, a brown bird with a red beak and pointy-head circles and loops before landing on the open window's sill.

"Look, Tilly!" she says. "It's a cardinal."

"Oh, Sylvie! Don't move. I need to get closer." Tilly motors up behind her as quietly as her wheelchair will allow to avoid scaring the bird. "A female. Hello, dear," she says to the bird, "did Gertrude send you? I know she wouldn't miss one of our luncheons."

"Oh!" Sylvie shifts her weight on her walker to ease the pain in her hip, and the bird flies away.

"You scared it!" Tilly grunts and turns her chair around. "We just started our conversation."

"That's what I want to talk to you about, Tilly," says Sylvie, righting herself. "I smell lilacs."

"They are lovely this time of year. Where did you see them?" Tilly pulls a small notebook and pencil from a pocket in the wheelchair and starts taking notes. "What color were they?"

"This is not for your blog post, Tilly. This is just between us."

"Oh," says Tilly, putting her pad down on her lap. "You think it is her, don't you?"

Sylvie leans close. "Who?"

"Elcira." Tilly squints, looking past Sylvie. "That bird is still out there. I can feel it."

"You think the lilacs mean Elcira is here with us?" Sylvie looks around, as if she could spot a ghost among the members.

"Not here, maybe. If she was here, I would know." Tilly rubs her hands together as if conjuring a spell.

Sylvie reaches into the pouch attached to her walker and pulls out a handkerchief wrapped around a key and slips it into Tilly's hands, hoping no one notices.

Tilly opens the handkerchief and her mouth opens wide, making an "O".

"Where did you find this?"

Sylvie leans close to speak into Tilly's hearing aid. "In my rose garden. I was digging up a deep root from a vine and it was tangled in it."

"Could this be the missing key?" Tilly brings the handkerchief close to her eyes. "When did you first smell the lilacs?"

"You think finding the key brought Elcira back?" Sylvie grabs the handkerchief, wraps it tightly around the key, and returns it to her pouch.

"You need to tell Millie," says Tilly.

"You need to tell me what? And it's Mildred, not Millie." Mildred passes by Tilly's wheelchair and gives Sylvie a peck on her forehead before whispering in her ear, "You know she's crazy, right?"

"Sylvie found something in the garden," says Tilly.

"You told her?" Mildred snaps her head back so hard, the silk scarf slips from her hair to her shoulders, revealing her white ringlets and a few errant strands.

"Now, Millie, calm down." Sylvie looks about the room and notices several members coming close enough to overhear. "Far too many empty chairs these days. We could move these luncheons to the carriage house. What do you think, Millie?"

Mildred shoots her a stern glance.

"I mean Mildred," says Sylvie. "Isn't that where Elcira started the club? We are coming up on the two-hundredth anniversary. Maybe she could visit us."

"Very funny," says Mildred. "I thought she started the club in the main house, but what difference does it make, anyway?"

Tilly gives Sylvie a thumbs-up gesture.

"I guess it all depends on the wedding," says Sylvie.

"You have to bring that up?" says Mildred. "This wedding is going to be the death of me."

"That's what Gertrude used to say about these luncheons," says Sylvie.

Kendal

Coffee wraps itself around Kendal Lightfoot's tongue like an old sock as he rocks with the rhythm of the keyboard. Something isn't right. A gnawing in his side precedes the grumble, and a hunger bubble frees itself from somewhere within his gut. He needs more than burnt coffee.

The main spring from the support of his chair cries out with a rusty twang as he rides the chair backward and abruptly impacts the compact fridge. Cool air usually falls from the open box, but today it fails to make its way to his sandaled feet. Barely lit shelves look grungy with their thin film of unknown growth. "Chrissy? Is anyone going to the deli?"

He guesses the lack of response means his assistant is out there in her iPhone-ian stupor, surfing the Net with music pumping into her ears.

The light through the blinds scatters the dust kicked up by his sudden movement. Sparkles distract him, but he remains focused on the task, writing this week's feature article on community opposition to the proposed low-income housing complex downtown.

"Hey! Did you hear me?" He leans back, letting the spring sound out its coiled pains. Rubbing his palms along the arms to dry them adds to the wear of the burgundy leather, long since polished to a pale tan along the entire length.

"I was busy." Ears still plugged, jaw in motion and eyes cast off like headlamps in the darkness, Kendal's over-sized assistant blocks the doorway in ill-fitting shorts and a halter that only stretches in one direction. "There's a woman here to see you."

"What?" Visits were seldom happy occasions, especially at the office, though there was little alternative these days. Rolling to the couch in the corner he grabs the pillow and sheet and stuffs them in one of the empty file drawers. "Why didn't you say something?"

"She just showed up while I was on break. She's been sitting there, all dressed up like a teacher or something."

"An imagined simile on your part, I presume."

"Huh?" She pops her gum and turns away. "Whatever."

Kendal's first glimpse of the woman offers him nothing. She stands and smiles, hiding all clues to her identity behind glasses so dark she could be blind. A few braids of brown hair intertwined with blond extensions drip down before diamond-drop earrings that twinkle as she walks. *This is what Chrissy thinks a teacher looks like?*

Each runway step flashes a dark and firm thigh as her flowery white dress rides upward from the knee. Kendal presses his hands on the arms of the chair to stand, but his eyes linger at the curve of her legs and then roam to her thin waist, loosely buckled, not stopping until they rest on the thin straps that barely hold the sheer linen against her cocoa-colored skin "You're not a teacher, are you?"

"Excuse me?" She catches his hand as he approaches and squeezes it firmly. His eyes are captive slaves of the diamond hanging loosely in the hollow of her neck. She is too small and too tan to worry about a bra. "Good afternoon, Mr. Lightfoot."

"I don't believe we've met." He straightens, meeting her at eye level, tempted to let them slide down her neck. She walks past him to find a spot by the leather couch. As she sits on the arm, the linen flowers settle around her. She rests her palms on the arm of the couch as if the next move was to cross her legs. Kendal realizes he is staring.

The smile returns. She giggles. "I'm surprised you don't remember me," she says, removing her sunglasses and hooking them on one of the dress's straps.

"What the?" The growl from his gut turned the moment sour. A bead of sweat drips onto his eyelid, hanging there with ladybug defiance to his blinking. "Effie?"

"Aunt Tilly told me you wouldn't remember, but I said how could my old boss ever forget his prize pupil?"

"But you're… different."

"In what way?" she asks, catching the inside of her lip between her teeth as if holding back a smile.

"If I didn't know better, I would say you were Black!" He rubs his eyes.

"Let's save that for later."

Kendal leans forward in his chair and rests his arms on his desk. "Does your aunt know you've gone Black?"

Effie laughs. "You make it sound like a disease, Lightfoot. This is the real me."

"Since when? When you worked for me… No. This is a joke, right?"

"DNA testing confirms it."

As she approaches, her perfume kisses the air, rich like gardenias, covering up the staleness of the office.

"DNA doesn't suddenly change your skin color, Effie. Come here." He reaches to grab her arm and rubs his finger over the skin. "Make up? Paint? What is it?"

"It's the real me."

"I'm not as dumb as I look, Missy."

"Watch it!"

"Oh, come on! You're not going to accuse me of racism now, are you?"

"Look, Kendal. I need your help. You owe me."

"We settled that score last time, Effie. I don't owe you a thing. Besides, what difference does it make what race you identify as anyway? I can't keep up with this nonsense. Why not just identify as a…"

"A what?"

"Never mind."

"I need access to the paper's historical records."

"You're up to something. You can change your color, but you can't change your spots if that makes sense. You can get access to that online. What is it you really want?"

"Not the years I'm looking for."

"The digital files go all the way back to before the war, the first one."

"I'm talking about the investigation into Chester Cranberry's death and the trial of Elcira Cranberry."

"I don't even know if that stuff still exists, Effie. If I remember correctly, there wasn't a trial. There was an investigation, but it was left unsettled. What do you need that for? Don't tell me that's where your Black history comes from. What percentage are you then? Are you even one percent Black?"

"I just need to find out for myself."

He gives a hearty belly laugh. "I have to admit, your approach is unique. Do you know how many people have tried over the years to prove they are the rightful heirs of the Cranberry Estate? Get in line. Everything was left to his wife, and all the illegitimate bastards who tried to stake a claim have failed to make a case. Besides, it was two hundred years ago. You can't change history."

"I believe Elcira murdered him. Slayer Rules, Lightfoot!"

"Slayer rules? What hat did you pull that out of?"

"The person who commits the murder cannot legally inherit the person's fortune."

"So you're a lawyer now?" He pushes his chair back from his desk and lifts himself up. "Forget what I said about changing spots."

"You haven't changed though, have you?" she says.

Kendal pushes against the arms of his chair to stand. "How do you plan to prove your case, counselor?"

As he approaches, Effie slides off the arm of the couch and backs up against the bookcase. "I don't need to prove it. I just need to raise enough doubt."

"You think you can restate history?" He comes close, the scent of gardenias tickling his nose. "You want to use the paper to sway opinion, don't you? This is not discovering the truth, is it?"

"Of course it is," she says, placing her hand on his shirt to push him back. "The time is right for the truth. All I need is to do a little research on Chester and find that blasted missing key."

"Ha!" Kendal backs off and returns to his desk. "Effie, as I said, that case is two hundred years old! There isn't a snowball's chance—"

"Watch me."

Sam

I can't believe she didn't respond." Maggie slams the car door. Sam scratches his head, fingering his curls while trying to understand the source of Maggie's anger.

"Your grandmother?"

The car alarm governing the seat belts begins its annoying series of tones. It will soon shift to a higher volume if Maggie doesn't lock herself in place.

"Who else?" she says. "I sent her the photo and text when we got engaged. That was last night."

Sam finds it hard to focus with the seat belt alarm chiming. "I think-"

"What?" She turns to face him.

"Maybe she just didn't see it?"

The alarm volume increases. Sam squeezes the steering wheel. The red symbol on the dashboard flashes with each sound of the alarm.

"She didn't look at her phone since dinner last night?"

"I don't know. Maybe it wasn't charged?"

"Sam, it's been almost twenty-four hours."

"Actually, I proposed after dinner, so-"

"Are you kidding me?" She throws her bag to the floor and puts her left hand in the palm of her right holding them up so she can admire the ring.

The seat-belt alarm chimes louder and faster.

"Maggie? Would you mind clicking your belt?"

"What?"

"The alarm." Sam reaches for her belt, and she pushes his hand away.

"You haven't listened to a word I said," she says. She grabs the belt and pulls but the clip won't reach.

"You have to let it go and pull it again."

"I know!"

"I'm just trying to help."

She throws the belt aside and drops her hands into her lap.

Sam turns off the engine and unhooks his belt.

"What are you doing?" she asks, her voice cracking.

A car behind them in the hospital circle honks its horn, and Sam lowers the window to wave them on.

"We can't stay here," she says, looking out the window at the security guard. "He wants us to move."

"We'll move when we're ready," he says, reaching for her hands.

She wipes her cheek with the back of her hand and then reaches for him. "Are you sure you want to marry me?"

Sam pulls her hands to his mouth and kisses them. "Do you have any doubt? I love you, Mags. What do you say we grab a bite to eat before I take you home."

"I don't know if I want to go home and see her."

"We can discuss it over dinner, okay?" He starts the car.

"Okay."

The alarm starts up again. Sam looks at Maggie, but she continues to stare out the window. He reaches across her and grabs the belt to click it in before doing the same with his.

As they leave the circle, Maggie's phone rings.

"Hello?"

The call automatically connects with the car's audio link and a woman's voice says, "Doctor Payton?"

"Yes," says Maggie.

"Sorry to bother you, but we have a patient in need of Audrey's Angels and none of the volunteers is available."

"Okay. I'll handle it. What patient is it?" Maggie looks at Sam and mouths, Sorry.

"It's a young man, homeless, no I.D., hit by a car."

"E.R.?"

Sam steers the car toward the emergency room entrance.

"Yes. I can meet you there and take you to him."

"I'll be there in a minute." Maggie ends the call.

"I'm going in with you," Sam says.

"You don't have to. This is my responsibility."

"Was. We are one now."

At the emergency entrance, Maggie jumps out while Sam hands the valet his keys and pockets the ticket.

He runs to catch up with her, but she passes the guard before he gets there.

"I'm sorry, but you can't go in there." The guard stands behind a podium like a judge.

"Sam, come on," yells Maggie. "It's okay, he's with me."

Sam gives the guard an *I-told-you-so* smile and joins Maggie, who uses her I.D. badge to open doors and part crowds on the way to the patient's room. A nurse meets them in the hall.

"Doctor Payton, I'm the one who called you. I'm sorry to bother you. Usually, one of the volunteers can get here quickly when we call, but we don't have much time and there is no one for him."

"This is my fiancé, Sam Castleby," Maggie says. "I just recruited him as a new volunteer."

"Great. We have to hurry."

Sam and Maggie follow the nurse, squeezing around beds and emergency medical professionals clogging the halls. Bells and chimes are going off with lights flashing over doors, and physicians are attending patients or inputting information in computers, staring at the screens.

Sam takes a deep breath as he enters the room. A thin curtain divides the room in two. Glass walls and doors with curtains provide the only privacy. An aide attends to the young man in the bed, though she isn't really doing much other than monitoring his vitals, which are barely registering life.

"We are here for you," says Maggie, holding his hand with hers while stroking it with her other hand. She looks at Sam and he pulls a chair close for Maggie to sit bedside. He then grabs another from the adjoining room and mimics what she is doing on the other side of the bed.

"You are not alone," she says.

The aide taps her on the shoulder. "Español," she says.

"Usted no está solo," says Sam, leaning close to the man's face. "Estamos aquí para ti. Nos quedaremos contigo."

"Thank you," says Maggie.

The monitor registers a slight change.

"Is that good?" asks Sam.

Maggie frowns.

The young man opens his eyes and stares past Sam, or through him at the ceiling. He tries to lift himself up and he mouths something unintelligible.

Sam wonders if that is a good sign, but Maggie's face registers something very different.

"Todo está bien. Dios está contigo." Sam feels Maggie's hand on his arm.

The man lowers his head and closes his eyes again.

They sit with him, stroking his hands and wiping his brow until the shallow breathing stops.

Sam looks at Maggie and realizes both her hands are on the man's arm. Who the heck was holding his arm?

Jacqueline

L eaning against her walking stick, Jacqueline begins caressing the fine white limestone of the mausoleum with her free hand.

"Here you are, my prize gelding, the only resident of the Preston Hudson Perpetual Garden of our staid Old Cranberry Baptist Church. You didn't think I would leave you in that urn on the mantel, did you? No, you always enjoyed being the center of attention, and now, you stand apart from all those at rest around you. I can't take credit for the gate. Wrought iron is Tilly's contribution, and I must admit it is a nice touch. It's just silly to worry about someone stealing your ashes, though, isn't it? Praise the Lord for all you gave me, and may you rest in peace for a long time before I have to see you again."

She tips her bonnet toward the sun to shade her nose. Her roving eye catches a glimpse of someone running. It is the minister scurrying along the gravel path from his office over the bookstore toward the Church.

Jacqueline couldn't remember ever seeing the young pastor in such a state of dishevelment, his shirt tail flying behind him like a loose sail when tacking.

"Oh, Douglas. Yoo-hoo!" Jacqueline waves and steps toward him, as far as the stone path will allow her Prada heels to venture.

Must be wary of the gravel. She pauses, assessing the consequences. What tidy tale will this hesitation prevent her from telling at tea?

The young man continues on his way, as if he hasn't heard her, and that, she knows everyone would find hard to believe. After all, she thought, when Jac-lene Hudson speaks everyone listens, even Tilly, who has trouble hearing the living but seems to be able to tune in to the right channel when it comes to voices from worlds beyond. Jacqueline wonders if Tilly ever hears from her Preston.

"Do dead men tell tales, after all, Preston? Tell me, then, what could have happened in there anyway, for our young, deliriously dashing director to run across the courtyard with his proper attire anything but?"

Jacqueline takes comfort in talking to her dead husband, as long as he doesn't make his presence known. So far, he hasn't, but today she has the sensation that someone is close, too close for comfort. She looks back toward the car and her driver. He is nowhere near, but she has a sense that someone is.

"Preston, don't you go following me around, now. I am much more comfortable with you staying put right here. You will get used to it, of that I'm certain."

She opens her fan and taps the air toward her face, shielding all but her freshly re-sculpted eyes as she pursues the stone path back toward Harold at the car. With a blink and little control of her wandering eye, Jacqueline nearly misses her, just barely catching the pale of her thigh as she jogs from the side steps toward the fence before slowing to a fast walk. Her hair is tied back, and it sways as her white shorts wiggle and her loosely covered midriff flashes with each bounce and jiggle. Even with the visor pulled over her eyes, there is no mistaking her.

"Oh, Margaret!" Jacqueline waves her fan in the air. "Maggie Payton, is that you?" Jacqueline inches along the walk, slipping through the shade of the sweet gum trees with their green, spiny balls that serve no useful purpose when matured to a dull, dry brown, scattered along a path, other than to wrench an ankle or wobble a wheel of one of those motorized wheelchairs, like the one Tilly commandeers.

Maggie holds her phone up to her face and Jacqueline is sure she is pretending to be talking to someone or admiring herself to avoid her advance.

With a healthy intake of mid-summer pollen and sweet honeysuckle, Jacqueline prepares to break through her concentration while waving her fan at Harold, signaling him to follow in the car.

"Yoo-hoo, Maggie. Ah, my dear, how good you look."

Jacqueline mutters, "Preston, these young women nowadays don't have a blessed clue about the world they live in. As I told Tilly, I fear that folly has finally flowered in the face of these fine felines, given they trade in their claws and fangs for corner offices and shorter life expectancies, just like the men they marry. Only that's where the true folly lies. How sad when they see how swiftly their beaus take up the virtues of gentlemanly sport like you did and forget all about bringing home the bread when it is so much easier to let Mommy do it."

Maggie has no choice but to cross Jacqueline's path on her way to the street. Jacqueline rests all her weight on her walking stick and stiffens her arm to plant herself directly in Maggie's line of sight. With only one good eye and too much vanity for a hearing aid, Jacqueline chooses to leave nothing to chance. She fills her lungs one more time. "Oh, Maggie, dear! I'm so glad to see you. Do stop for a moment and chat."

Too close to turn back, Margaret gives a wave, raises her chin to the air and pulls two small white plugs from her ears. "Mrs. Hudson, what a pleasant surprise."

Maggie's gaze shifts from eye to eye, something Jacqueline is well accustomed to experiencing.

"Oh, you are not good at lying, dear. Your nose scrunches up when you try it. I remember your mother used to do the same thing; God rest her soul. What a terrible loss for you. I am sure she wanted to be here for your wedding. To think that COVID could take someone so young and leave so many of us more mature ladies to carry on. Good genes, I guess. Don't you think?"

"It is amazing that someone your age could have avoided the disease. We lost so many younger and stronger than you. Just goes to show you that isolation worked for some."

"I'm surprised you didn't get sick, working in the hospital and all, but then, you weren't even in your mother's room, were you?"

"Mrs. Hudson-"

"If I had more time, I would give you a few pointers for your upcoming nuptials. Once you let him know all your secrets, you're done for. You would prefer to jog on through without having to stop and humor an old busybody like me, now admit it."

"So well said. I'm on my way to meet Sam now. I'll be sure to let him know of your offer to coach me. Unless you would like to join us for lunch? You could pick up the tab."

"No. No. Not today, dear. I wouldn't want Harold to follow us around in the car. Even with the air conditioning, he does tend to get overheated. He's a good man, but not devoted like Cecil was. When I was your age back in Kentucky, service was tradition, like weddings and funerals, the two great social occasions for our class, don't you agree?"

"I am sure I will see you at one or the other." She removes her visor, unwraps a cloth band from her wrist and pushes her hair back to slip it on her head before replacing the visor.

"So, you must humor me, dear, and tell me whatever did you do to our poor Pastor?" Shifting her weight to the other side, Jacqueline points toward the bookstore. "He seemed to be in a hurry."

"I don't know what you mean."

With the sun almost directly above, Jacqueline finds it hard to follow her eyes. She can only assume that Maggie is uncomfortable because only one of Jacqueline's eyes moves.

"You were just with him in the church, so there is no use acting coy."

"I beg your pardon, Mrs. Hudson, but I really do not know what you are talking about."

"No need to apologize, dear." Jacqueline turns to hide the slight lift in her cheeks. "I will try to speak more clearly."

30

"With all due respect, I don't go to this church. I only came here to help plan–"

"Not a wedding, then? I did see Ephedra Devine enter the bookstore. She's been studying law, you know. Did you have need for legal advice?"

"I really should be getting along. If you are so interested in why she is here, ask her yourself."

"Well, I just might do that, then."

As she steps onto the grass between the fence and the walkway, Maggie's sneaker taps Jacqueline's walking stick, causing her to lose her balance, and fall into the strong arms of the younger woman. Maggie's phone bounces off Jacqueline's shoe and lands in the grass. As she bends to pick it up, a piece of paper escapes from the pocket of her outfit and drifts to the ground.

"Good Heavens." Jacqueline wastes no time righting herself. She brushes her jacket and plants her stick firmly on the paper, pushing it into the grass. A smile blossoms on her face as she adjusts her bonnet.

"I'm so sorry. I didn't mean to knock you over. Are you all right?"

"Yes. Yes. No fuss. No bother. You just go along. I'll be fine."

Jacqueline raises a gloved hand and turns toward the street where Harold is waiting with the car. "Give my best to your young man. I do hope to meet him soon. Perhaps at tea?"

As Maggie makes her way past the end of the fence, Jacqueline lowers herself with the aid of her stick and retrieves the note.

"Well, Preston, my dear departed thoroughbred, what could this all mean? Tilly's niece, Ephedra, may be the most forthright young thing in Old Cranberry. Surely, she has bigger fish to fry than Maggie. Unless, of course, there is more to this wedding than I thought."

She opens the paper and reads the note.

Tuesday, 7:30. Spangles in East Arlingville.

As she climbs into the car, Jacqueline taps her walking stick on the glass between her and Harold. "Not attractive, is she Harold, with her mouth open and that silly band yanking her hair from her sweaty forehead?"

"No, ma'am." He scratches a small patch of tightly cropped hair on the back of his neck where his cap cradled his skull. "No telling what these young ladies are up to, Ms. Hudson."

"I don't know what's to become of the female race, Harold."

"It's gender, ma'am," he says.

"Maybe we can get some young blood in our club and show them how to carry themselves. Such a pity that she is passing herself off without a plan, a descendant of such a well-established family and all."

"Are you talking about her marriage, ma'am?"

"Are you paying attention, Harold? Didn't you notice how she ran out of there? What a shame. I believe she was trying to hide a midday encounter with our poor Pastor Tilton. Now that would make for interesting conversation at one of our club luncheons, wouldn't it?"

"Yes, ma'am."

"Maybe I should talk with him."

"Is that so? Come to think of it, I did see him running from his office before she came out."

"Yes, Harold. This is definitely much more interesting than crocodiles on the golf course." She felt the smile raise her cheeks high.

"But the consequences could be just as dangerous to a man with his eyes on the hole."

Jacqueline tries to swallow the laugh. "You surprise me, Harold." Pleasantly, she thought. She may like this one better than Cecil.

As she settles in, a chilling burst of air on her ankles and legs makes her shiver.

"Harold, the air conditioning is blowing too hard back here."

"Sorry, Mrs. Hudson. I'll turn it down."

"I shouldn't have to tell you these things, Harold." She places her gloved hands in her lap and sits quietly, the way she was taught as a child.

Mildred

SUNDAY

Mildred checks her phone for messages. The last one was from Maggie. Mildred still hasn't responded. She sits on the edge of the bed and types.

Could we meet and talk about this?

She is about to send it but then reads it again. Delete.

You look so happy. Let's get together tonight.

Better. Delete.

Oh, dear, I am so sorry I didn't respond sooner. Call me.

Send.

That done, she goes to her dresser to slip on her espadrilles. Not there.

She gets down on her knees and checks under the bed. Not there, either. Where could they be?

"Remember," she says aloud. She always takes them off at her dresser, where she can find them the next day. But she has been upset about the wedding. Maybe that's it.

With one hand on the railing, she descends the stairs into the foyer. Her bare feet tease her senses, not all nerve endings firing as she takes each step, making her feel unsteady. She needs her espadrilles.

Down the hall, the doors to the library are open. They are never open, at least they haven't been since she closed and locked them, shutting away the memories within. The last family member to use it regularly was Audrey.

Each step begins with her toes, as if she is testing the water before entering. Assured that the marble tile is solidly underfoot, she advances and takes another step. She's not so cautious in her shoes. They are cozy, an extension of her senses, dispersing the tingle of the nerves so the entire foot is more aware of the floor, more assured of each step. It's as if the remaining nerves that have not died off can take over, sensation traveling along the sole to those nerve endings that can still dance with delight when stimulated.

One door is open fully, while the other is ajar. A key with its tassel hangs from the lock.

"Josie?"

No response. Josie would have left hours before.

"Maggie?"

She reaches for the door handle to pull it shut but notices something under the desk. Her shoes.

She leans on the edge of the desk where the leather inlay meets the mahogany trim and cranes her neck toward the chair. It is empty, but pulled away, as if whoever was sitting there just left. The espadrilles are where she would have removed them had she been the one sitting there. But she hadn't. She hasn't been in this room since Audrey took ill.

She slips them on, bracing herself on the desk, and her hand slides across a paper, causing her to lose her balance, depositing her in the chair. The paper sticks to her damp hand. She lifts it from the desk and peels the paper from her palm.

It is a map of the property. Old, from when the house was built in the mid-nineteenth century.

Beside it is a quill pen and an open jar of ink. Where had they been hiding?

There is a black ink smudge on the map where her palm touched the paper. Whatever was written there is now illegible. The blotch left behind is where the garden and old oak are today.

She heads toward the powder room to wash her hands and spots an open book on the leather armchair beside the bookcases. She steps closer to see what book it is when a figure in white glides past her through the foyer and out the patio doors.

"Who's there?"

She chases the figure onto the patio and onto the stone path through the hedgerow, but the figure is too fast, too far ahead.

Mildred stops to catch her breath, her inked hand to her chest. Thump, thump. Her heart is pumping in her throat.

She pushes open the gate and sits on the garden bench. Looking up, she sees Sylvie standing on her patio, mouth open, her arm extended, pointing to the bench where Mildred is sitting. A hand grabs Mildred's hand and then pushes it away.

"Did you see her?" Sylvie asks, shaking.

"Who? Who is it?"

"I don't know." Sylvie drops into a chair. "I need a drink."

Mildred joins Sylvie who is pouring blackberry brandy into two shot glasses.

"Is this all you have?" asks Mildred.

"It's what I always drink when I've—"

"Seen a ghost?"

"I'm so glad you saw it, too. I sometimes wonder if I am losing my mind, Mil-dred. Oh, that sounds so dreadful. Can't I call you Millie?" asks Sylvie.

Mildred downs her meager drink and pours another. "You're usually the more susceptible one. She moved too fast to tell what she was."

"She? Are you sure it was a she?" Sylvie pours her second and downs it. "I'll sleep well tonight."

"I won't," says Mildred. She walks to the edge of the patio and looks around. She was in my house. Mildred holds up her hand, showing Sylvie her palm.

"Did she do that?"

"No, I did. I put my hand on wet ink on the desk in library." Mildred waits for that to register with Sylvie.

"I thought you kept that locked. Who could have left ink on the desk?"

Mildred looks at her palm. "The map. I need to look at the map again."

"What map?"

"She, he, or whatever that was, marked up a map. Maybe it was an *X*."

"Where on the map? Do you think there may be a buried treasure?"

"There," says Mildred, "where you were pointing when I sat down."

"That's where I found the key." Sylvie's eyes open wide. "I have to call Tilly."

Maggie

The Pediatric Cancer Unit of Southern Connecticut Hospital is on the fourth floor between the Cancer Treatment Center and Advanced Elder Care, where patients with severe memory ailments receive palliative care. The only advantage to the location is its proximity to the domed atrium, where patients and their families can sit among fountains and trees and enjoy a slice of nature together while waiting for treatment.

Doctor Margaret "Maggie" Payton loves to meet her patients here rather than in a hospital room. It makes them feel less confined, more alive. Today, though, she is the one in need of a little support. Every swoosh of the glass doors causes her to look up, hoping to see Sam enter. When he finally arrives, he runs the gauntlet, stepping around a couple shuffling along with a rollator, and jumping over a child's push-toy.

"So, what's wrong?" The lanky young man with curly black hair that he is always playing with as he listens, looks like he is lost.

Maggie reaches out before he reaches her. "I need a hug."

He holds her and finds himself patting her back. "Let's sit and talk."

"I don't have a lot of time," she says. "I was hoping you'd get here earlier."

"I'm sorry, but-"

"I need to talk to you about your mom." She interrupts him and drops herself down on one of the stone semicircle benches which double as planters. He takes a seat next to her in the shade of the ornamental pear tree, and he looks skyward as if expecting a message from above.

"What happened? Is she okay.? Where is she?"

"No. Everything is okay. I'm sorry. I'm just so upset I don't know what to do." She pulls a tissue from the pocket of her uniform.

"Maggie, talk to me." Sam reaches for her hand.

"Today is one of the days she volunteers, and we always talk afterward. Sometimes, she brings the patients here to rest after their treatment, and we have a chance to shoot the breeze.

"And?"

"After her patient was wheeled to the lobby to go home, she told me about a woman who doesn't want her family to know she has cancer. It's pretty advanced, and she has successfully kept it a secret. She wants to just let it take its course."

"That's tough. Mom didn't give her a hard time, did she? You know how she can be. She is such an advocate for treatment, having seen so many women- well, you know."

"It's Aunt Sylvie."

"Oh, no!" Sam shakes his head. "Does your grandma know?"

"That's it. I need to tell her, but Sylvie told your mom in confidence, and I am sure we will be getting together for dinner to talk about the wedding. In a way I'm glad Grandma hasn't gotten in touch with me. Now I don't know what to say to her."

"My mom would never say anything to your grandma, Maggie. You know that."

"This sucks." Maggie turns away. A man with a walker struggles to get up from a bench. A young woman grabs his arm and smiles at him.

"We'll figure it out," says Sam, stroking her hand.

"What? What are we going to figure out?" She doesn't look at Sam but keeps focused on the young woman assisting the older man, helping him walk.

"Do you want to postpone the wedding?"

Maggie snaps her head and stares at him. "Where did that come from? Are you even listening to me?"

"I'm having trouble understanding."

"They will both be at the dinner." She pauses, and Sam struggles to connect the dots.

"We don't need to include Great-Aunt Sylvie," he says.

"Sam, she's family. I call her Aunt Sylvie, just like Grandma does. The three of us are all we have left. She will want to be a part of the planning."

"If she wants to keep it confidential, she won't say anything." Maggie's look makes him feel like he said something stupid.

"She has no filter," says Maggie. "She will blurt out something when she sees your mom."

"You think she inwardly wants your grandma to know?"

A woman with a rollator struggles, and her husband helps her sit on its seat facing him. They pass by, staring into each other's eyes.

"She won't be able to keep it a secret long." Maggie's head follows the couple. She takes a deep breath and bites her lip.

"I think you need to let your grandma know."

A man pushing a rollator heads toward them. Maggie stands to help him navigate around them. Then she bends to whisper to Sam.

"I can't tell her. That would be dishonoring Aunt Sylvie's wishes. She's a patient at the hospital here. I can't say anything."

"Well, I can," he says.

She sits next to him and bends close. "No, Sam, you mustn't. I shouldn't have even told you." She looks around to make sure she is not being overheard.

"You would keep secrets from me?"

"Don't be so insecure," she says, waving her hand at him as if the comment was not hurtful.

"Insecure?" He stands.

"Where are you going?" She reaches for his hands and pulls him back to his seat. "You can't do that, Sam."

"Do what?"

"Walk away from an argument." She realizes her voice is louder. People are watching them.

"Is that what we're having here?" He steps in front of her.

"Sam, please." Maggie bunches up the tissue in her hand. "It's hard enough—"

"Without your mom? It's been four years since she passed, Mags."

She bites her lower lip and looks away. "That hurt."

Sam kneels before her and holds her hands. "Maybe we can talk to my mom. I know it's not the same."

"No, it's not. Not a day goes by, Sam. You never got a chance to meet her. She was so full of love and joy."

"I'm just trying to help."

"There's nothing you can do." She pats his hands with hers. "I should have been with her."

Sam looks around at the islands of patients and family members, seeking a clue for how he should react, how he could help her.

She looks down at their hands. "I was here in the hospital all night, Sam, and I didn't do this." She lifts their clasped hands.

"But you were with other patients, Mags. There was a pandemic. People were dying."

She looks at him, and he realizes what he said. *It was your job.*

"What's more important? Work or family?"

Sam scratches his head, letting his curls wrap around his fingers.

Maggie touches her cheek with the tissue.

He pulls out his phone and makes a call.

"Mom? Do you have plans for dinner tonight?"

"What are you doing?" Maggie asks.

Sam holds his finger to his lips. He clicks on the speaker.

"Maggie and I would like to come by and maybe bring pizza. It will give us a chance to relax and talk about the wedding."

His mother responds, "Your father has a meeting tonight, so I am free."

"Good. We'll come by at—"

Maggie says, "Seven?"

"Seven thirty," he says. "Love you."

He hangs up.

"Okay," he says. "We'll deal with this and then go after the bigger fish."

"What do you mean?"

Sam kisses her hands cupped in his. "My dad."

"Your dad? He doesn't seem to be a problem. You always know where he stands, right?"

Silence.

"Sam?"

Tilly

Tilly Parker's motorized wheelchair hums its way toward Gertrude's casket. She had hoped to be the first to arrive. She always likes to be first, hoping she will encounter a spirit or at least some sign that the deceased's spirit is near. What would Gertrude's spirit look like? Certainly not like this woman. She is tall and slender, standing by the spray of roses near the window. Her long black hair is draped over the shoulders of an off-white midi-length, long-sleeve dress, looking more like a costume than a modern outfit. White stockings and wide-heeled pointed matching shoes completed the ensemble. As Tilly approaches, the woman turns to face her. She smiles and curtsies.

The front of the woman's dress is black lace in a rose pattern at the bust with black buttons down each side to where the satin reveals the same rose pattern lace below.

"Do I know you?" asks Tilly.

The woman turns back toward the spray of roses on the stand by the window.

Tilly starts to move toward her. The room, filled with the sweet, almost nauseating aroma of so many flowers, suddenly takes on the aroma of lilacs. Cool air falls around her as if from an overhead fan. The motor on her wheelchair chokes and dies.

Tilly pushes the button to restart it, but nothing happens.

The woman floats by and encircles her before heading to the casket where Gertrude lies. Tilly turns her head, unable to turn her wheelchair, but she cannot see what the woman is doing.

She tries the button again and again. Then with a blast of air, the figure flies past her and disappears as it reaches the window.

Tilly is suddenly aware of the soft music playing through the ceiling speakers and though the air conditioning is on, beads of sweat form on her brow and neck. Her wheelchair hums and jerks forward. She motors over to Gertrude and is barely able to see over the side of the casket.

"Oh, Tilly!" Sylvie pushes her walker toward her. "What a lovely touch. You put one of my roses in Gertie's hands. Thank you."

"I-I-I didn't do it," says Tilly looking back and forth from the rose to the spray by the window.

"I'm glad we're alone," says Sylvie, "I need to talk to you."

"Let's go where no one will hear us."

"Tilly, it's just you, me, and Gertrude, and she won't tell anyone."

Tilly looks back at the window.

"She just left."

"What are you talking about? She's right here." Sylvie grabs her walker and lifts it to make it easier for her to lean on the kneeler. "I won't dare get down on my knees, not with this hip of mine."

Tilly backs her wheelchair away from the casket and motors over to the window where the woman was standing. She reaches up to touch the roses, letting her fingers glide along the petals. A chirping sound causes her to remove her hearing aid to check the battery. It's fine. Returning the hearing aid, the chirping resumes.

"Tilly, look out the window," says Sylvie, hobbling toward her, favoring her left leg.

Tilly rotates her wheelchair in time to see a cardinal flap its wings and take flight.

"I swear it was talking to you, Tilly." Sylvie is breathing heavily when she arrives.

"Sit, Sylvie," says Tilly.

"What's wrong? You usually get excited to see birds come so close." Sylvie sits and rests her arms on the arms of her walker.

"Birds and butterflies are signs that the spirit of someone close to you is still nearby, watching over you."

"Really? Every bird and butterfly?"

"I don't know. That's what my mom told me when I was a little girl. I treasured that thought. For years when I would see one I believed granny was nearby."

"I never met her. I don't think I did," says Sylvie.

"No, she passed when I was young. But I would see her in my room at night, smiling at me. For the longest time, she said nothing. She just smiled and watched me fall asleep. But then, when I had my accident, I heard her call my name, and she pulled me out of the road as a truck was coming. The truck destroyed my bike, but I survived."

"You never talked about your accident," says Sylvie.

"The accident happened because I was starting to lose control of the muscles in my legs. I thought I was just tired, so I pushed myself. After that, I never saw her again. I convinced myself it was just my imagination until I started feeling the presence of spirits. I know people think I'm crazy."

"I don't think you're crazy," says Sylvie.

"I think the jury may still be out on that," says Mildred. She bends over and pecks at Sylvie's cheek.

"You're impossible sometimes, Mil-dred."

"Actually, Tilly," says Mildred. "I wanted to ask you something." She looks around. "Jacqueline is at the doorway signing the guest book, so I will make this quick. Do these spirits of yours, can they write things or move things around?"

"You see," says Sylvie, "I think I saw something too in my garden. Maybe you're not so crazy after all."

"Or maybe we all are," says Mildred.

44

"Oh, how preciously lovely to encounter the three of you all together like this," says Jacqueline, tapping her walking stick lightly with each step as though it serves a greater purpose than an ornamentation. "I ran into Maggie at the church. She had been talking with Pastor Tilton about this that or the other and then the poor young man made a mad dash across the grounds as though he had seen a ghost."

The three look at each other.

"And guess who I saw heading toward the cemetery?"

"Gertrude?" asks Tilly, rotating her wheelchair toward Jacqueline, bumping up against her walking stick.

"What? No, silly, it was your niece, Ephedra Devine, of all people. What a lovely young woman, and such an amazing transformation. She's changed the color of her skin. Imagine that. She wears it well, though, not like some. I wonder what we should call her. Is it still Trans if it is changing a race?"

Tilly lets her hand slip and the wheelchair jerks forward, knocking the walking stick out of Jacqueline's hand. "Dear me, I am so clumsy with this new contraption. You know, it is a lot more powerful than it looks."

"I guess size isn't the determining factor," says Jacqueline. She sticks her nose in the air and walks off.

Mildred steps forward, taking an envelope from her purse. "Tilly, as the outgoing president of the garden club, I apologize for the demeanor of our incoming president."

"She's not the only one to comment," says Tilly. "Why must people be so cruel?"

"I guess she stands out more now," says Mildred. "I have to put this on the tree over by Gertrude. Come with me, Sylvie."

"They didn't do such a good job on her, did they, Mil-dred?"

"Would you stop emphasizing that second syllable when you say my name?

"I never saw her wear that color lipstick. What is it, pink?" asks Sylvie "And what about that dress? What were they thinking at the home? They had plenty of time to plan. I should hope to die so slowly."

Tilly taps her hearing aid and adjusts the volume while she watches Sylvie place the card on the brass card tree beside a large bouquet of flowers.

A string-bean of a woman approaches, dressed in black slacks and blouse with white sneakers. Her hair is thin and wiry, her scalp showing through. She waddles toward Tilly with her cellphone in front of her face.

"Tilly," she says with a mouse-like squeak in her voice. "I got a good picture of Gertrude for our newsletter. You want to see it?"

"Abigail, we can't put that in our garden club newsletter," says Tilly, adjusting the height of her chair to see eye-to-eye.

"Why not? We have quite a list of members who don't come to these events."

"Abigail Summers, It's a wake, not a charity event."

"I know but look." She shoves her phone in Tilly's face.

Tilly grabs the phone and pulls it close. She uses two fingers to enlarge the photo and inspects every corner. She points to a cloudy white section of the picture. "What is this?"

Abigail pulls the phone back and readjusts the magnification with her fingers. "Oh," she says, matter of factly. "That's her spirit."

Tilly lowers the seat of her chair and lets the words sink in, as Abigail goes off taking photos and chatting with guests.

The music becomes faint. Tilly plays with the volume on her hearing aids, but to no avail. Hearing aids are not practical for focusing on one conversation. The human ear is much better at it. She removes them, and everything becomes distorted, a hum.

With a tissue, she wipes the hearing aids clean. Suddenly, a gloved hand covers hers, and she looks up to see the face of the woman in the satin and lace dress. Her skin is pale but has a sheen to it, giving it a silvery look. She holds her other gloved hand to her lips, signaling to Tilly not to speak. Tilly looks around, but no one seems to notice the figure who glows from within.

"Gertrude tells me you should be able to hear me. Is that right?" Her voice is soft and mellow, like two women speaking in harmony.

"Gertrude said that? Who are you?"

"Elcira Cranberry." The woman repeats the curtsy she did earlier. "Which one is my great-great-great-granddaughter?"

Tilly raises her hand and points to Mildred at Gertrude's casket.

"Mildred." she says. "We met earlier. She dresses well, doesn't she? Thank you, Miss—"

"Parker. Tilly Parker."

"Until next time." Elcira takes a step back and wisps off like a cloud.

Tilly replaces her hearing aids, and the noise in the room returns. "Mildred! Sylvie!" She motors off to tell them before she convinces herself it never happened.

Maggie

Maggie clutches the ice-cold bottle of Rosé in one hand and rings the doorbell.

"Just go in," says Sam, following behind with the pizza box.

Maggie hesitates, so Sam reaches around her and opens the door. "We're here, Mom."

"In the kitchen." Harriet Castleby's voice is soft and sultry, like a sexy starlet from the forties.

Maggie follows Sam from the foyer, through the French doors, and then through the living room. The last time Maggie was here, the house had more of a lived-in look, with pillows, magazines, and coffee-table books in disarray. Now it is surprisingly pristine. The dining room table is set with full place settings for eight. No papers, laptops or mail. Why so elaborate? It's just the three of them with pizza.

Harriet meets her as she enters the kitchen and gives her a strong bear hug. The woman is much shorter than Maggie, which explains why Sam's stature is less than commanding. She looks like she could have just come from the stylist, her hair colored brown with highlights designed to look natural. It doesn't. The pearl-drop earrings she was wearing this morning are gone, leaving her earlobes bare, made more obvious by the dark hair, sprayed and tucked in place around the ears, ending in a flip at the neck. Did she really think this mid-century look was for her? Maggie looks down at her shoes, expecting to see bobby socks, but Harriet is wearing fluffy slippers and a skirt too short for modest seating on a stool. Maggie can't help think that Sam needs to move out of this house. Now.

Sam puts the pizza box on the island and grabs Maggie's wine. "We brought your favorite, Mom," he says, robbing Maggie of the opportunity to gift it.

"Come, sit." Two red cheeks border Harriet's smile. "I already started," she says, reaching for a half-empty wine glass from the counter.

Sam opens the wine bottle and pours some for Maggie.

"Mrs. Castleby, the house looks different. Don't take this the wrong way, but it looks like You're planning to have a dinner party."

"Oh, you know James. He likes to have his clients come by for drinks, so I want the place to look nice."

"It looks like a picture in one of those luxury living magazines."

"Thank you. I'll tell him you said that." Harriet stands across from the couple and holds up her glass. "To the two of you."

They toast and sit on the stools.

"We really didn't get a chance to talk very long at the hospital," says Maggie, jumping right into the conversation she needs to have.

Harriet pushes an errant lock of hair behind her ear and sways a bit on her stool. Sam steps around the island and puts his hands on her shoulders, leaning down to give her a hug from behind.

"Maybe we should have some pizza," he says. He grabs the plates Harriet had put out and fills each with a slice.

"Just one for me," says Harriet. "I have a five-K on Saturday. It's not much, but I like to keep active."

"You look fabulous," says Maggie. Really? She can drink, but not eat?

"Yeah," says Sam. "You two could be sisters."

Maggie reaches over and pinches him.

"Sam, you're a terrible liar," says Harriet. "Your nose crunches when you lie."

"I noticed that," says Maggie.

"When?" Sam grabs his nose, and the three laugh.

Maggie grabs a slice of pizza and offers it to Harriet, who takes it, folds it, and takes a small bite before dropping it on her plate. "So, you want to talk about the wedding plans?"

Maggie catches Sam looking at his mother.

"Well," says Maggie, "I want to talk about Aunt Sylvie first."

"What a dear old lady. I added her to our church prayer list. That way, everyone will be praying for her." She takes another sip of wine.

"My grandmother doesn't know about her condition," says Maggie. "And I'm not sure what to do."

Harriet puts down her glass and leans on the island. "She needs to know, Maggie."

"I can't tell her because she told you in confidence. You shouldn't be telling anyone."

"I told Maggie I could tell her," says Sam.

"No!" Harriet sits up. "And what would you say to her? Think, Sam. It's clear that it has to come from Sylvie."

"I agree," says Maggie.

"So, it's settled. I will take her name off the prayer list, and we won't tell Mildred." She grabs her pizza and takes another small bite.

Maggie puts up her hands. "Now, wait a minute. There's a bigger problem here. We are all going to be together for dinner to celebrate our engagement and talk about the wedding plans. Aunt Sylvie is bound to make a fuss over you, the way she does at the hospital. She loves you. My grandma will know something is up. How would Aunt Sylvie know you?"

"Oh, we can come up with some story, my dear," says Harriet, suddenly alert and in control. "Lord knows, I can tell a tall tale." She turns toward Sam. "I've managed to lead your father around, haven't I?"

"I don't know what that means, Mom." Sam tilts his head and looks at Maggie.

"Sam, dear, you have a lot to learn." She looks at Maggie and puts her hand on Maggie's hand. "Give me until tomorrow. I will come by the hospital and let you know what I come up with."

A door opens and closes. All heads turn toward the sound coming from the garage.

"What a pleasant surprise," says James, dropping his briefcase on the floor and running over to Maggie. Sam is scratching his head, playing with a curl. James slaps Sam's hand away as he passes.

"Mr. Castleby," says Maggie, receiving his hug. His breath smells of alcohol.

"James to you," he says. "Pizza? That's the best you could do, Sam?"

"Now, James, leave the boy alone."

"I'm not a boy, Mom," says Sam. He folds into himself as he always does around his father.

"I'm sure your mom didn't mean it that way," says Maggie, "did you, Mrs. C?"

"Oh, stop whining, Sam," says James, grabbing Sam's shoulders to massage them. "Lighten up."

They are so different, Sam and his dad. She tries to remember if her dad was that way with her. Her mother certainly wasn't. She made Maggie feel special, like she could do or be anything she wanted. Maggie turns to Sam and says, "Maybe you should take me home."

"Nonsense," says James, reaching for a glass from the cabinet behind Harriet. He pulls out a bottle of Makers Mark bourbon and pours a healthy glass. "There is still a lot of pizza left."

"I think Maggie is right. She has to get up early tomorrow," says Sam.

Harriet stands and comes around the island to give Maggie a hug. "I'll see you tomorrow."

James gulps his drink and puts the glass down hard, causing some of the bourbon to spill over the side. He licks the bourbon off his fingers and smiles, his mustache and beard creating a cave-like appearance against the dull white teeth.

"Why do you always drag her away when I come home?" He turns to Maggie. "You are going to make something out of him, I'm sure of that. It's what women do, right dear?"

Harriet pours the rest of her wine down the drain in the sink and puts her glass down on the table in front of James. "I'll see you tomorrow," she says to Maggie.

James grabs his glass and walks out without hugging his son.

As Maggie walks to the front door, she realizes Sam is not behind her. She pauses at the door and looks back. His mother has her arms wrapped around his neck, and she is kissing him on the forehead.

Maggie stops in the living room and looks around again. James didn't say anything about the table being set with their best bone china. This is not for a dinner party. This is for a showing. They are planning to move.

Mildred

Pastor Tilton's kind words about Gertrude followed by prayers read from his black book dissipate in the drone of the air conditioner and the hum of Tilly's wheelchair as it struggles to find a spot to rest and shut down. Mildred's thoughts are everywhere but here. She doesn't believe in ghosts. Even as a child, those stories of spirits and unexplained phenomena all seemed more humorous than possible. There must be an explanation for Tilly's sightings. Of course, this is Tilly, now, so one must takes them with the proverbial grain of salt, and yet, Mildred has seen something as well. Could it be a hallucination? It couldn't be that Elcira's ghost is actually here, among them, could it? Why? Why now, after all these years? The house has never been haunted before, has it? What is she going to do?

Pastor Tilton closes his Bible, turns to the casket, and kneels before Gertrude to silently pray. With his head bent, he seemed to disappear into his suit. He stands, turns around, opens his arms to offer a silent prayer to the guests, and then walks down the aisle between the rows of folding chairs to the entrance to the room. All eyes are on him, partly because he is tall, basketball player size, some would say because of his skin color, and quite handsome, with his hair neatly braided in tight cornrows with ends forming coiled Rasta locks. He could be a rock star or a rapper, if it wasn't for the collar and black suit. Mildred gets up and follows him, catching up to him just before leaving.

"Excuse me, Reverend," she says.

"Douglas," he says, "you don't need to be so formal, Mrs. Cranberry."

"Mildred," she replies. "Do you have a minute?"

"Sure." He gestures toward an empty adjoining room. They enter and sit in the nearest folding chairs. "What is troubling you?"

She sits. Her fingers busy themselves nervously, pulling at the black skirt, crumpling it in her hands until her slip is all that covers her knees. "Do you believe in ghosts?"

"The Holy Ghost, of course," he says. "So, yes."

She releases her skirt and spreads it out to straighten the wrinkles. "Does God send them, or do they come from somewhere else?" Mildred twists and folds a tissue in her hands.

"Did something happen?" He leans forward, closing the space between them.

"I feel like I'm losing my mind," she says. "This morning, I couldn't find my shoes. They weren't where I always leave them. I found them in the library, which is always locked. The door was open, and the shoes were under the desk." The words keep coming out quickly, probably faster than Tilton can follow. His eyes dart back and forth as if looking for an excuse to avoid the issue.

"Obviously someone put them there." He places a finger on his chin.

"I know I didn't," she says.

"Why do you think it was a ghost?" She can see the disbelief in his eyes, or is it something else, fear maybe?

"I saw a figure run out the door and down the path, though it wasn't running. It was more like gliding, and there was an aroma of lilacs. We don't have lilacs on the property. Not anymore. They used to be on the property line, but that was years ago, and I don't even remember that."

"I'm sure there is an explanation for all of this," he says, leaning back as if the conversation was making him uncomfortable.

"There's more. Whoever it was left a mark on an old map on the desk in the library. The ink was fresh."

"All the more reason to believe someone is playing a prank on you." He leans close and stares at her. She expects him to say more, but his expression becomes blank, uninterested.

"So, you're saying a ghost couldn't do that?"

"I'm saying I doubt it's something supernatural." He opens his Bible. "Why don't we say a prayer for guidance."

"You think I'm crazy, don't you?" She stands and looks down at him, wishing he would offer something, anything, to make sense of this.

"I think you believe you saw something, and you're confused."

Mildred stares at his mouth as he speaks, but the words don't register. She wants to tell him about Tilly's vision, but he will not be much help.

She turns to exit the room and runs into Sylvie and Tilly. They are an odd pair one in a chair and the other standing beside her, just a little bit taller. In the hall outside the room where guests are paying their last respects to Gertrude, they are like guardians, flanked by streams of people entering and leaving.

Sylvie, leaning on her walker, speaks loudly into Tilly's ear, "I want a closed casket."

"For whom?" she asks.

"For me, silly, when it's my time. Then they won't have to try to puff up all my wrinkles and creases. And I don't want Abigail taking pictures of me to post on social media or put in the newsletter. Good God."

Mildred notices Sylvie's fingernails and taps her hand. "Did you forget to wear your gardening gloves again?"

"Oh, Millie, dear, you know I always have trouble with that. Make sure they clean the dirt from beneath my fingernails, will you? Of course, if the casket is closed and I get cremated, it won't matter, will it?"

"I should live so long as to worry about that." Mildred reaches out to hold Sylvie's arm. "You're shaking. Are you cold?"

"I'm always cold. I'm a summer baby, remember?"

"You always say that, but it doesn't make any sense." Mildred puts the back of her hand to Sylvie's forehead. "You're a bit clammy. Maybe I should take you home."

Sylvie moves and passes gas.

"Oh, Auntie!" Mildred waves her hand. "I definitely need to take you home."

"Wait, I want one of those baseball card things with Gertie's name on it."

"They're not baseball cards."

At the stand near the door Pastor Tilton signs the guest book.

"Ladies," he says, bowing his head slightly. "Are you leaving?"

"Aunt Sylvie is a bit tired. I thought I would bring her home."

Sylvie grabs one of the cards from the podium with the guest book and puts it in her purse. She reaches up to grab Pastor Tilton by the lapel. "You will do what you did for Gertie for me when it's my turn, right? Tell me you will."

"Of course," he says.

"Auntie, don't be so forward."

"It's all right, Mildred." He turns to Sylvie. "Would you like me to stop by for tea? You can tell me what you would like when the time comes."

"Oh, yes!"

Mildred is shocked to hear how excited her aunt sounds. She looks back into the room. "Did Tilly leave?"

"I don't think so," says Sylvie.

As they go down the handicap ramp, they spot Tilly in the parking lot looking up at the moon and stars.

"Tilly?" Sylvie clomps her walker toward her friend. "Are you okay?"

Mildred follows and walks around to face Tilly. She appears to be in a trance.

"Tilly?" Sylvie shakes her shoulder, and Tilly reacts with a start.

"Oh, Sylvie. Mildred. The strangest thing just happened. I saw Gertrude and Elcira together."

"Where?" asks Mildred.

Tilly points up at the sky. "There."

Mildred

Mildred sees a light on in Maggie's room as she drives past the main house on her way to the carriage house to drop off Sylvie. She will have the long overdue chat with her granddaughter, but first, she needs to get Sylvie settled. Her head is no longer clammy, but Sylvie is drifting off to sleep and waking herself up, so Mildred knows she has to work fast before her aunt becomes an unmovable object.

"Come on Auntie, help me help you," says Mildred. The sudden change in her aunt's health was frightening.

"Are we home?" Sylvie squints and lifts her arms so Mildred can grab them.

Mildred opens the walker and places it in front of Sylvie. "Grab on, Auntie," she says, and pulls Sylvie's arms to get her to stand.

"Good," says Sylvie. "I'm tired."

"We're almost there," Mildred says.

Step by step, they make their way to the front door of the carriage house, a short trip that Mildred could do in fewer than ten steps. Together, with Mildred focusing on holding Sylvie up, it is a trek.

"We have one big step at the door, and then we're in," says Mildred, preparing Sylvie for the next move. Can she do it? How can she do it?

At the door, Mildred pushes it open and helps Sylvie lift the walker so the front feet are inside and the tennis-ball-covered feet are at the edge. Sylvie strains to lift her leg, but it won't clear the step.

"I can't lift it, Millie," says Sylvie.

Mildred reaches behind the knee and lifts, then pushes her behind to get her to put weight on the leg.

Sylvie starts to fall backwards, causing Mildred to step back. As Sylvie falls, Mildred grabs her under her arms and pulls upward.

"Stand! Auntie, put weight on your feet." *Please be able to stand.*

Mildred manages to hold on and pull Sylvie up over the step and into the foyer.

"I'm sorry, Millie." Sylvie struggles to grab hold of the walker, while Mildred guides her forward to the first available chair. The two fall into the chair together, Sylvie on Mildred's lap. Mildred lets out a long, heavy breath, one she had been holding for who knows how long.

"We did it," says Sylvie. "I'm so sorry."

"It's not your fault, Auntie." Mildred catches her breath, still holding tight to make sure Sylvie doesn't slide onto the floor. That would be worse.

"I think I need the rollator. It's in the closet."

Mildred works to free herself from Sylvie, squeezing herself out of the chair letting Sylvie slide down into the chair. She opens the closet and pulls out the rollator, a walker with a seat. If she can get Sylvie on the seat, she can wheel her to bed. "Auntie, do you think we should go to Emergency?"

"No!" Sylvie straightens up in the chair. "I'm not going to die in the hospital."

"Die?" Mildred kneels before her. "Who said anything about dying?"

"That's what happens at my age," she says, "you go in and don't come out. I don't want that, Millie."

"Don't worry, Auntie."

After much struggling, Mildred gets her to bed. She goes to the kitchen to get a glass of water for Sylvie, but on her return, Sylvie is snoring.

She sends a text to Maggie.

Spending the night in the carriage house with Aunt Sylvie. See you in the morning.

She waits, but there is no response. Eight forty-five. Maybe she has an early shift in the morning.

Mildred prepares a turkey sandwich and a cup of tea. In Sylvie's bedroom, Mildred makes herself as comfortable as possible in an armchair.

The look on Tilly's face when she was staring up at the moon haunts her. Tilly is the one person Mildred would expect to be comfortable with a vision, and yet she looked frightened. Mildred finishes her tea and places the cup on the night table beside the bed. If it really was a ghost, maybe it is gone now. Mildred imagines all the ways that outcome could be true, and she settles on Elcira came for Gertrude and took her home.

She closes her eyes and starts to drift off.

"Mildred, dear."

The voice penetrates and wakes her. Mildred runs to Sylvie, but Sylvie is snoring away.

Mildred walks through the house, checking every room, locking every door, closing every window. She walks through the kitchen and spots her teacup in the sink. Back in the bedroom, she checks the night table.

I'm losing my mind.

Maggie

The only sound in the house this early in the morning is the gentle swoosh of the ceiling fan over Maggie's bed. She longs for the day she will roll quietly out of bed while her husband continues to sleep peacefully, making gurgling sounds. But definitely not snoring. She could not deal with that. A CPAP machine, maybe, but snoring? No way. She wonders if Sam snores in bed the way he does in the car when she is driving at night and he has drifted off. Sometimes, she just doesn't know where his head is. It bothers her that he still lives with his parents, but here she is in her grandmother's house. It will be hers soon, and then what?

Will she and Sam sleep here, in this bed, with Grandma next door? She snores, and she gets up during the night to pee. Hmm. She didn't hear her during the night. Maybe she got in late. Yes, there was Gertrude's wake.

Standing over her bed, with two options laid out before her, she wonders which outfit she should wear for her meeting with Doctor Harlan, the hospital's chief administrator. She had heard of Maggie's idea for a dedicated children's cancer center and asked Maggie to meet her in the hospital cafeteria for breakfast. Either she will be praised or reprimanded for raising money for a project that has not been approved. What did Gladys Hopper say? It is better to ask forgiveness than permission—something like that.

She chooses her hospital whites and leaves the pantsuit and blouse on the bed. She is not one to change at the hospital, as the nurses and aides do. Some doctors do it as well, such as the young ones who go to the gym first and then run in the park after their shifts. She likes to arrive ready for work. How many times has she encountered a young cancer patient walking from the hospital garage with mom or dad in tow? Better to be prepared for an encounter.

With a pair of clogs in hand for later in her shift, and dress shoes with slip-resistant soles on her feet, she steps carefully past her grandmother's room. Maggie stops to press an ear against the closed door. Not a sound.

She checks the time and flips through the summaries of messages on her watch. There is one from Grandma, but she doesn't have time to read it now. She locks the front door, knowing Aunt Sylvie and Grandma use the doors on the back patio most of the time, and walks down the long drive to her car, which she always parks close to the road. She looks up at her grandmother's bedroom window. Still no lights. See you later, Grandma.

She makes a left, bringing her past the carriage house, where Mom's car is in the driveway. Why would she drive there? She usually just walks. Maybe they have an early meeting?

She stops at the corner and turns around. Pulling up in front of the house, she checks her watch. She can still make it, if she runs in and out.

The door is locked. It's never locked. She rings the bell and knocks on the door.

Footsteps, the lock disengaging, the door opening.

"Maggie, oh, thank God." Mildred is shaking.

"Grandma, what's wrong?"

"She's not waking up. I don't know what's wrong. She was fine last night."

The two run to Sylvie's room.

"Grandma, go in my car and get my bag."

Maggie takes Sylvie's pulse, checks her eyes and feels her forehead.

Mildred returns with the bag and places it on the bed.

"Call 9-1-1," says Maggie.

"Oh, no."

"Tell them to let the hospital know Doctor Payton is with her and that we need an ambulance. Tell them that you're Sylvie's niece and she needs immediate care."

Mildred grabs her phone and leaves the room.

"Auntie? Auntie, can you hear me?" Maggie is tapping on Sylvie's chest. She pulls out her stethoscope and listens to her heart and lungs. *Can't keep this a secret any longer.*

Mildred returns. "They are on their way."

"I will go in the ambulance with them. You take my car and meet me there. Go now, and park in the circle at the ER. Valet will take it from you."

Mildred hesitates. "She doesn't want to go to the hospital."

"What?" Maggie looks at her. "She will die here."

"That's what she wants." Mildred starts to cry.

"Just go. I'll take care of this."

Mildred takes the keys and goes.

Maggie's phone rings. It's Doctor Juliet Harlan, Chief Administrative Officer. Instead of breakfast, Maggie should be prepared to make a presentation to the heads of the departments.

Breakfast would have been easier, less formal, but with this emergency, she would have been late, possibly missed it all together. Maybe this is for the best. The spirit moves in mysterious ways. She remembers her mother telling her that. Some spirit, taking her in the prime of her life. But isn't it always too soon?

She pulls the covers off Aunt Sylvie. She has soiled herself. She can't let her go this way. She grabs a washcloth and runs warm water over it in the bathroom sink. Back at the bed, she checks Aunt Sylvie's pulse and breathing. She needs to work fast. After removing the panties, she rolls her great-great-aunt's body just enough to wipe her clean, puts on a clean pair of panties, and then covers her with a fresh nightshirt. This will do for now. At least she will be decent, as Aunt Sylvie would say.

Her mom told her to never leave the house without clean panties. Mission accomplished.

Mildred

The last time Mildred arrived at the emergency entrance of the hospital, she was wearing a surgical mask and was told she couldn't enter due to the COVID19 pandemic. The last time she saw her daughter, Audrey, alive, two EMTs were pushing her fold-able stretcher through the ambulance entrance and disappeared as the automatic doors closed. What a difference a few years makes.

The valet isn't going to let her leave the car, since she doesn't have a patient with her, so Mildred mentions Doctor Payton's name and the doors open for her. No one stops her, required her to wear a mask, or use sanitizer on her hands. At the check-in desk, she is given a visitor pass and told to wait for the ambulance. The wait is not long. Mildred doesn't even have to find a seat in the waiting room.

Everything happens so quickly, too fast for Mildred to process, and within minutes of their arrival, the EMTs are handing off the patient to nurses and aides, and Sylvie is rolling. Maggie is talking with the nurses, rushing to the nurses' station in the center of the busy Emergency Department where glass-enclosed rooms are divided by a thin curtain, allowing two patients to be treated simultaneously in each. Mildred feels like everything is moving so fast and she is frozen in time, or moving so slowly, someone is bound to bump into her sending her sprawling across the brightly lit floor.

Watching Maggie take charge, coordinating more than directing, Mildred realizes she really has no idea what Maggie does. This is her granddaughter. How could she not know? Has she been that busy? Doing what? Garden club meetings, luncheons, social events, tea with Sylvie, is that what her life is all about? No wonder they have so little to talk about when they do, and now what? Now that Sylvie is, what? Sick? Dying?

She enters the room where Sylvie is surrounded by white coats, and carts are pressed up against the bed. Maggie steps back, letting them take over.

Bright lights, bells, and beeps all around her keep her from focusing on Sylvie and what is happening to her. What is happening to her?

Sylvie lay still, wires and tubes attached to one device and then another. After the attendant reads the printouts and whisks off, wires and contact pads remain abandoned on her chest, arms, and legs.

People in blue and red uniforms and doctors in white coats come and go, each adding an order or comment or a note to the chart before walking back out. Few manage a mumbled introduction and what might have been a smile behind an N95 mask.

Everything is a blur.

An aide takes tubes of blood of different colors, shakes them and places labels on them. She scans the wristband on Sylvie's arm and takes some of the tubes away, leaving others on the metal cart.

Mildred keeps her eyes on the abandoned tubes, wondering who and when someone will take them.

"Don't they need them? Why did they take her blood?" She tries to get Maggie's attention. Maggie looks at her watch.

"Doctor Payton, please sit down. You're getting in the way," says the aide.

The white lab coat returns and comes over to Mildred. "This is going to take a while. We have a lot to do and too little space in here.

Why don't you two sit in the ER waiting room? I will come out and get you."

Maggie grabs Mildred by the hand and guides her out.

"Do you want some water?" she asks.

Mildred nods and follows. She cannot speak. Walking away, she looks back at the wall of rooms, each displaying the same chaotic scene, and people rush by, almost touching her, making her feel unsteady on her feet.

At the check-in desk, a young man bends down to talk through the small hole in the glass, while the woman with him holds a little girl to her chest. The girl is crying with interruptions of coughing.

Mildred connects with the young girl as she passes. A memory surfaces of her holding Audrey and comforting her when she was sick as a child. Mildred takes the water from Maggie and studies her granddaughter's face.

"I am so proud of you, Maggie. I can see your mother in you," she says, "she was so proud of you. I had no idea how much you are needed here."

"Grandma, please," says Maggie, blinking her eyes and looking up to the ceiling.

Mildred rubs her palms along the arm of the chair, her thoughts jumbled and interlaced between Maggie and Sylvie. A television on the wall in the corner creates some distraction, with what seems like an endless stream of commercials and chatter. The people sitting in chairs along each of the walls look lost in their own fears and concerns, some talking quietly in another language, possibly Spanish, and one woman holding rosary beads. Most of the men are dressed in work clothes, as are some of the women, with uniforms or logos on their shirts. One woman smiles at her, and Mildred recognizes her. Sofia colors her hair at the salon. And the man in the corner may be one of the men who works for her landscaper. Suddenly, the world shrinks.

Maggie touches Mildred's hand and stops it from rubbing back and forth on the arm of the chair. "Are you okay?"

Mildred looks at her hand and then focuses on Maggie's face.

"She's very sick, Grandma."

Words won't come. Mildred just looks at Maggie's mouth as if the words will be visible and clear when they appear.

"She has bone cancer, and she has refused treatment."

"You knew this?" Mildred pulls her hand away and punches her lap.

Maggie reaches for her hand. "I couldn't—"

"Why couldn't you?" Mildred stands and steps away, feeling her knees weaken.

As she walks past, Maggie taps her on the shoulder, "I have a meeting. I'll be back."

"What? You're leaving?"

Mildred stands by the double doors that lead to the ER, doors that won't open without swiping an ID badge. She knows she can't reenter, and she is not sure she wants to.

The young girl with her parents at the check-in is crying, tears flowing down her face. Mildred wants to do something, but what can she do. The girl suddenly turns to face her, eyes open wide, and the tears stop. Mildred feels a draft of cool air coming through the doors. She turns to see if she is in the way, but the doors haven't opened.

Looking back, she sees the young girl smiling and waving to where the guard sits in the hallway. Mildred heads back to her seat. As she passes the girl, she sees there is no one in the hallway. The guard is not at his post. Who did the girl smile at?

Maggie

The administrative offices in the hospital are not located on a special floor like in major corporations in big cities like Manhattan. They are scattered throughout the hospital, usually close to the department or departments they oversee. The food services administrator's office is in the basement, where the kitchen and cafeteria are located. So, it takes some time to familiarize oneself with the layout, especially since changes are continuously being made. Some things can't change, like Purchasing & Receiving and Emergency, but as personnel up top changes, offices expand or contract based on the degree of importance and reputation. Doctor Juliet Harlan's office is one floor above the children's cancer unit, with a bank of windows overlooking the atrium where Maggie spends much of her time.

She runs from the elevator, firmly clutching her white lab coat, project portfolio, and iPad. She has been hoping for this opportunity, and now she is late for the meeting, which could provide the most significance to her career.

Standing before the mahogany door, she dons her lab coat, presses it flat, and checks her name tag to make sure it is straight. She knocks on the door of Doctor Juliet Harlan, Chief Administrative Officer.

"Come in, Doctor Payton."

Maggie recognizes the scratchy female voice immediately. Juliet's bout with throat cancer as a resident gives people the impression that she needs to clear her throat.

"I am sorry I'm late, Doctor Harlan," says Maggie, closing the door behind her.

"We were just about to adjourn, having covered all of the old business. I believe you know everyone here." She motions for Maggie to take a seat at the conference table.

The office is the size of three standard C-level offices to accommodate the large number of private meetings required to run an expanding hospital complex. Maggie nods to the group, pulls out the chair from her spot and places the iPad on the table. "I prefer to stand if you don't mind."

In response, Juliet leans against the frame and sill of one of the tinted glass windows overlooking the atrium. "Please proceed."

Maggie connects with each department head individually by introducing herself and her program concept. "For those of you whom I have not had the privilege of working with over the past ten years, I have lived in Old Cranberry my entire life, except for four years at college, followed by medical school. I was ecstatic to fulfill my residency requirements here at what was then called United Hospital, and I feel I have grown as the hospital has grown in scope and depth of service to the community."

Several of the department heads scratch notes on their yellow pads. No one is using an iPad or laptop.

Maggie props up her iPad on its stand and turns it toward the group. Instinctively, they lean forward. "I apologize," she says, "I had hoped to arrive early enough to set this up on the screen, but I had to rush my great aunt to Emergency, where she is now."

Several eyes look up.

"I only mention that in case my cell phone goes off and I must leave." She syncs her phone to the iPad to control her prepared images and tables.

"Thanks to improvements in the detection and treatment of cancer in general, fewer children are being diagnosed each year than a decade ago, while an aging population and early detection have resulted in a twenty percent increase in cancer diagnoses in adults and the elderly." Charts on the iPad show the changes.

"The impact of these changes is hard to spot without a close look at how we treat cancer patients. If we walk right now to the open courtyard on the fourth floor, just outside that window, we will see patients and their families meeting and waiting for treatment in a positive, natural setting. We will see mostly wheelchairs, walkers, and rollators, with a few children's toys scattered here and there."

Several heads turn toward one another, and Juliet looks out the window. A few heads bob in agreement.

"I can see that myself," says Juliet. "It is getting quite crowded down there."

"I am sure everyone will agree that we need space for our aging population," says Maggie, "but we also need a dedicated space for the children who require just as much care, if not more, and are being displaced at a time when they are most frightened and confused."

"May I ask a question?"

"Yes, Doctor Lin," says Maggie, addressing the head of pediatrics.

"If you had all the money you would need to build a dedicated children's cancer center, where would you put it? Old Cranberry is being developed into a sea of luxury homes with every available lot being split and developed."

Maggie swipes her finger across her phone to flip through several slides. The one that appears is a rendering of a new building on beautiful park-like grounds. "This is where I will build it. On the old Cranberry Farm."

Mildred

Mildred stares at the rosary beads in the hands of the woman in the chair across the room. One by one, the beads roll between her fingers while her lips mime the words. Mildred's fingers copy the motion, rubbing, rolling, spinning invisible beads of hope and the words of the prayers she learned at her grandmother's knee play in her ears, without thought, without effort. Does anyone hear them? Do they make a difference? Do they do anything more than occupy time and space?

A white coat blocks her view, and she looks up.

"Mrs. Cranberry, your aunt would like to see you." His voice is gentle and calm, almost frighteningly so.

"Oh," she says.

Mildred checks around her to see what she needs to bring. Pocketbook, phone. She stands and starts to walk, a little unsteady on her feet.

"Do you need a walker?"

"No. No. But my granddaughter is not back yet."

He grabs her arm and says, "We will let her know she can come to the room."

At the opening to the small room, Mildred stops and leans against the glass. The doctor motions for her to enter, but the message doesn't reach her feet yet.

Sylvie's eyes are closed, and her mouth is hung open. She has oxygen delivered through nasal prongs on a tube that wraps around the ears. Mildred looks at the monitor, hoping to reconcile the difference between the readings and what she sees.

The doctor leans over Sylvie to talk to her, "Mrs. Rose? Sylvie? Your niece is here."

Sylvie gasps and closes her mouth. Her eyes open slightly, and she turns toward the doctor.

"I'm here, Auntie," says Mildred, her voice shaky.

Sylvie rolls her head on the pillow. Mildred moves closer. She looks to the doctor for help understanding Sylvie's condition, but the small man remains silently focused on Sylvie, checking her pulse and listening to her breathing through his stethoscope.

"Millie?" Sylvie's voice is a whisper.

Mildred leans closer.

"I don't want to die here, Millie. Take me home." She reaches for Mildred's arm.

"Mrs. Rose, you are in the Emergency Room. I am Doctor Pavel. You are very weak, as you know. I want to keep you here overnight and see if we need to admit you in the morning."

"I don't understand," says Mildred. "She was fine last night."

"Mrs. Rose, may I talk plainly about your condition with your niece?"

Sylvie looks at him and then back at Mildred.

"I want to go home," says Sylvie.

"You are fully within your rights to sign yourself out, but I strongly advise against it," he says, returning his stethoscope to his neck. "You need hydration and some blood. We have started the hydration and have ordered the blood. You will be here for several hours for that and then we can talk again."

He turns to Mildred. "Do you know if she has a healthcare proxy on file here? Does she have an advance directive?"

"I don't know. We never talked about that." Mildred's hands are shaking as she pulls out her phone. "Maggie may know. I can text her."

"What might I know," says Maggie, entering the room with iPad and portfolio. "Hello, Doctor. I am Sylvie's great-grand-niece, Mildred's granddaughter."

"Doctor Pavel," he says, "I am the on-call overnight. I will be leaving this morning, but I just explained that Mrs. Rose needs blood and hydration before we can determine if she can go home."

"Home?" Maggie asks, looking at Sylvie and then Mildred. "Is she well enough to go home?"

"I want to go home," says Sylvie. "I won't die here."

"Auntie, it's me, Maggie." She kisses Sylvie on her forehead. "Leave it to me. Let's do what the doctor says, and then we will work out the next steps."

Sylvie turns her head and stares at the corner of the room over the door. Her eyes open wider.

Mildred strokes Sylvie's hand and pulls up a chair. "I'll stay with you, Auntie. I won't leave you alone."

Sylvie points to the corner of the room where she is looking. "We're not alone."

"What do you mean?" Mildred looks where Sylvie is pointing.

"She's here with us, the lady in white." Sylvie's voice is weak, almost a whisper.

Mildred looks at Doctor Pavel. He motions for Mildred to follow him, and he leaves the room.

"Let's go to the family lounge," he says, "we can talk there."

Mildred follows, her feet numb, her hands shaky, and her thoughts a kaleidoscope of images, none positive.

Doctor Pavel turns one chair around so they can face each other. "Would you like some water or coffee?" he asks.

"I'm good," she says, taking a seat. She folds her hands in her lap.

"I am sure you have many questions for me," he says. "Let me start by saying that your aunt is very sick."

"I don't understand," she says. "When did this start?"

"I guess she didn't share any of this with you. I can tell you that the initial diagnosis was three months ago. I believe she fell and injured her hip?"

"Oh, that was at the garden club luncheon," says Mildred. "She did complain about the hip and went to her doctor. She knew then?"

"There were some tests and an MRI. You didn't know about those?"

Mildred bunches up her skirt with her hands. "What can you do for her now?"

"We can make her comfortable," he says, as though he is talking about a sofa or a pillow.

"What does that mean?" Mildred pulls her hands together and presses them against her lips. "Will she get strong enough to walk on her own? Can she live alone? Do I need to get someone in to care for her? Will she need around-the-clock care? We can arrange that."

"I will have the Palliative Care Team come and meet with you and your aunt."

The door opens, and Maggie walks in.

"Oh, Maggie," says Mildred, reaching for her.

"I wanted to talk to the nurse before joining you here," Maggie says.

Doctor Pavel stands and gives Maggie his chair. "I will give you two some time to talk."

Mildred breaks down and sobs.

"Grandma?" Maggie puts her arms around her.

"They're not going to do anything for her, are they?" Mildred wipes her eyes with a tissue.

"She is very sick." Maggie stands before her, one hand on Mildred's shoulder.

"I need to get her home. Can you help me do that?" Mildred asks, tears streaming.

"If that's what you want."
"It's what she wants."
"Then let's go tell her."

Effie

MONDAY

Effie's heels tap out a warning to anyone listening that she has arrived.

"Come on in, Ms. Devine. I'm glad you could make time to come by." James places both hands on the walnut conference table and poses over his model of the Cranberry Estates community he hopes to build.

"I called you, remember?" she says, noticing that this is one of the few offices in his establishment that show any signs of life.

"I knew you would," he says. "Everyone wants to see the future of Old Cranberry."

"Everyone?" She holds her head to the side, giving her earring energy to swing. "I assume you mean your investors, or should I say creditors?"

"You mean to tell me that if you had this much prime property in the wealthiest county in New England, you wouldn't develop it? You don't look like someone who would pass up an opportunity to reach for the brass ring."

Effie rests her hands on her hips. "What does that mean?"

"Should I say brass key?"

"You have been doing your homework," she says, easing her shoulders slightly.

He spots the large plastic tree that has fallen over near the carriage house in his model and reaches in to right it. "You will not goad me into saying, 'I didn't get to where I am–' Oh, but I did say it, didn't I?" He smiles, showing more teeth than warranted.

Effie walks around the model, taking a closer look. "How long did it take you to build this?"

"I didn't build it myself, though I could have, of course. I farmed it out. There are plenty of talented students looking for internships."

"So, it could be faulty?"

"Why do you ask?" He steps closer to her, causing her to back away slightly. "Are you saying you younger folks are not that talented?"

"I assume you would have done better, given your decades of experience." She steps around him and bends down for a street-level view. She expects his eyes to follow her, and she is not disappointed. "Yes, definitely student quality, but not bad. So, tell me, why did you leave the carriage house intact? I would think that would have made a great park-like entrance to your gated community."

"Gated?" He laughs and bends to meet her eyes. "How Twentieth Century of you. What do residents of Old Cranberry need to worry about?"

"Meaning?" She holds her gaze on his eyes, her brows furled.

"This isn't The Bronx, Ms. Devine."

"Or Harlem, perhaps?"

"I see what you're driving at."

"I'm not the one driving, Mr. Castleby. But to answer your question, I would do something radically different if this were my property."

"Like what?" He stands and walks toward her, like a used car salesman, sensing a possible sale.

"You'll see."

"I will, huh?" He walks over to the credenza and grabs a handful of business cards and brochures. "Take these with you. I would love to have a shot at your dream when you are ready."

She chuckles and continues to walk around the model, counting entrances. "A bit cramped, don't you think?"

"Au contraire, Mademoiselle." He unfolds one of the brochures to reveal a collage of photos of the interior of one of his developments. "This is an example of what we build. The smallest unit at this site is a one bedroom with thirteen hundred square feet and high ceilings."

She glances at the page. "Low-income housing, I see."

"Are you serious? Though it is one of the more affordable units in town."

"Affordable for whom?" She reaches into the model, measures the open space with her hand, and then does the same with the parking lot. "Is this all the parking you plan to have?"

"Very astute of you to notice," he says, puffing up his chest. "There is additional parking under two of the buildings."

"So these are all attached homes?"

"Those two buildings are. The rest are single-family homes with their own garages."

"So, the apartments in those two buildings are what you would call affordable? Is that how you get around the planning board's ten percent affordable housing requirement?"

"You've done your homework."

"Who decides what is affordable? Or is it like pornography, you know it when you see it?"

He laughs and takes a step closer. She counters by stepping around the table and putting his model between them.

"Too bad you won't get a chance to build this play-land for wealthy white folks."

"You know we can't limit use like that, Miss Devine. That would be unethical."

"And illegal?"

"Of course." He leans over the model, bringing his face closer to hers. "Why wouldn't you want this in Old Cranberry?"

Effie shakes her head. "You are clueless, aren't you? I thought you were smarter than that. If it was just for the money, sure. Go ahead and build what will bring in the largest profit."

"So, what's it about then? For you, I mean. If this was your property, which it isn't." He steps around the table again, trying to get close to her.

She leads him to the other side, bringing her closer to the door. "You will find out when I am in a position to call the shots. I'm not there yet, but I will be soon."

"Look, I love to hedge my bets whenever I can, but I have every confidence Mildred will live up to her promise to hand over the property to her granddaughter when she marries."

"So, when did you start planning this project? Before your son asked Maggie to marry him?"

"How long have you been working on trying to get your hands on it, Ms. Devine?"

"I guess Sam just happened to run into Maggie at the hospital, having no idea she would inherit a windfall?"

"I'll admit that I've been working on this for a while, but I won't admit to orchestrating it."

"Well, that doesn't guarantee you will get it." Effie pulls a document from her bag and drops it on the model. "You should read this."

James picks up the document and starts to read it.

"It's a copy. I have the original."

"Chester Cranberry's will. I've seen this before. I believe everyone in town has at one time or another. You're not the first person to contest it. He left everything to his wife when he died, and she inherited it."

"Ah, but there is a condition. If Elcira predeceases him or if she is otherwise unable to inherit the estate, it goes to his male heirs."

"But she didn't die before he did. No one could prove that she killed him."

She lifts her chin and smirks. "If someone could, then Slayer's Rule would kick in."

"What's that?"

"A person cannot benefit from their crime. The estate would go to the next of kin or whoever is named."

James laughs. "So, it winds up in the same hands. What's the big deal?"

"Not necessarily," she says.

"But you just said it goes to the children."

"His male heirs."

"So, you think your ancestor is one of those heirs?"

Sam tosses the paper on the table and walks over to the window.

"There was no trial. The case was dropped. Lack of evidence. It's still a cold case. Which means it can still be solved."

"A two-hundred-year-old cold case?"

He points to the buildings visible beyond the trees. "Every multi-family mansion was once on a sprawling farm, just like the property Mildred is holding onto. Eventually, the families sold and made a fortune, and we built half of them."

"So this is your last hurrah?"

"The pandemic hurt everyone. This will get us back in the game."

Effie walks over to him and leans close to whisper in his ear. "You can have your wedding, but the property will be mine."

James starts to laugh, but she turns his head toward hers and stares into his eyes.

"I can prove Chester was killed by his scheming wife, and as one of his descendants, a portion of that property is mine. Chester raped Deborah Townsend and she had a son, Henry, my great-great-grandfather."

"You're nuts!" He shakes his head and walks away. "What proof could you have?"

"I know the key exists."

"The legendary, infamous, mysterious second key? Ha!" James looks down his nose at her. "Where is this key? Can you prove it was the same key Elcira used to lock herself in the potting shed? You see? I know the story. I studied it myself, along with every one of the cases brought to the courts over the years from descendants who felt they deserved a piece of the pie. Mildred has defended her property like the Swiss Army. It will go to Maggie when she marries, and that is who will decide."

"You will see when I get my hands on that key," she says.

"Oh, so you don't even have this mysterious key of legend. You're chasing ghosts. You'll never prove that Elcira was the Lizzy Borden of her day just because you find an old key. If you do find it, that is."

"I will prove I am a rightful heir to the estate, just as much, if not more than Mildred."

"Good for you." James waves his hand at her. "Go chase your ghosts. I have work to do."

"We'll see who laughs when I get the property." Effie grabs her papers and starts for the door. She stops and pulls another paper from her pocketbook. "I'm getting a court order. You want this property just as much as I do, maybe even more, so remember this moment when you have to come crawling to me for a deal."

"Ooh! I'm shaking. But don't forget, if you inherit the property, we can talk."

Mildred

When Mildred and Maggie arrive at the room, an orderly and an aide are pushing the bed with Sylvie out into the hallway.

"What are you doing?" Mildred rushes to stop them, her stomach tightening. "We're taking her home."

Stopping the bed from fully exiting the room creates a traffic problem, with nurses squeezing to get past and EMTs waiting with a moaning patient in a collapsible stretcher. The aide turns the bed sideways letting the EMTs pass, but now the bed is blocking the entrance to the room. An aide tries to exit from the side of the room where a new patient has been hooked up to monitors. She pushes the bed with her hip and squeezes out.

Sylvie reaches out to hold Mildred's hand.

"We can't stay here like this. I have to take her to her room. She's being admitted," says the orderly.

"Auntie, you want to go home, don't you?" Mildred asks Sylvie.

"Home," says Sylvie, squeezing Mildred's hand. "I don't want to die here."

Maggie plants herself in front of the bed.

83

The orderly bends to address her. "I have my orders. You will have to speak with the doctor."

"I spoke with Doctor Pavel a few minutes ago," says Maggie.

The aide pushes her way between Maggie and the bed. "He's not the admitting doctor. You need to talk with Doctor Swan."

"I'm going to take her home," says Mildred. A chill comes over her as she struggles to think of how she will care for her aunt. In the same instant, she tries to push away the fear. The knot in her stomach twists. She wishes this was all a dream.

"You need to talk to the doctor," says the aide.

"You don't understand," says Mildred. "This is my aunt. She wants to go home. You can't keep her here." *And I will find a way to care for her at home.*

"Please move aside so I can move the bed. It's in the way." The orderly pleads with Maggie.

"Put the bed back in the room," says Maggie.

"Millie?" Sylvie pulls on Mildred's hand. "I have to pee."

Mildred turns to the aide. "She needs to use the restroom." Her fists clench, fingernails digging into her palms.

"You can go ahead and pee, Mrs. Rose. The PureWick will catch it." The aide pats Sylvie on the shoulder.

"Put her back and call the doctor. Now." Mildred stares the aide down. The knot in her stomach feels like it will burst.

"What's the problem here?" A male nurse who makes the orderly look puny barks his question at Maggie.

"Apparently, Doctor Swan admitted Mrs. Rose without her consent," says Maggie.

"Oh, I doubt that, Doctor. But let me check into it, and we will resolve this quickly." He turns to the orderly. "Put her back in the room for now. We can't block the hallway. We're way too busy. I'll get Doctor Swan."

The orderly wheels the bed back, grabs his orders, and leaves.

"I'll be back," says the aide, leaving without hooking Sylvie up to the monitor or oxygen.

"They've left her on the tank because they plan to move her again," says Maggie.

"Can we take her out of here?" Mildred strokes Sylvie's head, pushing her hair away from her eyes. *Then what?*

"Thank you, dear," Sylvie says.

Mildred's chest tightens. Listening to the monitors buzzing and the hiss of the oxygen when she leans toward Sylvie makes her wonder what she will need at home. Could she do this? Could she have done this for Audrey? Should she have kept her home? Had Maggie wanted that, and she insisted? She has trouble remembering. It is as if everything is a dream, a bad dream.

She smells urine and notices that the tube running from the wick to the suction container isn't pulling the way it should. She lifts the sheet and checks Sylvie's legs. They are wet. She presses the buzzer attached by a long cable to the wall. A light goes on over the doorway. People walk by but no one enters.

"Where's the orderly or nurse? Who's supposed to be taking care of her? Why isn't someone coming?"

"Can you use your influence to find out what is happening?" Mildred pleads with Maggie.

"Sit down, Grandma," says Maggie, remaining calm. "I'll get the nurse."

She steps into the hallway and walks toward the large square bullpen-like space in the center of the floor, where doctors and nurses are hovering over computer screens, and patients without rooms are lined up in the aisles. It looks like controlled chaos.

Maggie returns with a male orderly who pushes the button on the wall to turn off the light and uncovers Sylvie.

Mildred and Maggie step out while the orderly adjusts the wick system, and lifts Sylvie to change her sheet and hospital gown. Mildred stares at him, trying to imagine doing this herself at home.

"I don't know how we are going to manage, Maggie. Can you look at her chart?"

"Everything is in the system, and I don't have access with my ID."

The orderly adjusts the curtain and waves for them to enter.

Maggie comes close, leaning over the bed. "Auntie, you know that if you go home, you will die. We cannot treat you there."

Mildred gasps. She didn't want to hear that.

Sylvie smiles and reaches up to touch Maggie's face. "You are so sweet, child."

"Mrs. Rose, I'm Chaplain Nguyen, and this is Nurse Lovett, the team lead, and Linda Crocker, a community health worker. We are part of your palliative care team."

The trio enters and stands at the foot of the bed, blocking anyone and everyone from entering or exiting the small space in Sylvie's half of the room.

Mildred looks at them and then turns to Maggie for an explanation. "I don't think we need their help, right?"

"Are you a relative of Mrs. Rose?"

"We both are," says Maggie, taking a firm, authoritative stance. "Doctor Swan has authorized our aunt to be admitted against her will. As a member of this hospital staff, I find that a bit disappointing, to say the least."

"I see," says the chaplain. "Do you mind if we talk to your aunt?"

"It is up to her," says Mildred. "Auntie, do you want to talk with these people?"

"I have to pee."

Nurse Lovett walks over to Sylvie and peeks under the sheet. "You have a wick, Mrs. Rose. You can just pee and it will be captured in the container on the side of the bed."

"It didn't work before," says Mildred, stepping as close to the nurse as she can. "My aunt is not comfortable peeing in her bed. Are you?"

Sylvie leans back and closes her eyes. A gurgling and sucking sound indicates she listened to the nurse.

"Now it seems to be working," says Mildred. "So, you can all leave now."

The chaplain signals to the others to follow him. "We will come back later."

"Good," says Maggie.

"Good riddance," says Mildred. "Wait here."

"Where are you going?" asks Maggie.

"To get a wheelchair," Mildred says, "I'm taking her home."

"Grandma, no. Let me work this out."

Mildred keeps walking without turning back. At the entrance to the ER, several wheelchairs wait for incoming patients. Mildred grabs one and heads back, only to find herself locked out at the double doors.

"Can someone let me in?" she asks whoever would listen. "God help me, please."

After several minutes, the doors open to let someone out. She looks up at the ceiling. "Thanks."

"We have to think this through, Grandma," says Maggie, standing beside the bed. "Aunt Sylvie is hooked up to an IV and has a type of catheter. We can't take those with us."

Mildred looks at Sylvie. All expression drains from Sylvie's face.

"I can't go home?" she asks.

"I'm taking you home, says Mildred. I will find a way."

"Let me at least call to make arrangements for a bed and nurse to meet us there," says Maggie.

"How long will that take?" asks Mildred.

"I'll say it's a rush." Maggie leaves.

"Okay." Mildred leaves the wheelchair at the door and walks over to Sylvie. "We'll get you home where you belong, Auntie." She fights to hold back tears.

Sylvie touches Mildred's face and wipes a tear from her cheek. "Don't forget the key," she says.

Elcira

O nly a few clouds dot the sky, and yet it is drizzling. Umbrellas, mostly black, a few black and white, and one red, go to the grave site at the Old Cranberry Baptist Church where Gertrude will be laid to rest. But Elcira knows that Gertrude is no longer with that body that caused her so much pain and suffering. Tiily knows Gertrude is gone. She saw Elcira take her home. From now on, Gertrude will make her presence known in other ways unless called back to serve another purpose, like Elcira.

She can choose to be seen just as she can choose what form to take when she is seen. Most like to see a willowy figure in white when their time comes. Right now, Elcira has some time. Sylvie is not ready. She floats among the headstones and markers in the oldest section of the cemetery, where she buried Chester, where her children buried her, and her grandchildren buried them. Some of the markers are so worn, it takes her some time to figure out who they are for. Many, she never knew when she was alive, but only met them in death. She was there for them when it was their time to go, just as she is here now. A thin coat of water from the drizzle coats the tops of the stones. She forces it down to darken the face of the stones, revealing what remains of the names and dates. She wipes each one with her gloved hand, pushing away the water. One by one, she finds each of her children. Susan Cranberry Hopper and her husband, Maxwell. What a lovely wedding that was on the great lawn, late in the day, with torches lit along the path to their waiting carriage.

Martin, Tootsie, Wally, Tubby, Felix and Sally, she found them all, deciphering the eroded lettering where possible to determine the dates of their deaths. Felix, the oldest, lived the longest. His wife, Lorraine is not buried beside him. Those were the Civil War years. Most of the rest of the stones in this sectioned-off area are his descendants, with the exception of three, Lila and Dana, Elcira's twin sisters, and her father, Lincoln Engels, whose death was another mystery. Elcira finds their stones near the stone corner post in an area marked off from the rest of the cemetery. Today, the rectangle is marked by corner posts of cement with metal rods connecting them to each other, just a few inches off the ground, enough to trip over. A tarnished copper sign tells visitors this is the Cranberry Family Cemetery. In Elcira's day, this was the spot on the very lowest point of her property. She had planned to build a proper mausoleum closer to the main house, away from the man whose death links her forever to this place, but like secrets that are never revealed, some plans never get fulfilled.

She bends and picks up two smooth stones, putting them on the headstones of Lila and Dana. "I may need your help," she says. Suddenly, a crow swoops down and knocks off one of the stones. Another crow joins in and knocks the other. It rolls over to Chester's headstone nearby. Elcira chuckles and smiles. She knew they would choose a form-fitting their mischievous nature. "I don't need you now, Sisters," she says, shooing them off. They circle overhead and then fly over the umbrellas, cawing. Maybe that will prove to be a mistake. They are hard to handle, those twins. But they love to have fun.

Elcira steps over Chester's grave, superstitious about waking him. That would be a very sticky situation indeed. She looks toward the main house on the hill above the pond. Progress has paved roads, built homes, and sprinkled the dale with wealthy residents who have developed traditions and legacies of their own. The road from the church winds its way to the carriage house and beyond, to the long drive of the main house and the park-like estate.

Mildred has served her heritage well. Elcira could see some of herself in the woman standing guard at the end of a long line of strong Cranberry women, defending all she holds dear. Is it time to let go? Or will the tradition continue? Mildred will need to learn more about what it took to hold onto this land, how it held a family together, and almost tore it apart.

This is what has pulled her back here, another battle, she's sure of it. She usually ferries someone home and leaves, but a strange attraction holds her here. It must have something to do with the missing key.

She approaches as the men in black carry Gertrude's coffin to its resting spot.

"She's gone home," says Pastor Tilton, carrying his black book in one hand and an umbrella in the other. "Hers was a good life."

Did he know that for a fact? He's so young. How can he know anything about Gertrude's life? All he knows is what the ladies of Elcira's old garden club passed along. Those are the keepers of the secrets, the keepers of tradition.

Jacqueline pushes her way forward, her red umbrella bumping its way through the crowd while her walking stick jabs the wet grass. "Gertrude was the oldest member of the garden club. Sylvie holds that title now. Where is she, anyway? And where is that annoying niece of hers?"

Tilly's wheelchair motors its way behind the crowd. Elcira chooses to stay out of sight, knowing that Tilly has spotted her before.

"I expected Mildred and Sylvie to be here," says Pastor Tilton. "I thought Mrs. Rose wanted to say a few words for her friend."

"Friend?" Jacqueline laughs. "Is that what this club is all about? It's amazing it has survived so long."

Jacqueline positions herself at the graveside. "It just goes to show you. If Mildred cannot bother to show up to usher off the most senior member of our club, perhaps it is time she step down and let someone younger and wiser lead. Forget the afternoon teas. We need to get back to being a real women's club."

Elcira chuckles. If she only knew what it was like in her day. They wouldn't have put up with someone like Jacqueline. What is the bee in her bonnet anyway?

Several of the women prattle away, leaving poor Pastor Tilton standing in the rain with an open Bible and no real audience.

"Let us pray," he says, attempting to get their attention.

Jacqueline manages to grab someone's ear. Elcira can hear her commenting about everything from the weather to the way the sun glistens off her husband's limestone vault.

Elcira slips behind Jacqueline to where the young, dark-skinned woman stands resting her umbrella on her shoulder while tapping on and swiping her phone. She is the only one not dressed in black, with facial features similar to Deborah's, Elcira's friend, Deborah, is not buried here, though she would have been if Elcira had been alive when Deborah died. Deborah is buried in the Negro burial ground at the edge of the property, where the fields couldn't be plowed.

She visited Elcira when Elcira was sick with consumption, called the White Plague back then. It was Deborah who picked out this dress Elcira is wearing. "She will not be buried in black," Deborah said. She was by Elcira's side every day until the end. It is important for someone to be there for you when you go.

Elcira reads the text on Effie's phone.

I need your help to get the key so I can prove that Elcira killed her husband.

Elcira flips her wrist to knock the phone from Effie's hands. It lands in the grass at her feet.

"What the?" Effie turns entirely around, confused.

Nobody there.

Effie picks up the phone and dries it off with a tissue from her purse.

She stares at the screen and drops the phone again.

Elcira chuckles.

Below the text message is a new one.

Let's have some fun, shall we? - Elcira.

Mildred

Mildred stares at the wheelchair, remembering how difficult it was to get Sylvie from the car to her bed at home. A wheelchair can take her to her car, but then what? Will Maggie be able to come with her and help her get Sylvie into a hospital bed at home? If they can manage that, maybe the home care people can take over.

Sylvie opens her eyes and mumbles something.

"Do you want water?" asks Mildred, touching her hand. It's cold. She rubs it with both of her hands. Sylvie turns her head toward Mildred, blinking her eyes as if wincing in pain. She then rolls her eyes upward. Mildred reaches for a cup on the sink behind her and fills it with water. She offers it to Sylvie but she doesn't sip. The water drips down Sylvie's mouth onto the sheet.

"I'm not sure how we are going to do this, Auntie," she says, feeling her chest tighten again.

When Maggie returns from meeting with Security, the look on her face tells Mildred something is wrong.

"You're not going to believe this," says Maggie, pushing the wheelchair out into the hall. "They won't let us take her out in the wheelchair. We need an ambulance."

93

"Problem?" Sylvie looks at Mildred.

"We can deal with it, Auntie," Mildred says. She turns to Maggie. "Can we deal with it? What do we need to do?"

"We need Doctor Swan to release her." Maggie drops into the chair and checks her watch. "I have to call in if I'm not going to start my shift."

"Go," says Mildred. "Just tell me what to do." Mildred can't believe she hears herself saying this.

"Aunt Sylvie," says Maggie. "You definitely want to go home, right?"

"Yes, dear." Sylvie looks at Maggie, and then upward again, as if following a light or shadow. Sylvie's mouth forms a faint smile.

Mildred rings the buzzer and asks for Doctor Swan. "I'll get a release. Will the hospital provide the ambulance?"

"They will if we can show that we have the proper care at home." Maggie pulls a piece of paper from her bag. "This is the number for the home care agency we use for cancer patients. Call them and mention my name. They are excellent."

Mildred searches her bag for her phone and notices she has several messages. "Today was Gertrude's funeral. I totally forgot."

"Oh," says Sylvie still looking past Maggie. "Poor Gertie. Was it a nice funeral?"

Maggie looks at Mildred. "Is she talking to me?"

"I don't think so," says Mildred. "We didn't go, Auntie. We were here with you."

Maggie checks her watch again. "Text me if you need me." She walks over to Sylvie and kisses her on the cheek, then gives Mildred a hug and whispers in her ear, "I don't want you to be alone."

"We're not alone, dear," says Sylvie.

"Nothing wrong with your hearing," says Maggie. She stops in the doorway and throws Mildred a kiss.

Mildred touches Sylvie on the shoulder and then walks over to the window to make her call, keeping her eye on Sylvie, who seems to be in less discomfort as she continues to look toward the door.

Just as Mildred is finishing her call with the home care agency, an aide walks in and attends to Sylvie, unhooking the oxygen from the tank and attaching the hose to the wall connector, setting it for the proper flow.

"What are you doing?" Mildred rushes to Sylvie's bedside.

"The tank will be empty if I don't switch her over." The aide reconnects Sylvie's cables to the monitor. "This way we can keep an eye on her."

"But she is going to be released," says Mildred. "Does she really need oxygen?"

"I don't know anything about her being released, and you will need to talk to the nurse about the oxygen." She puffs up Sylvie's pillow, checks the container of urine and then the wick, and leaves.

"Is Doctor Swan coming soon?" Mildred asks, but the aide walks away without responding.

In the hall, orderlies shuffle patients back and forth, lining the walls with gurneys and stretchers awaiting treatment or triage. Emergency Medical Technicians gather at the central nurse's station. The patient in the other half of the room, partitioned off by a curtain, moves out to make room for the next patient. Mildred paces back and forth, looking out for Doctor Swan.

A nurse passes by the room, and Mildred grabs her arm. "I need to talk to Doctor Swan. Could you get her for me?"

A security guard grabs Mildred's arm and pulls her away. "You need to be patient, or I will remove you."

Mildred pulls her arm back. "I would like nothing better, but I am taking my aunt with me."

The guard calls for backup and grabs her arm again.

"What are you doing?" Mildred's knees grow weak.

"I warned you," he says. He starts pulling her.

"Let go of me!" Mildred fights back, but she is not strong enough to resist.

The guard pulls the wheelchair close and pushes Mildred into it.

Mildred grabs her phone and texts Maggie.

They're kicking me out. Help.

Immediately Mildred's phone rings.

"Grandma, where are you?"

Mildred puts the call on speaker because the guard is pulling at her arm. "I am being escorted out of the E.R."

"I am just bringing you to the waiting room, that's all," says the guard. He wheels her through the double doors.

"Take me off speaker and put him on," says Maggie.

Mildred gives the phone to the guard. He keeps a lock on her arm.

"Yes, Doctor," he says, "I understand, but she is being difficult and the E.R. is overcrowded. I can come and get her when Doctor Swan is free."

The guard's rigid facial features melt. He hands the phone back to Mildred.

"Maggie?"

"He's overstepping, and he knows it. I will be down there as soon as I can get away. In the meantime, sit tight."

"What about Aunt Sylvie?" Mildred looks back at the double doors separating her from Aunt Sylvie. "I don't want to leave her alone."

"Give me a little time," Maggie says. "I have to go."

"Just sit here," says the guard, pulling her arm to direct her into a chair.

"You are hurting me," says Mildred.

He releases her, steers the wheelchair into a corner of the room, and heads back to his post at the entrance to the Emergency Room.

All eyes in the room are on Mildred. She straightens out her skirt and puts her phone in her purse. The visitor badge stuck to her purse gives her an idea. She gets up and walks over to the guard at his post.

He raises his eyes from his paperback without raising his head.

"Ladies room?" she asks.

Without looking at her he points. "Down the hall, make a right, second door on the left."

"Past the E.R.?"

"Yes. See where those EMTs are?"

"Thank you," she says.

At the end of the hall are the doors to where the ambulances unload. Two EMTs are escorting a patient on a stretcher through an entrance to the Emergency Room, not far from Sylvie's room. Of course. They have another way to get in, one that avoids the guard.

The doors close and lock just as Mildred arrives. She looks back. The guard is watching her. She points to the restrooms, he nods, and she walks toward them, out of sight.

There, outside the unisex restroom, she waits.

After a few minutes, the doors to the E.R. swing open with a crash as an EMT pushes a stretcher through and turns it so he can direct it through the doors to the ambulance. Mildred steps aside, circles the stretcher, and slips through the doors, hoping the guard hasn't seen her.

Holding her purse in front of her face to show the visitor pass, she returns to Sylvie's room.

As she enters, she feels someone or something push her out of the way and exit, knocking Mildred against the wall. She looks to see who that was.

"Auntie? Are you okay?" asks Mildred, righting herself.

"Millie, I'm so glad you're here. She was here looking for the key. I put it in my bag. We can't lose it." Sylvie's heart monitor is erratic.

Mildred runs to her and holds her hand. "You're shaking. Who was here?"

Mildred's own heart is pumping feverishly in her chest. She puts her hand on Sylvie's forehead. It is cool and clammy. No fever. Could it have been a hallucination? But who pushed her?

"I think it was her."

"Who?" asks Mildred, using her fingers to comb Sylvie's damp hair away from her face.

" Elcira."

Kendal

Monday

The view of the courthouse from the diner across the street is impressive. Every window along the old-style railroad car design faces the building, which receives the morning sun as a golden sheen on the granite stones. They are etched and pitted to reflect the light unevenly rather than create a blinding light that snorts traffic.

Kendal enters holding the door handle with one hand and the door frame with the other, steadying himself for the walk to the table where Effie is sitting. A booth wouldn't do. He needs a solid chair that he can place far enough from the table for him to be able to breathe and eat. Effie nods to him and waves him to come as she sips her coffee. Kendal grabs the back of several occupied chairs as he makes his way to the table, ignoring the looks from the patrons he disturbs along the way. He pulls out the chair and calls the waitress over.

"Do you have something sturdier than this?"

She looks at him and the chair and chuckles. "Nope. Don't break it, or it goes on your bill."

He makes a face and grumbles. As he drops onto the chair he makes a sound like a balloon deflating. He checks his pocket watch and turns to Effie. "So, what's so urgent?"

Kendal yanks at his jacket to cover the stain on his shirt as he adjusts his ass in the chair. "I have a one o'clock."

"Not even a hello? After all that we've been through?"

He catches her looking him over. "What?"

"Nice outfit. Is that how you are going to your one o'clock?" She puts her cup in its saucer and raises a hand for the waitress.

He looks at his lavender and tan checked shirt, which he is wearing untucked, even though it was not one of those designed to be worn that way, and adjusts his corduroy jacket. He shrugs and raises his hands. "You know why I agreed to be here. Tell me, what did you find?"

The waiter comes by, and Kendal orders a coffee.

Effie pulls some papers from her bag and places them on Kendal's place-mat. "I've been doing my investigative work, just as you taught me."

Kendal flips through the papers and his brow wrinkles.

"Henry Townsend?" He lifts a document and reads. The waiter arrives with his coffee, placing it beside the place-mat on the table before him.

"It's my great-great-grandfather's death certificate." She smiles. "Look who is listed as the father."

"It says Chester H. Cranberry. Do you have a birth certificate as well?" He scratches his head.

"No," she says. "Nothing on file. Back then, not all births were recorded, especially for Black folks."

"He was a Cranberry? But his name was Townsend?" He sips his coffee and then pours some sugar from a glass dispenser. He stirs, sips, and pours some more.

She waits for him to look at her. "Deborah Townsend was his mom. She had sex with Chester, but she never married."

"Wait," he says, reaching for more sugar. "She had sex with him, or he raped her?"

"What difference does it make?"

"Are you serious?" He pushes the coffee aside and studies the papers more closely. "I don't think this will hold up in court, Effie. And if you do find a birth certificate, I bet my collection of Howdy Doody memorabilia that it won't have Chester's name on it."

"You have a Howdy Doody collection?"

"Never mind." He folds the paper and hands it back to her. "Where did you find this? Are there more documents about Henry and Chester? Is it even real?"

"Oh, it's real. Pastor Tilton gave me access to the church archives. They are in the process of digitizing them. Mrs. Hudson funded the project."

"Jacqueline Hudson?" Kendal adds cream to his coffee. "Why would she do that?"

"Something to do with her husband, Preston, I think. Anyway, I was just as surprised as you to see these records survived. And Chester's name is on it. You don't think this is incriminating evidence?"

"It's enough for a journalist to make a headline, but that's about all," he says.

"With this, I can get a court order."

"Whoa, Nelly! Just because you think you can link yourself to Chester doesn't mean you are entitled to a part of his estate." He flips through the rest of the documents.

"I don't want a part of the estate. I want it all." Effie whips her braids and smiles.

"I see you found a printed transcript of the judge's ruling on the matter of Elcira's alleged guilt. Did you find any original court documents or just these newspaper clippings?" He reads the document and sips his coffee, abandoning it again after tasting it. "This coffee is worse than in my office, which says a lot."

"Most of the records are clippings from your paper. You did good work back then."

"Don't be funny."

"Admit it, you're old as a California Redwood."

"Did you read through all of this?"

"Of course."

"Then you know it's inadmissible. Elcira was found innocent of the murder."

"Insufficient evidence was the reason the judge let her go. They couldn't figure out how Elcira could have killed Chester with two pitchfork stabs through his vitals in the barn and then wind up locked in the potting shed when the only key was in Chester's pocket."

He reaches for his coffee and then pushes it away again. "You're not digging up that old wives tale about her having a second key, are you? No such key was ever found."

"That's because they didn't look for it, at least not in the right place."

He looks at the menu and then checks his watch. "And where do you think they should they have looked?"

"The outhouse."

He puts his coffee down. "Are you telling me she swallowed the key?"

"They didn't do a cavity search on her."

"You have a wild imagination, Miss Devine."

"Well? It's worth looking there, isn't it?"

"I'm not saying you have something here, Effie, but knowing you like I do, I'm sure you can spin a story some folks are likely to believe."

"Thank you. I think." She grinned. "Next stop, the courthouse. Judge Philips likes me."

"Wait a minute," says Kendal. "Philips has thrown out cases like this before. Besides, he's, you know." Kendal circles his ear with his index finger.

"All I need him to do is allow me to look for the key."

"On Mildred's property?" Kendal laughs. "Now I get it." He points his finger at her, circling her head and face. "The spray tan, braided hair, and puffy lips are all part of the deal, right? You think you can convince Philips that you are the rightful heir because you are descended from Henry, and he probably wouldn't give you the time of day if you still looked like the Effie I hired as an intern years ago."

She smiles at him and picks up her papers.

"Okay, Miss Devine," he says. Kendal knows her too well to let her go off without supervision on this. Besides, there may be a story in it, and he could use a boost in circulation. No one wants to buy newspaper publishers anymore, but a story about a two-hundred-year-old cold case could get national interest and maybe a movie deal. "I'm going, Kendal. I'll pay at the counter." Effie stands. Her chair flies out from under her, scraping the floor and stopping several feet back.

"Kendal! You're impossible."

Kendal leans across the table, his jaw free to hang loose. "I didn't do that."

Effie flips him off and leaves.

Kendal gets up and walks around the table, looking for an explanation.

"Can I help you?" asks the waitress.

"I'm good," he says. But he is not good. He trained Effie. He knows what she is capable of. She has always been a bit of a loose cannon, easier to control when she was a high schooler. He looks at his watch. He has some time before his one-o'clock. Maybe he should have a talk with Jacqueline. What is she trying to dig up about Preston? Maybe he was wrong to ignore the goings on of that ladies' garden club. It seems all of these women have secrets that could make for interesting stories.

Sylvie

MONDAY

Sylvie counts her breaths, her eyes on the clock on the partial wall outside the room where she has been planted all day. Each time the second hand reaches twelve, she starts again. One. Two. Three. If she is not distracted, if no one comes in and talks to her, prods her, sticks her, or blocks her view, she can make the full loop. But each time she tries, she fails to keep count for the minute. How many breaths in a minute is good? Thirty-nine? Twenty-five? Certainly not less than that. Or should she be noting any dramatic change? If it drops too low, will she be able to remember why she is counting? Ten. Eleven. What was the total the last time?

"Mrs. Rose, do you remember me? I'm Chaplain Nguyen."

The olive-skinned gentleman with the black hair and beard isn't wearing a mask. Should he be? The woman in white standing behind him doesn't speak.

"Can we talk, or should I get your niece?" He points to the empty chair as if Mildred will magically appear there at will.

"She was kicked out," says Sylvie. "But I think she's back. Maybe in the bathroom. Can you see who is behind you?"

He turns around. An orderly is pushing a gurney past the doorway. "He works here," he says.

"Her," she says. She raises her hand slightly and tries to point.

He grabs her hand and wraps his fingers around her wrist.

"You're hands are cold. Do you want a blanket?"

"I want to go home." Sylvie can't take her eyes off the woman. "I saw you before," she says. She knows who it is she sees. It is the woman she has seen in a beautiful dress of gray and white with lace, and at other times like this, in white, floating, looking like an angel.

"Yes," says the chaplain, "I was here earlier."

Sylvie drops her hand and lowers her head onto the pillow. Another woman enters and walks through the woman in white. "I know who you are," says Sylvie to the woman in white.

"I am Nurse Lovett. I was here earlier as well. How are you feeling?"

The woman in white is Elcira. Sylvie watches her slip through Nurse Lovett and the bed, stopping at Mildred's chair. Sylvie remains glued to her.

"She is having trouble concentrating," says the chaplain. "Perhaps she has been sedated."

Elcira reaches for the bag holding Sylvie's clothes.

"It's not in there," says Sylvie. "I moved it."

"Who are you talking to Mrs. Rose?" asks the nurse.

Mildred rushes into the room and bumps into the couple. "Oh. What's going on here?"

"We thought we could have a meeting to discuss Mrs. Rose's care," says the chaplain.

"You did, did you?"

Elcira slips out of the room.

"She's gone," says Sylvie. "I'm glad you're back, Millie. These people keep me from counting my breaths."

"Why are you counting your breaths, Mrs. Rose?" asks Nurse Lovett.

"Thirty-five a minute? Is that good?" asks Sylvie.

Mildred turns to the pair and points to the door. "I tracked down Doctor Swan and convinced her to sign a release for you, Auntie. We are leaving."

Sylvie feels her whole body ease into the bed. The painkiller they had been giving her leaves a dull throbbing in her leg and abdomen, but she's going home. She can relax.

"I must advise you against such an action. It is totally unwise in her condition."

"Chaplain Win, is it? If you knew me better, you would know that wisdom is not my strongest attribute," says Mildred. "Now, if you don't mind, I have an ambulance waiting outside, so please call the nurse to unhook my aunt."

Mildred looks at Nurse Lovett. "Can you do it? Or do you just stand around looking pretty?"

Nurse Lovett stomps her heel and leaves, followed by the chaplain.

"I guess looking pretty was the job description. Now, Auntie, what were you saying?" Mildred leans close and adjusts her pillow.

Sylvie reaches under the sheet and pulls out a brass key. "Put this in your purse, so she can't get it."

"Who?"

Sylvie opens her eyes wide and stares at the door.

"Oh," says Mildred. "Is she back?"

"She will be. I think she'll be coming with us." Sylvie takes a breath and stares at the clock again. One. Two.

The commotion picks up as people enter and leave, unhooking this, switching that, pulling and poking, and all the while blocking her view of the clock.

"They're here," says Mildred, as two paramedics arrive with a travel gurney.

"We have the orders," says the taller man, his muscles stretching his uniform.

"I'll switch your oxygen and transfer the I.V.. Then we can lift you up and get you out of here," the shorter one says. His uniform is stretched as well, but not because of muscles.

"Twenty-one. Twenty-two."

"What are you doing, Auntie," asks Mildred.

"Counting breaths," she says. "Now where was I?"

Sylvie looks back at the clock. "One."

Mildred

As they emerge from the hospital Emergency entrance, where the private ambulance is waiting, Mildred feels the sudden change in temperature, from the air-conditioned hospital air to the humid afternoon heat. The sun is sitting low in the western sky, painting the surrounding buildings an orange-yellow, almost surreal. While the paramedics load Sylvie into the ambulance, Millie hands the valet the ticket for her car; She turns to look at Maggie on her phone at the doors to the ER.

"You coming?" she asks.

"I'll get an Uber," she says. "I'll meet you there."

When Mildred arrives at the Carriage House, there are several cars in the driveway, including an Access-A-Ride, indicating that Tilly is there. Mildred parks her car on the street to give the ambulance room to unload Aunt Sylvie and eyeballs the cars as she walks past. One car stands out. It is Jacqueline's black Escalade. Harold is not at his usual post behind the wheel. Most of the garden club must be here.

As she opens the door, Tilly's motorized wheelchair approaches. "I called the hospital, and the nurse said you were taking Sylvie home, so here we are."

"I don't understand," says Mildred. She follows Tilly into the garden room, with its glass doors open, extending the room out onto the patio and across the lawn to the rose garden. "You set up the hospital bed in here?"

One of the healthcare aides rushes over to her. "Mrs. Cranberry, I'm Elsa, and that's Petra over there. We will be here tonight until the morning, and then we will be relieved. Someone will be here around the clock. I believe that is what you ordered."

"Yes," says Mildred looking over the two women who might be mother and daughter. Elsa, the older one, has a few missing teeth, and Petra has a butterfly tattoo on her left arm.

"Mildred, I know Sylvie likes to look at her roses, so I told them to put the bed here." Tilly spins her wheelchair around to admire the view.

Jacqueline taps her ebony walking stick on the tile floor as she walks the perimeter of the room toward the patio, avoiding the bed and Mildred. "I was so sorry to hear that Sylvie was in the hospital. I guess it couldn't be helped that you both missed the funeral. Pastor Tilton did a fine job."

Before Mildred could respond, the paramedics wheel Sylvie in and use the pad under her to lift her onto the hospital bed. Immediately, the aides swap out the oxygen tank for the oxygen concentrator, a suitcase-sized machine that pulses fresh oxygen through a tube to the patient with a swoosh and click that is continuous.

Sylvie waves for Mildred to come to her. Mildred leans close enough to hear Sylvie whisper, "The key." She holds out her hand.

Mildred hesitates but doesn't want to cause a scene, so she wraps the key in tissues and slips it into Sylvie's hand. She places it under her leg.

Mildred scans the room to see if anyone noticed, but all are busy putting flowers in vases, clearing the table of clutter and opening the doors from the room to the patio.

"Tilly," says Sylvie. "Come here."

Abigail walks over swaying side to side like a lame duck. She holds her cell phone up and takes a selfie with Sylvie.

"Abigail, please," says Tilly, pushing her out of the way with her wheelchair. She leans as close to Sylvie as she can, facing the opposite direction. Standing on the patio, Jacqueline leans on her walking stick, facing the garden.

What's Sylvie up to now? She seems stronger since she arrived home.

Sylvie reaches under her leg and hands the key to Tilly, saying, "Hold this for me."

Mildred rushes to Sylvie's side, blocking the view from the patio. She whispers, "Auntie, what are you doing?"

Sylvie looks up at Mildred with wide eyes. "You have enough to worry about."

"But, Auntie," says Mildred. This is not smart. They should hold onto the key here.

Maggie arrives and puts her bag down on the floor. "Oh, my! You're all here."

Sylvie falls back into her pillow, the head of the bed raised so she can see the last rays of sunlight turn Jacqueline into a sinister shadow.

"Doctor Payton?" The older aide approaches her. "We have instructions to medicate as needed."

"We can hold off and give everyone a chance to spend some time with Auntie," says Mildred. "Is that okay, Maggie?"

"Yes," says Maggie, removing her white coat. "Let's make this a party."

Tilly pushes a button on her wheelchair and music starts to play. "It's the Eagles," she says. "My favorite."

Mildred backs away to give Sylvie some space. Tilly starts singing out of tune and Abigail joins in. Sylvie smiles and then winces. She's in pain. Mildred scans the room, and she believes this may be everyone's chance to say goodbye to her aunt. In the mirror over the fireplace, Mildred watches the scene as if it is on a TV screen and imagines it will be how she remembers this moment. A figure in white appears behind her and leans over the bed. Mildred snaps her head around to see who it is, but no one is there.

Jacqueline taps Mildred on the shoulder, causing her to jump.

"Bad timing, isn't it?" asks Jacqueline. What did she mean by that? Knowing Jacqueline, it could mean anything. It's her way of trying to catch Mildred off guard, unaware. This rivalry has been going on too long, but since Preston passed away, it has escalated. What did she discover? Would she have built a monument to his life in the cemetery if she knew? Maybe she didn't know then.

Jacqueline doesn't wait for a response but starts walking toward the front door. Suddenly, her walking stick slips from her hand, and she falls against the fireplace mantel, catching herself in time.

"You did that," she says to Mildred.

"I am nowhere near you, Jac-lene." Mildred feigns concern. "Petra, perhaps you can escort Mrs. Hudson to the door?"

"Of course." The young aide runs over, but Jacqueline grabs her walking stick and stands with regal arrogance.

"I can manage myself, thank you."

At the door, Jacqueline bumps into Harriet and Sam.

"Oh, Mrs. Hudson, I'm so sorry," says Sam, but she keeps going without saying a word.

Mildred turns to Sam. "Did you see Harold out there? He wasn't in the car when I arrived."

"No," he says.

"I'm back here, Mrs. Cranberry," says Harold. I was staying out of the way. "I guess I had better follow her before she starts yelling for me."

Mildred wonders if Harold saw Sylvie give the key to Tilly. That key in Jacqueline's hands could spell disaster.

Harriet walks over to the bed and gives Sylvie a big hug. "I'm so sorry, dear," she says.

"You two know each other?" asks Mildred. She looks at Sam and Maggie.

"We met at the hospital," says Harriet.

Sam stiffens up and looks at Maggie.

"I am always the last to know what is going on," says Mildred. She

110

leaves them, walks out to the garden bench, and sits, letting the cooler evening air slip over her.

Why is Jacqueline here? What is she plotting? This can't be about the garden club. If it was, if it had to do with her wanting to take over as president, she would have shown some compassion and concern for Sylvie in front of all her friends in the club. She barely acknowledged her. And why was Howard lurking in the background?

She closes her eyes and takes a deep breath. Lilacs. There it is again. Why does she smell lilacs, and what are these strange visions? It has to be that someone is trying to drive her crazy. Well, it's working.

Mildred

TUESDAY

Mrs. Cranberry."

Mildred awakens to Petra shaking her shoulder. A bit disoriented, she looks around the room and realizes she is in Sylvie's bedroom.

"Mom and I are leaving. Philomena here is taking over."

Mildred lifts her head. The woman behind Petra is nearly double her size in height and width. "How's Aunt Sylvie?"

"She didn't have a good night, as you know, but she is resting now," says Petra.

"I will keep an eye on her," says Philomena, her voice deep and hollow. "I had to park down the street because of the truck and police cars."

"What?" Mildred sits up and swings her legs from the bed. She is still in her clothes from the day before, having spent most of the night at Sylvie's side.

Without stopping to check on her aunt, Mildred runs to the front door. She opens it to see a tall, Black officer about to push the doorbell.

"Mrs. Cranberry?" He produces a document for her. "I have a court order from Judge Philips to search your property."

"What? Let me see that." Mildred grabs the paper and scans it. "Ephedra Devine?"

"Yes, she's the one who sought the order."

"What are you looking for?" asks Mildred, while continuing to read the order. "You are going to dig up my property to find a key?"

"I know," he says, turning to point to the backhoe being unloaded from the flatbed trailer. "All this for a key. Seems odd to me, but that's what it says."

"You can't do this. I have a very sick woman here and she cannot be disturbed." Mildred opens the door wider so he can see Sylvie in the hospital bed.

"I'm just following orders, ma'am." He steps back from the door. "We'll be out of here as soon as we can."

"No, no. No. You will not dig up my aunt's garden. It will kill her." Mildred leaves him at the door and runs for her cell phone to call Judge Philips.

One of the contractors comes to the door and sticks his head in. "Ma'am, could you move your car so we can bring the backhoe around to the back?"

Mildred ignores him. The phone rings several times without an answer. It doesn't go to voicemail, but does get picked up by someone else.

"I need to talk to Judge Philips, now." Mildred stomps her foot.

"Millie?" Sylvie points to the garden. "My roses."

Men in yellow shirts, brown pants and work boots stand around the rose garden, holding shovels.

"I'm sorry, but Judge Philips is unable to come to the phone right now, and he will be in court all day."

"When will he be in court?" Mildred walks to the door to the patio and opens it to yell at the workers. "Don't you dare start digging. I am getting Judge Philips to cancel this order."

"He will be in court from nine o'clock on," says the woman on the phone.

"I will be right down there to catch him. Don't let him go in until

I get there." Mildred hangs up the phone and turns to Philomena.

"Keep Aunt Sylvie comfortable while I run down to the courthouse."

"What's happening, Millie?" asks Aunt Sylvie.

"They are looking for your damn key."

"But it's not there," she says. "Tell them."

"What does she mean? How does she know it's not there?" the officer asks.

"What if I told you she already dug it up?" asks Mildred, looking to avoid having Sylvie's garden destroyed.

"That would be fine," he says. "Then you can just give it to me, and we can leave."

"No," she says, suddenly seeing an option she hadn't realized. "The order here doesn't require me to do that."

"Hmm," he says, rubbing his chin. "I have to check with the court on that."

"I was just about to go down there, but I trust you can do that and leave us alone. Judge Philips will be available until nine. Get him before he goes into the courtroom."

"So, what do I tell him?" he asks.

"That's up to you."

"I'm going to leave the men and equipment here while I straighten this out."

"And pay for a whole day of them doing nothing? I don't think your superiors will be too happy with you."

"You're right." He walks away and gives a hand signal to gather the men.

Mildred can't believe that worked. The only problem is now they know the key is not there. Tilly has it, and she is Effie's aunt. Bad timing is right. Could Jacqueline have known?

"Auntie, I have to go get that key," says Mildred.

Sylvie drops her head back into her pillow. Mildred opens the door and realizes she is still in yesterday's clothes and hasn't even brushed her teeth or hair.

After changing and freshening up, she gets in her car and pulls out of the drive determined to get that key.

As she pulls away, she notices something in her rearview mirror. It looks like a white garbage bag, maybe attached to the bumper, billowing in the wind. She pulls over and gets out. Nothing there. Perhaps it blew away.

The entrance to Tilly's first-floor condo is the only one in the development with a handicap ramp, so it is easy to spot. Mildred pulls the car into a visitor spot and walks up the ramp. The door opens, and Tilly approaches in her wheelchair. In her hand is a remote.

"I saw you pull up," says Tilly. "You want the key, don't you?"

"How do you know? Don't tell me one of your spirits told you."

There is an aroma of incense and possibly marijuana. The living room is dark, with shades pulled and only a little sunlight visible around the edges.

"Someone named Philomena called for Sylvie."

"Why did she give you the key?" Mildred walks around her, looking to spot the key on a table or counter.

"She told me the key is the only way this nonsense about the property will be put to bed. I am sure that is why Elcira is here. She cannot rest until the key is back where it belongs." Tilly tilts her head as though listening to voices. "Then, again, she could be here to take Sylvie home, like with Gertrude. But I saw a cardinal this morning, and I'm sure Gertrude sent it to let me know she is with me. It gets so confusing."

Mildred leans toward her. "The key?"

Tilly motors over to the kitchen and opens the freezer drawer. She pulls out a plastic container. "I put it on ice. Literally."

Through the transparent container, Mildred can see the key is in a block of ice. "This is all bizarre. Are you saying that I can make Elcira go away if I put the key back in the ground?"

"I think so," she says. "But maybe not."

"So you don't know. But if I put it back, they will dig it up and take it."

Tilly hands her the container. "Here."

Mildred reaches for it and then hesitates. "I can't have it."

"You can keep it here. It will be safe in my freezer. No one will look for it there." Tilly puts the container back in the freezer and covers it with a bag of cauliflower rice.

"But what about your niece?"

"She doesn't stay with me." Tilly spins her wheelchair around. "Jacqueline has put her up."

"That explains a lot." Mildred follows Tilly back to the living room. She looks for a place to sit, but magazines and books occupy every available space.

"It's my fault," says Tilly. "Too much clutter for her. Since Effie came back, she's changed."

"I've noticed." Mildred leans close to Tilly, her hands on the arms of the wheelchair. "I can trust you, right?"

"Mildred! We've known each other a long time, since before David was born."

"I'm sorry, but I believe this attempt to get the key is all Jacqueline's doing. I need to find a way to settle this stupid battle with her once and for all. It's gone on too long."

"Are you sure you are willing to do that? You know word will get out."

Mildred backs away from Tilly's wheelchair.

"Sylvie wants me to get the club to help. I can do that without letting Jacqueline know. I can also call my son David," says Tilly.

"I don't know about getting the club involved. They pretty much let Jacqueline do what she wants, but I was going to ask if I could talk to David. He is always in court, mostly in Manhattan."

"He has a local client, someone big. He has been working locally for a couple of weeks."

"We can't let Jacqueline know what we're doing, though," says Mildred, walking back to the door.

"Keep your phone charged. I'll call you when I have a plan." Mildred steps out into the sun, feeling her face flush with heat. Walking down the ramp, she spots two black crows perched on the telephone line behind her car. That can't be a good sign.

Mildred's phone rings.

"Mrs. Cranberry, this is Officer Lloyd. I was at your home this morning. I am here with Judge Philips and he wants to talk with you."

Mildred drops into the driver's seat of her car and puts the call on speaker so she can put the phone down.

"I understand you have a problem obeying my court order," says Judge Philips in a gravelly voice.

"Your order is to find a key that is no longer on the property so you can have the equipment removed," says Mildred.

"I'm afraid that's not how this works," he says, "but there is a way to resolve this."

"Good," she says, feeling victorious.

"I am amending the order."

"What?"

"It now says they can search the property for remnants of the old potting shed."

"What do you mean, remnants? What specifically are you looking for?" She can feel the blood rushing to her face.

"Apparently there were two keys to the lock on the shed, one that was recovered on the body of Chester Cranberry and one that is missing. If we can find the lock, we can see if the key we have in the archive fits it. If it does, then I will amend the order to find that second key, which is somewhere in your possession."

"Are you kidding me? You are going to dig up my property for a two-hundred-year-old lock? It would be so corroded and rusted that it couldn't have survived. And it definitely won't work."

"I am sending Officer Lloyd back, and the operation will commence immediately."

With that, the call disconnects.

Mildred dials Tilly. She needs to meet with David immediately and get him to write a restraining order."

The two crows caw loudly and fly away.

Mildred

Mildred takes long, forceful strides down the hallway, checking the office doors for a name she recognizes, anything "Castleby" but specifically, "James Castleby," the owner of this business. She can hear her steps echo and feel her stomach grumble. The bustle of business is hauntingly absent, even though it is a weekday. She needs to get in and get out quickly and not leave Aunt Sylvie for too long.

"Can I help you?" A young woman approaches. "Do you have an appointment?"

"Do I need one? There's no one here."

"It would be better if you'd scheduled an appointment. The team is busy at job sites." She pulls her hair back over her ears, making it look like she intends to listen.

"Really?" Mildred makes no effort to hide her feelings. "You're that busy, are you? Too busy to take my calls, so I decided to come down and see what I'm up against."

"I don't like your tone."

"I get that a lot lately. I must be going through my changes." She looks around at the empty offices. "Where can I find Castleby?"

"Which one?"

"The bastard who's men and equipment are digging up my garden. That one!"

"I'm sorry, but you need to calm down."

"Why? Are you going to call security?" Mildred laughs. "Good luck with that. It looks like you're ready to close up shop."

"What's going on here?" James marches toward them. "Oh, Mildred. Good to see you. Please come with me. I want to show you something."

"Now that wasn't too hard, was it?" Mildred scrunches her face at the unhelpful assistant and follows James to the conference room, where a model of a multi-home community sits on the table.

"Look, James," she says, not looking at his model. "I need to get back to my aunt. She is very ill."

"I'm sorry," he says, walking around to the other side of the table.

She is about to accuse him for authorizing his men to dig up her property when she notices some familiar details in the model. "So this is what you think you will build on my property when Sam and Maggie marry? A bit presumptuous, don't you think?"

"Not at all," says James, pointing to the model. "I just like to be ready for opportunities when they arrive."

"And how long were you waiting for this opportunity to just fall in your lap?" She walks around, looking at every detail.

"Mildred, I know how much work it is to manage this much property. Wouldn't it be better for Maggie to have a solid financial foundation for her future?"

"How much do you stand to make off this?"

"What do you mean?"

"Don't do that, James. You're too smart to play dumb with me."

"My company would build it, naturally. The revenue would pay for the construction and provide a healthy income for years to come. They will be able to live quite well."

Mildred puts her chin in her hand. "So, if you only care about my granddaughter's future, I will make it easy for her to start a new life. I

119

will sell the property now and give her the money. Then she will net more since she won't have to pay for the construction."

"No!" He reaches for her arm, but she pulls away. "It is the homes we build that will bring in the money. Each one will sell for six figures, maybe even seven for some, and we can fit over one-hundred-and-twenty homes on that property."

"So, if this is such a great deal, why didn't you present it to me rather than plot behind my back?"

"Are you kidding?" He laughs. "The whole community knows your feelings about tradition and keeping Old Cranberry as it was. But look around you. It has changed a lot, even with all you have done to hold onto the past."

She falls silent.

"Besides, you and I need to work together."

"Why?"

"Because this crazy person is planning to steal the property from you."

"Who? Effie? She is becoming a real pain in my ass. That's why I came here, to get you to call off your backhoe and put my garden back together."

"What are you talking about?"

"I was awakened this morning to a construction team trying to dig up my garden."

"That isn't me. None of my guys are on your property. She took one look at this model and laughed in my face, saying she will get the property from you and build something very different."

"You showed her this model before showing me?" Mildred turns to walk out, angry that she can't get him to call off the dogs.

"Effie doesn't have the money to battle for this property, so you don't have to worry."

"You don't either, but look what You're doing?" she snaps back at him. She remembers Jacqueline saying she saw Effie at the church. If she was digging up church records, this could be a bigger problem than she thought. Jacqueline. It must be Jacqueline who is funding her.

"I think I know who is behind this," says Mildred. "There is only one person with the money and vindictive nature to want to dig up my garden."

"Effie's got Lightfoot in her pocket, you know. Did you see today's paper?" He walks over to the credenza and grabs the newspaper to show her. "Go to page four."

Mildred opens the paper and starts reading. "Young Black Attorney Seeks Reparations for Centuries of Abuse? What? She's a lawyer now?"

"If you read on, it says she hasn't passed the bar, but she went to law school."

"Tilly didn't mention any of this. However, she is her adopted child. You would never have known she was black then."

"She was always a bit black. So, you can't fault her for claiming her heritage."

"She's full of it, and you know it." Mildred pulls out a chair and sits down.

James does the same and sits. Several moments pass without a word.

"I think we need to work together. We can stop her nonsense and then plan the future for our kids," says James.

Mildred looks at her watch and jumps up. "I can't spend any more time on this. I need to get back."

"But agree with me."

"I'm not agreeing to your plan."

"I'm not asking you to. Let's just call a truce for now."

"It's clear what she's up to. According to the article, she is looking to make this a referendum. With Lightfoot's help, that will attract national media. They will both become media stars and here, in Old Cranberry, we will look like a bunch of white privileged racists. What will that do to those property values you mentioned?"

"We need a good lawyer. I know someone who has worked with me on my projects."

"No," says Mildred, standing. "I can't let this go to court. I need to nip it in the bud. And if I need a lawyer, I'll get my own."

"You don't trust me."

"Would you?"

"What are you going to do?"

"I don't know yet. I need to talk with Maggie."

"This Effie is a sheep in wolf's clothing, if you catch my drift. She's using identity to send a message and possibly start a movement, and that could work today. Can we agree to work on this together?"

"I feel I am signing a pact with the devil."

"What a nice thing to say to a future in-law."

Jacqueline

Tuesday

Jacqueline taps the glass separating her from her driver and waits for him to acknowledge her.

Harold doesn't respond at first, making Jacqueline uneasy. The windshield wipers flip right to left and then pause. Jacqueline taps her foot counting off the seconds before he turns to acknowledge her.

"Yes, Ms. Hudson," he says, without turning around. "This is the place. Spangles in Arlingville."

His hesitation makes her stomach churn. The wiper blade makes another swishing motion, sliding the tiny droplets to one side or another.

"But it's an ice cream parlor!" She stares out the side window, looking for some sign that it is the right place. The droplets run toward each other, combining to speed up their descent. "Are you sure this is the place?"

"It's what you had on that piece of paper. Seven-thirty, Tuesday. It's Tuesday, and in a few minutes, it will be seven-thirty."

She places her face against the smoked glass window, not wanting to open it and reveal to anyone looking that she is inside. "But- There must be some mistake. This is no place for a liaison."

"It is if you're a child, ma'am," he says, pointing to a group of young women surrounded by kids.

She couldn't be wrong, could she? Would the young doctor choose an ice cream parlor for a rendezvous? She could hear Harold snickering even through the glass partition. Help. They have no respect. It's not like back home in Kentucky, where everyone knew their place. No one in service would do what he is doing, ignoring her like this. How rude. If she had half a mind, she would… what? She needs Harold, and he knows it. She's alone in this town, always has been, even when she thought she wasn't.

Jacqueline's lips press tightly together, twist to the right and then to the left as she runs the possibilities over and over in her mind. "Maybe she won't show, with her great aunt in such a poor state of health." She is looking for a reason to leave.

"Isn't that Doctor Payton leading the pack?"

"So it is," says Jacqueline. The wiper blade makes its pass, pauses and then, after an uneasy silence, passes again. "Go see what's going on." She taps again, and Harold opens his door. He steps out and leaves his door open while he reaches for her handle and opens hers.

"Do you want to stand at the door and watch? Or perhaps I can go in and FaceTime you?" He looks down at her as she looks up and down as if studying him. He opens an umbrella for her.

He's goading her. "No, Harold. I will go see for myself. No point in making a scene. It's bad enough I have to go in."

"Yes, ma'am." As she walks away, he says, "I would love a sundae, though."

As Jacqueline walks across the street, a car pulls up, and a heavy-set man emerges, lifting his sports jacket over his head as if he needed protection from the light rain.

Kendal? she whispers to herself. Now, I really need to know what is going on.

The noise inside is deafening, with bells and clangs accompanying slaps of clappers on the wall of pinball machines to her right. She skulks along the wall, keeping her walking stick from touching the floor, thinking she needed to avoid making a sound. She walks as far as the video game machines and leans against the closest one to take a picture with her phone.

"Mrs. Hudson, what a pleasant surprise!" Maggie says. "How did you hear about our fundraiser? Or are you here to get some ice cream?"

Jacqueline struggles to hear her over the din. "Er - Of course, dear. I couldn't have you raise money for such a good cause without getting in on the act." What is she trying to pull? Several tables of parents are sitting at one end of the room, farthest from the pinball machines and video games, while the children in wheelchairs, on crutches, and one in a reclining chair are giggling and chatting with each other, taking turns to toss balls into baskets or shoot water guns at balloons.

"Come, say hello to the parents. They will be so pleased to have such a wonderful benefactor as you help with their children's serenity garden at the new cancer center when it's built. I plan to talk about this at the next Garden Club Luncheon."

Jacqueline places a finger in one ear as she passes the shouting kids and noisy machines, following Maggie to one of the tables where parents and children are sitting with Kendal Lightfoot.

"Mr. Lightfoot, you know Mrs. Hudson, I believe." Maggie steps to the side so all can see Jacqueline.

"Of course, Maggie. We go way back, don't we, Jac-lene?"

"Way back indeed, Kendal." She smiles, eyeing his jeans and t-shirt. "A bit macho for you, don't you think?"

"I had a sports jacket, but it was wet, so I took it off," he says before licking the ice cream dripping from his cone. "Maggie told me all about this new children's garden planned for the hospital, and I think we should spread the word about it in the paper. Could I get your thoughts on the project?"

"And where do you plan on building this garden, Maggie?" Jacqueline closes her wandering eye to focus on Maggie's face.

One of the fathers approaches the table with two cups of ice cream in each hand, plastic spoons sticking out of them. "Who had the chocolate?" Hands raise, and he doles out the treats to the cheers of a boy and a girl, each wearing a colored scarf where their hair used to be.

"Mister Jackson, here has two children, twins, receiving chemotherapy."

"The existing atrium is just too crowded," he says. "It's overrun with elderly patients. This new garden will be perfect, and the children will be able to grow plants so they can focus on life and feel like they have some control," he says, choking up at the end. "Thank you, Doctor."

"So, are you interested?" asks Maggie of Jacqueline.

"But there is no room at the hospital," says Jacqueline.

"We will find space in the new children's cancer center," says Maggie. "With a large enough donation, we could name the garden for you or maybe for your husband, Preston. It would really be something to brag about at the Garden Club luncheons."

Jacqueline bites her lower lip. The sting of that comment lingers. Maggie is clever, but this sounds like Mildred's hand is in it.

Maggie looks at Kendal and then Jacqueline. She turns away, her hand covering her mouth.

"Doctor Payton?" One parent waves for Maggie to join them at their table. Jacqueline inches toward them so she can stay within earshot. "Children, what do you want to say to Doctor Payton?"

"Call me Maggie. You can all call me Maggie." She wipes a tear from her eye.

"Maggie?" One of the young girls, wearing a bow where her hair should be, motions for Maggie to bend close to her. "I love you!"

She kisses her on the cheek.

"You have done so much for our kids," the mother says, "not just the ones going through therapy, but their siblings as well. The play area you created makes coming to the hospital fun, and that is saying a lot. Thank you."

"I couldn't have said it better," one of the fathers chimes in.

"Many parents have complained that the children don't have

enough open space to play with their toys or sit together while they wait for their siblings, so the time is right for a children's garden."

"It's a fabulous idea," says one of the mothers.

"What do you say we have some ice cream?" Maggie looks at Jacqueline and smiles. "You too, Mrs. Hudson. And how about inviting your driver, Harold, in?"

Jacqueline finishes scratching her name on a check and hands it to Maggie. "You dropped that note on purpose, didn't you?"

"Now, would I be so cunning as to do something like that?"

"I believe you would, my dear. I believe you would." She picks up her phone and makes a call. "Harold, come in and get your sundae."

Mildred

TUESDAY

Mildred stares at the sandwich the aide, Philomena, prepared for her before leaving at the end of her shift. The mother-daughter team of Elsa and Petra adjust Sylvie's position in the bed and take turns attending to her. Sylvie has been quiet, except for her labored breathing, and the swoosh, click, thud sound of the oxygen concentrator. Several times, the repetition lulled Mildred to sleep.

Mildred's phone buzzes from its charging station on the mantel. She lowers her feet on the recliner and pushes against the arms to stand, her legs a bit tingly from lack of movement.

"I'll get it for you," says Petra, running to the fireplace. "Hello?"

Mildred leans against the frame of the bed to steady herself.

"Yes," Petra unplugs the phone and brings it to Mildred. "It's a pastor?"

Mildred takes the phone and goes back to her chair. "Pastor Tilton, thank you for returning my call."

"I got your message. I can come right over."

"Thank you."

Anything I can bring for you?

"No. Just come. Quick."

She ends the call and checks her messages. Nothing from Maggie.

Elsa checks Sylvie's pulse and increases the flow of oxygen.

Mildred bends over Sylvie and grabs her hand. "I know you can hear me, Auntie. Pastor Tilton is coming to see you."

She expects Sylvie to squeeze her hand, but it remains limp and cold in hers. Mildred looks at Elsa.

"Talk to her. It is good," Elsa says.

"Auntie, Maggie will be here soon. She is with the cancer kids and their parents having ice cream. Remember when Maggie was two and we took her for ice cream on the avenue? Audrey lifted her up to the counter so she could see all the flavors and Maggie was determined to have butter pecan."

Sylvie's hand closes around Mildred's and her eyes flutter.

"That's your favorite, too, isn't it?" Mildred's eyes fill up. She blinks away the tears.

Elsa whispers in Mildred's ear, "She can hear you."

Mildred replays memory after memory in her head, searching for the right words to share, recalling those precious few times they spent together as a family, all of them, while Maggie was growing up, while Audrey was taking night courses, when Alfred died.

"I wish we had spent more time enjoying life, Auntie. It seems all we talked about was the club and your roses."

Petra answers the doorbell.

Pastor Tilton approaches the bed, placing his book on a nearby chair. He nods at Mildred and leans over Sylvie.

"Auntie, Pastor Tilton is here."

"Hello, Sylvie. I promised I would come and visit you. I want you to know You're not alone."

Sylvie's eyes flutter, and she slowly turns her head toward him.

The sing-song rhythm of the oxygen concentrator is now out of pace with Sylvie's breathing, which has noticeably slowed. Her neck muscles strain with each breath, and Mildred counts as Sylvie had done in the hospital.

Pastor Tilton grabs his book. As he recites the prayers, his words seem to float between Mildred and Sylvie, not touching either.

"Whaaaah!" Sylvie cries out. Her eyes open wide, and she looks straight ahead between the pastor and Mildred.

"She sees something," says Mildred.

Elsa walks around the bed to join Mildred, passing through whatever Sylvie is looking at. "This is normal."

"Normal? Crying out like this is normal?" Mildred strokes Sylvie's hand. "I'm here, Auntie."

"It is part of the process," says Elsa.

Sylvie leans back, half-closing her eyes.

"The process? You mean—"

"Sylvie, may you find peace that passes all understanding, in the name of the Father, and the Son, and the Holy Ghost. Amen." Pastor Tilton anoints Sylvie.

Mildred stares at him, her eyes wide and accusatory. "You're letting her go?"

"Whoa! Whoosh who-oh!" Sylvie shouts and sits up again, this time looking frightened, her face almost pressed up against Mildred's.

Mildred puts her hands on Sylvie's face. "Calm down, Auntie. I am here with you."

"Moe mom Moe mamma whooh!" Sylvie's voice is deep, stronger than expected giving how she has been breathing.

"What is she saying?" asks Mildred, looking at Pastor Tilton and then Elsa. She stands and flaps her hands.

Elsa comes around behind Sylvie and wipes her brow while using her fingers to comb her hair from her face. "Don't be afraid. You are safe. You are loved."

Mildred catches her reflection in the mirror over the fireplace. Standing beside her is a woman with dark hair tied back, partially covered by a bonnet. She is dressed in a cream-colored dress with a black lace top and bottom. "What the—?"

Sylvie turns to the woman and in a low voice says, "Moe ma me lay Moe mom. Wah, wah, me, Moe mamma."

Mildred looks to where the woman in the mirror should be, but no one is there. She looks back at the mirror and turns to Pastor Tilton. "Look," she says, pointing to the reflection.

Pastor Tilton looks at the mirror and then back at Mildred. "What do you see?"

"Stand up. Come here and look."

He walks around the bed and stands beside Mildred. "I see you, me and Sylvie."

"She's gone," says Mildred. "She was just there."

Sylvie calms down a bit and closes her eyes again.

"I'm here, Auntie. Don't be afraid. I won't leave you." She turns to Pastor Tilton. "Thank you for coming."

"I don't need to rush off," he says. "I can be here for you."

"For me?" Mildred's knees shake. She sits down and looks at Sylvie.

Elsa says, "I can give her something to—"

"To what?" says Mildred, "keep her calm? Hasten her death? Take her from me?"

"Mildred, she is just trying to help," says Tilton.

Tears escape onto her cheeks. "I can't do this."

Tilton grabs her hands. "We will do it together."

As Mildred strokes Sylvie's hand, she counts Sylvie's breaths.

One.

Outside, in the garden, the old oak tree waves its leaves and branches in the wind. A flash of light illuminates the yard in an eerie black-and-white image of the garden bench and a dinosaur-like backhoe ready to gobble up Sylvie's roses. Drops of rain tap out a pattern on the glass doors, and the first clap of thunder rolls in the distance.

Two.

The pause lengthens and lengthens.

Come on, Auntie, breathe. Mildred leans close and kisses her aunt on the forehead. Just one more breath, one more minute?

Elsa steps away from the bed, and Mildred's body folds in half. Pastor Tilton uses his thumb to leave an oily mark of the cross on Sylvie's head.

Outside, the rain slapping on the patio stones sounds like a thousand hands clapping as if the performance has just ended.

Mildred

The morning light weaves its pattern on the tile floor like a spider planning to capture its prey. Mildred studies Sylvie's fingernails as she holds her hand.

"Petra," she says without looking up. "Could you get me my purse?"

She dutifully delivers the black leather handbag to Mildred, placing it on the bed beside Mildred's hand.

Mildred removes a clear zippered pouch from her bag and selects the curette appropriate for the job. Spreading a tissue on the bed sheet under her hand, Mildred leans close and touches Sylvie's hand.

"They will take care of that," Petra says.

"No," says Mildred. "I will do it." She takes a deep breath, holds one of Sylvie's hands gently in her own, and breathes on them. Delicately guiding the edge of the metal tool along the underside of Sylvie's nail, she takes her time, working from the inside out, scraping across the underside of the nail, dropping flecks of garden soil onto the tissue.

Elsa can be heard scratching away on a pad of paper with her pen while speaking on her phone through her Air Pods. Mildred doesn't need to hear what she says to know what she is doing, completing required paperwork, making arrangements, and letting all the appropriate authorities know what will still take some time to sink in for Mildred.

Maggie may still be around someplace, but Pastor Tilton has been gone for some time, not sure really how long. It was raining when he left. Soon it will be chaos, but now, as in the peaceful silence of two dear friends gathering over tea, it is just Mildred and Aunt Sylvie.

She gathers up the tissue and places another on the bed. Gently, she rests Sylvie's right hand beside her and takes up the left.

Petra starts to lower the head of the bed, but without saying a word, Mildred stops her.

Sylvie's hair is stringy and needs a comb. "Her favorite brush is on the dresser in her bedroom. Could you get it, please?"

Petra looks at Elsa, who nods her head.

Mildred reaches the fourth finger and touches the rose on Sylvie's ring. It occurs to her that she doesn't know what her aunt wants. Should she leave it on her or take it off? Why didn't she think to ask?

Maggie carries two teacups on saucers from the kitchen and walks out to the patio, where she places them on the round table.

"I don't know if I want tea," says Mildred.

"Come," says Maggie. "It's tradition. We need to honor her in a way that would make her happy."

Maggie is not dressed for work. She is wearing a bright yellow sundress and sandals, as if she is headed to the beach. She takes a seat with her back to the garden so that Mildred will have a view of Sylvie's roses.

Petra hands Mildred a brush and Mildred gingerly brushes Sylvie's hair.

"Why didn't you tell me how sick she was?" asks Mildred, talking to Maggie, but focusing on Sylvie's hair.

"She didn't want me to," says Maggie.

"We don't keep secrets, right?"

Maggie sips her tea and returns the cup to the saucer. "We never have, have we?"

Mildred places the hair in her hand and uses her palm to guide the brush. "I have been honest with you from your birth, child."

"And with Mom?"

"Why do you ask?" Mildred stands and holds onto the back of the chair. She puts her bag and the brush on the chair and takes calculated steps toward Maggie.

"Are you having trouble feeling your way?"

"I've been sitting too long," she says. She refuses to worry Maggie about the numbness in her feet. As Mildred reaches the table, her legs wobble, but she manages to drop into the seat and then adjust herself.

"No secrets, huh?"

Mildred stares at the tea in the cup. "No cookies? Auntie always had her biscuits."

Maggie stands.

"No," says Mildred, "stay here. I don't need them."

Maggie sits and reaches across the table to touch Mildred's hand. "This is harder than Mom, isn't it?"

"What do you mean?" Mildred pulls her hands away and folds them together as if in prayer.

Maggie leans back in her chair and looks up.

"Losing your mom was the worst day in my life." Mildred raises her hands to her chest.

"Until today?" Maggie leans forward. "I was so angry with you for not being with her when she died. I thought you couldn't handle it."

"But with COVID—"

"I know. It makes no sense. But you are so damn headstrong that I believed you could have found a way. Look what you did to get Aunt Sylvie home."

"Don't you think I did that because of what I didn't do for your mom? I didn't even know your mother's wishes." She thinks of Sylvie's ring and feels a wave of emotion rush against her.

"You raised Mom to be like you."

"And she raised you to be like her."

Mildred isn't sure if they are praising or blaming each other. "I am proud of you, Maggie."

"Why?" Maggie stirs the tea in her cup. "But we don't trust each other, do we?"

Mildred sighs. "What do you mean?"

Maggie shakes her head and sips her tea.

There is something troubling her. She feels Mildred has shown more love for her aunt than for her own daughter? Could that be it? She looks beyond Maggie to the garden.

"Do you think we can get permission to bury her ashes here?"

"On the property?" Maggie turns to look at the garden. "Where?"

"There, where she spent all of her time."

Maggie looks as if she wants to say something, maybe share one of those secrets they both claim they don't keep from one another. Mildred wants to ask her what is wrong, but the doorbell rings, and she hears Elsa run to answer it.

"They're here," says Maggie.

Mildred's hands shake. She doesn't want to let them take Sylvie, but she knows she can't stay here. Everything is different now.

Mildred stands, picks up her cup and saucer, and heads toward the kitchen.

When she returns, Maggie is at the door coordinating everything as usual. Mildred looks at Sylvie, still propped up as if looking at her garden bench. A cardinal comes and lands on the back of the bench and sings.

Mildred

Wednesday

From the second-floor balcony of the main house, the carriage house looks like a peaceful refuge nestled in a garden. The activity within is out of sight, but not out of mind. Maggie has taken charge, guiding all the medical and other professionals through the house that will soon become hers. For Mildred, a shower, a change of clothes and a chance to shut her eyes are the only agenda items she can handle, for now, anyway.

She discards the floral print blouse and blue Capri pants that had become a part of her during the past two days and covers herself with a terrycloth robe. At the door of the closet, she pauses, leaning on the frame for emotional support. A rainbow of color bordered by white on the left and black on the right, the blouses, skirts, pants, dresses, and gowns stand at attention on their hangers, while the sweaters and hats fill the shelves. The drawers are for accessories and underthings as she liked to call them. The organization of such items is not her doing, but the work of Josie, who has a propensity for such arrangement. Mildred is sure she has done a similar project for Maggie, though Mildred rarely intrudes on her granddaughter's privacy.

It is proper to wear black. But now? Perhaps people will be stopping by. Maybe it is best, in order to show respect.

Then again, they were all here last night. Would they come back so soon? But there is much to do. Black with a touch of red it will be. Sylvie will like that. She likes red.

In the bathroom, she finds a shower cap in the cabinet and tucks her hair up under it. She should wash it, but it will take too long to dry. She can go to the beauty parlor tomorrow, or Friday at the latest. The wake will be Friday, probably, unless there is a delay because she died in her home and not in the hospital. Maggie will know. She knows everything. There was a time when Mildred was the one everyone came to for advice, help, or to solve a problem. She ran this estate. Yes, it is an estate, too much for one person to handle, especially when that person is old.

Mildred undresses and holds her arms out in front of her, noticing the pillows of skin that droop down between her elbow and armpit. Gravity has caused other areas to look like melting peaks and sunken valleys. Her body is older than she is, or so it seems.

The water is too hot and then too cool, never the right temperature. Old pipes in an old house, serving an old matron. No wonder Sylvie didn't want to be bothered fighting it off.

After the shower, she should feel better. She doesn't. Tossing the shower cap in the sink, she wraps herself in the bathrobe and lays down on her bed.

The French doors to the balcony are open and she can hear a train in the distance. What would it be like to get on board and go far away?

She closes her eyes and imagines traveling in one of those glass-top luxury transcontinental trains from Toronto to Vancouver. No one would bother her for days, a week, or more.

When she opens her eyes, the light in the room has changed; shadows are longer, and streaks of light along the floor have moved like a sundial.

How long has she been asleep?

After dressing, she makes her way down the staircase and notices the door to the library is still open. Hadn't she closed it after finding the map on the desk? Maybe not, since she ran out to wash the ink from her hand. Then she saw someone or something outside. She must have left it open.

She pushes the doors open completely. Flecks of dust particles in the air dance on the sunlight from the windows. Memories return of Alfred smoking his pipe behind the desk and Audrey sitting in the wingback leather chair reading a book. It isn't a large room tucked away under the staircase. It is easy to ignore and forget, but entering causes the memories to flow like waves against the shore. She walks over to the bookcases and touches the spines of her favorites, the stories she read to Audrey when she was a child, the same stories and poems her mother had read to her. Dickens, Longfellow, Woodhouse, Woolf, Bronte, Alcott. She hasn't read these books for so long, she cannot remember when she last opened one.

And yet here is one, resting on the wooden smoking table beside the chair.

She bends to pick it up. Its pages are yellow with time, even though the book may have been closed and unread for decades. She carefully touches the pages with her fingernails. The cover is soft, and the paper is almost like worn leather.

She looks at the cover and reads the title page.

Life of James Mars, A Slave Born and Sold in Connecticut. Written by Himself

James Mars

In the margin of the title page is writing in faded ink. *Deborah Townsend, Cranberry Farm, 1865.*

Mildred looks up at the bookcase to see where this book may have been hiding. There is an empty space, thin enough to be the place where this book had been, between The *Underground Railroad in Connecticut* by Horatio T. Strother, published in 1962, and *The Underground Railroad Records*, by William Still, published in 1872.

When she was a young girl, her father would invite local businessmen and academics to enjoy cigars and brandy while discussing topics of interest to them. Mildred would sit on the stairs and sneak around to listen at the door, imagining what it was like to live in the past century, before progress had turned the lovely farmland into an upper-class community. She looks at the writing again.

Deborah Townsend, Cranberry Farm, 1865.

This Deborah Townsend lived here? Who was she? And why would she have this book? Has it been here all this time? Mildred grabs the chair to steady herself.

She places the book on the desk next to the map and sits in the chair behind the desk. What did she not see before?

The smudge of ink where she had placed her hand obscures part of the image, but she can see what must have been the potting shed. There is a mark she hadn't noticed before next to the structure. *RR.* Railroad? What would a potting shed have to do with the railroad?

Sam

Rarely is the morning quiet in the Castleby household, so Sam has no problem ignoring the shouting and clamor coming from the kitchen as it makes its way down the hall to his bedroom. Father's voice is always the loud one, with Mother's barely heard, but today, this morning, the volume continues to rise on both counts.

Sam unplugs his phone from the charger and checks his messages. One from Maggie.

Busy making funeral arrangements with Grandma. See you later. It is followed by a heart emoji. She hates emojis. What's changed?

Sam's father is pacing between the fridge and the counter, holding a pint of half-and-half in his hand. His coffee mug is on the counter, beside the morning paper, where it always is.

"James," says Harriet, "sit down and have your coffee."

"Don't you realize what this means?" James slams the pint on the counter, causing the creamy liquid to overflow the top and spill onto his shoes. "Damn it!"

Sam looks at his mom. She motions for him to take a seat at the far end, out of the line of fire, and she pours him a cup of coffee.

"Why didn't you tell me about this?" James yells at Sam.

"Good morning to you, too," says Sam, reaching for his cup.

"Show some respect, Sam," says Harriet.

"Respect?" Sam reaches for the half-and-half. "Are you done polishing your shoes with this?"

Harriet's eyes pierce through Sam.

"Explain yourself," says James. He reaches for his tie draped over the back of his chair, where his suit jacket is the only occupant. His shirt is unbuttoned, and his silver-streaked hair has not yet been introduced to a comb. "When did she decide to do this?"

He pounds his forefinger repeatedly on the open newspaper page, bending it at the knuckle so hard that it might snap off.

Sam reaches for the paper and pulls it across the counter toward him.

The headline reads *Board Approves Design of New Children's Cancer Center.*

"This is great news," says Sam, picking up the paper to read the article. "Maggie has been working for this a long time."

"So, you knew she was planning on building it on Cranberry property, and you never told me?"

"What?" Sam scans the article and folds the page back to read.

"Go to page ten," says James. "There is a rendering of the proposed building. Did you do that?"

Sam flips the pages and puts the paper on the counter, his mouth hanging open.

"I didn't do this," he says, his entire body sinking into itself.

"I'm sure there is some explanation," says Harriet. "Let me make you some eggs and toast."

"I'm not hungry, Mom," says Sam.

"But you must eat something."

Sam continues reading.

"She met with the board on Monday. She never said anything to me." Sam leans back in the chair and looks to his mom for sympathy.

"I am sure with Sylvie's passing, she has been too busy. Have you even seen her this week?"

Sam folds the paper and stands. He steps away from the counter and starts walking, holding the paper in his hand.

"Where are you going?" asks James.

He can hear his father yelling for him to stop and return, but he continues walking.

He closes the front door behind him and stares at the For Sale sign the Realtor has placed on the front lawn. Everything was going so well, but since Maggie agreed to be his wife, his world has turned upside down.

Behind him, the door opens, and his mother comes toward him. He waves her off and heads for his car. "I don't want to talk to anyone," he says, before closing his door and driving away.

Mother was there at the beginning, and there she is now, fading from view in his rear view mirror.

As he drives, he tries to make sense of his own feelings. He is happy for Maggie. She can finally have what she has wanted, but what about Dad? He has had his heart set on developing that property. He has been lining up funding based on his model and his plans. Maybe he was being too reckless and optimistic, but that's Dad. He grabs hold of an idea and runs with it.

He pulls over a block from the hospital. He hadn't planned on driving here, but maybe subconsciously, he had. He wants to see her, but she's not there. She's with her grandmother. How could she not share her plan with him? He can't park here, so he drives to the hospital and pulls into the garage. He rolls down his window and turns off the car. He could use a cup of coffee, but that will have to wait. He needs to read the entire article. Maybe that will help him understand. He refuses to let his emotions drive his actions like Dad does. He is more like Mom or wants to be.

At the end of the article, Maggie is quoted.

This is the most important thing in my life right now. As soon as I have title to the property, work will begin.

The most important thing in her life? What about marriage? Isn't that the most important thing? Or is marriage just a means to an end?

143

Maybe Maggie is right about him. Maybe he is too weak, too sensitive. Maybe neither of them is doing this for the right reason. He tosses the newspaper on the passenger seat and starts the engine.

It is time. He needs to go off on his own. He pulls out of his spot and drives up the ramp out of the garage. The white sun in the cerulean sky inspires him to drive. He will do what he wants to do and stop thinking about everyone else. After all, they don't think about him. They just want to use him to get what they want. No more.

Mildred

Thursday

As the car bumps its way across the railroad tracks and down the sloped lane, Mildred turns to the driver of the Access-A-Ride van and asks, "Are you sure this is where the funeral home is?"

Tilly's wheelchair is locked in place, the back up against the partition between her and Mildred. "Maria, my cleaning lady told me they do a really good job. All her friends use this place."

"You can't even see out the window, Tilly. How do you know if this is the right way?"

"I can see out the back," she says. "We just passed the bodega where Maria gets enchiladas."

"Muy bueno," says the driver.

The car turns onto a one-way drive bordering a large brick building that could have been a bank several decades before. A lawn green walkway awning leads guests from the parking lot to what looks like the preferred entrance. Mildred spots the name on the awning and the door to the entrance.

"De Nada? What does that mean?" Mildred stares at the entrance as though it could swallow her up and never spit her out.

"It's nothing," Tilly says.

"Seriously?"

"It's the Spanish equivalent of Fuggedaboutit," Tilly says.

"I'm not sure about this place."

The driver opens the rear doors and grabs a remote device attached by cable to the ramp's motor to ease Tilly's wheelchair out of the van. Tilly propels it forward to finish the trip down the ramp.

"Gracias," she says to the driver.

"De nada," he says.

"See?" Tilly motors past Mildred onto the carpet leading to the door. "I feel like I'm a celebrity."

"We will be about an hour," says Mildred to the driver.

"I'll text him when we're ready to leave." Tilly pushes the handicap button on a post and the double doors to the funeral home open for her. "Her majesty has arrived."

"At least they have handicap access," says Mildred.

"They all do. They know their clientele."

"I don't know about this," says Mildred.

"According to Pastor Tilton, this is what Sylvie wanted. She told him not to go back to the place that made Gertrude look like a rag doll."

"She was pretty bad, wasn't she?" Mildred follows Tilly into the building. A wide hallway greets them, and the overpowering aroma of gardenias causes her throat to tighten.

Tilly motors on, checking each room. "Looks like we're alone this time."

"Who did you expect? And don't tell me Aunt Sylvie!"

Tilly uses her fingers to zip her lips.

"Good afternoon, ladies." A short, dark-haired man in his fifties approaches and extends his hand. "Charlie Maguire. You must be Ms. Cranberry, and you are?"

"Tilly Parker."

"Parker? Are you related to David Parker, who used to play for Cranberry High? My son played on his team."

"That's my son. He works in the city, now. Big shot lawyer."

"Really? My son Vince works with me. He does a great job. A good face guy."

"Could we come in?" Mildred nudges Tilly to make a point.

"Of course."

As he leads them through the entrance, Mildred leans over to whisper to Tilly. "I set up an appointment with David to review some legal issues."

Tilly smiles but continues looking around as if expecting someone else to arrive.

"When you called, you mentioned having a wake for your aunt. Did you have a date in mind for that?" Maguire keeps his gaze on Mildred as he walks into his office.

Mildred settles into a chair, and Tilly motors beside her. "Could we do it tomorrow night?"

"That's cutting it close," he says, flipping through what looks like an appointment book on his desk. All of the pages appear blank.

"Millie, you want her to look good, don't you? Besides, I'm sure she wouldn't mind waiting if you aren't having a closed casket. That's what she told me."

"Oh?" Maguire pulls out a form and starts to fill it in. "I have already been in touch with the coroner. Procedure you know when the death occurs in the home. A lot of people are doing it that way these days. Doctor Payton arranged for the body to be transferred to them and will make all the arrangements to get her here."

"You don't have her yet?" Mildred bites her lip.

"No. So, the earliest we could do the wake is Saturday."

"She wanted to be cremated."

"Do you want to do that before the wake?"

"Millie, she didn't want people to see her looking dead."

"She will look great," he says. "Do you have a recent photo we can use?"

"If we decide we want a closed casket, can we do that?"

"If you want to do that, we can have her go right to the crematorium tomorrow, so we won't have to wait until Monday."

147

"Monday?"

"They aren't open on the weekend, so if you want an open casket for the wake on Saturday, everything gets pushed."

"Damn."

"Ms. Cranberry, we will do everything we can to make this as painless as possible."

Tilly turns her head back toward the door. "Sylvie is okay waiting a few days more. She's not in a hurry to go."

"She is dead, right?"

"Yes, Mr. Magoo," says Tilly.

"Maguire."

"Bless you, dear." Tilly takes out her phone and sends a text.

They make their way back down the hall and stop at the door to the parking lot.

"What was that about?" asks Tilly.

Mildred bites her lip and turns toward the door, not wanting to talk.

"It's because she wanted to be at home, isn't it?"

"I just feel like everything I do is wrong." Mildred sniffles. "Maybe we should have a closed casket like she wanted. But all her friends will want to see her."

Tilly turns her wheelchair around to face Mildred.

"And now, with this damn court order. What if they find the lock? We'll have to give them the key, won't we?"

"Is that what you want?"

"I don't want to lose everything. Why can't they leave me alone?"

Tilly reaches for her hand. "I think I need to give you back the key."

"Why?"

"Effie just texted me. She wants to stay with me for a while."

Mildred

After returning to Tilly's to retrieve the frozen key and her car, Mildred pulls her car onto the street, where the driveway to the carriage house and the long drive to the main house are blocked by a long, flatbed truck. It is a heavy-duty construction transport, being loaded with the backhoe that had been in the backyard. Two construction workers are securing the behemoth onto the truck with chains. Their yellow jackets and helmets seem more appropriate for a large building site than to dig up a prize rose garden.

"Are you done playing?" Mildred asks, circling the house to the backyard. She doesn't wait for an answer.

A uniformed officer steps out of the shadows to greet her with a smile. "Miss Canopy? I'm Officer Jenkins."

"It's Cranberry!"

"Mildred Cranberry?" He produces a paper and slaps it in her hand.

"Urgh! I fell for that one, didn't I? Care to do that again?" Mildred unfolds the document and holds it at arm's length. "I need my glasses," she says.

"It's signed by Judge Philips."

149

"He's been a busy man," she says, reaching for her purse. "What does he want now? Driftwood from the swamp?"

She dons her glasses and starts reading.

"Ma'am, it's a request for you to produce the key."

"Did you find the lock?"

"Once we moved the bench out of the way and dug there, near the rosebushes, we found what looks like could be a lock. We bagged it as evidence. A lock expert will be called in."

"You mean a locksmith?" She scans the document looking for the claimant. "Just as I thought. Ephedra Devine."

"There is a preliminary hearing on Friday morning."

"I can read, Officer. Did you happen to notice when the coroner left, or were you too busy digging in my garden?"

"I'm sorry for your loss, Miss, but we had to find the lock today so it can be analyzed in time for the hearing." He steps backward, preparing to leave.

"Fine!" Mildred starts walking toward the backyard and stops to look back. "You had better put everything back just the way it was. Or I will file some paperwork of my own."

Mildred starts shaking. The funeral, and now a court case, what next? Oh, the wedding, of course. Is that going to happen?

Mildred grabs her phone to answer a call.

"Maggie?"

"Have you seen the paper today?"

"I have not had time to do anything. I haven't even eaten."

"Good. Meet me at the diner for lunch."

"Okay, I have an appointment with a lawyer this afternoon."

"Grandma, it's important. I need to tell you this in person."

The call ends. Mildred wipes her eyes. "Now what?"

Don't look at the mess in the garden. Just go meet Maggie.

Mildred listens to herself and returns to her car. In the passenger seat, a transparent container is sweating from the humidity, and inside, a brass key emerges from the ice. Mildred makes a call from the display on her dash.

"David Parker's office," the woman who answers sounds young.

"This is Mildred Cranberry. I have an appointment with David here in Old Cranberry for two o'clock."

"Yes, at your home, right?" she asks, her voice suddenly softening. "I am so sorry for your loss."

"Thank you."

"Would you like to cancel?"

"No, but I would like to change the location to the diner across from the courthouse."

"I will let him know. I'm sure it won't be a problem. Can he call you on this number if it is?"

"Yes."

Ending the call, she tries to clear her thoughts. What could Maggie want? What was in the paper?

As she approaches the intersection, a woman runs out into the street in front of her. Mildred slams on the brake and brings the car to a screeching halt. The car behind her does the same, the driver leaning on his horn. The container is no longer on the seat beside her.

The man in the car behind screams, "What's wrong with you! The light's green!"

A school bus flies through the intersection without stopping.

Her heart is pounding so hard she can feel it in her throat. She looks at the woman, who smiles and disappears.

The school bus pulls over and turns on its flashing lights.

Mildred puts the car in park and gets out, staring down the angry driver in the car behind her. She shrugs, and runs over to the school bus, letting the cars behind her go around hers.

"Are you okay?" she asks, pounding on the bus driver's window.

One hand is locked on the steering wheel while the other is clutching his chest. He says nothing. Kids are crying.

He's having a heart attack. She runs back to her car and calls 9-1-1.

Then she texts Maggie. *I'm going to be late.*

Maggie

THURSDAY

The diner is a short walk from the hospital. While the mornings are getting cooler, the temperature rises to the high seventies or low eighties, and one can work up a good sweat when the sun is overhead. The nice thing about scrubs is they are cooler than most outfits, especially without a lab coat.

She checks her watch and sees the text message from Grandma. She will be late. What now? This is going to be hard enough for her without having to rush before her next appointment. Maggie was hoping to have a nice lunch and explain why she wants to break up the property for the children. Maybe they could work together on this. Probably not.

A woman approaches with a young girl in a stroller. Maggie smiles at the girl and the girl smiles back. She looks familiar.

"Good morning, Doctor," says the woman. "Gloria Grant. Amy, do you remember Doctor Payton?"

Of course, Amy Grant. Leukemia. She may need a bone marrow transplant if the treatments don't work. That's a lot for a young child to deal with, not to mention the mom.

"Good morning, Amy," says Maggie. She turns to the mom. "Are you going for treatment now?"

"Yes, will you be by?"

"After my meeting."

"Good. Say goodbye, Amy."

"Goodbye, Doctor."

Maggie watches them walk away. She imagines the days, weeks and months ahead for the girl. She needs this cancer center built now.

Grandma's car is not parked out front, so Maggie checks the parking lot behind the diner. No luck.

How late is late? Should she wait outside so they can walk in together or take a seat in a booth? Maybe one in the window.

She climbs the steps and opens the door. The checkout counter is before her, and on it is today's newspaper. Luckily, the article is not headlined on the first page. Maybe Grandma read the paper, and that's why she is late. Maybe she isn't coming.

"Would you like a booth?" The waitress holds a menu before her.

Maggie realizes she is holding up a line of patrons. "Sorry, yes. Could I have that one in the window?"

The waitress seats her and asks if she would like something to drink. Maggie orders a coffee and then wonders if she should have ordered tea. Grandma will probably have tea. It was their routine, Aunt Sylvie and Grandma.

Nursing the first cup of coffee, Maggie watches the clock in the bank across the street tick away the minutes. Soon it will be time for Grandma's meeting with her lawyer. What is that about? Aunt Sylvie's will? The property?

The waitress refills her cup and walks back toward the kitchen, passing the check-out counter. A man in a light brown suit with a pink tie and black shoes checks his watch. He looks familiar. Could he be one of the parents? Where else could she have seen him before?

The waitress escorts him past her booth, and she can feel him settle in behind her.

"Tea, please," he says, "Earl Grey if you have it." His voice is smooth and soft, like a pillow or a cloud surrounding her.

An image of a younger version of the man, without the mustache but with the same black curly hair, pops in her head. It can't be. High school was so long ago, and she had heard that he moved away. But he was color blind, and that would explain his choices.

"Maggie, is that you?" he asks, standing to take a look at her.

"David?" She presses her lips together, remembering she hadn't worn lipstick today. "Are you waiting for my grandmother?"

"Yes," he says, bringing his cup, and motioning to sit across from her.

"Please," she says. "Wait. Let me fix this for you."

She stands and adjusts his tie.

"I never was good at tying these things," he says. He loosens it a bit and then goes back to fetch his briefcase and newspaper. "I see congratulations are in order."

"Oh, yes. It's taken a long time, but I have wanted this for so long. It's all I've been thinking about."

"The engagement?" He looks puzzled. "I had no idea you were that serious with someone. You were always focused on work. I know what that's like."

She could feel her face blossom. "No, I was talking about the new children's cancer center. I thought you saw the article in the paper."

"I did," he says. "I particularly like the rendering. Did your fiancé do that? I assume his firm will do the construction." He sips his tea and returns the cup to its saucer.

She pushes her napkin close to her cup and then back to its spot. "To be honest, I had that done before I met him."

"And if you're not honest?" He smiles.

"You know me better than that," she says, staring at her coffee.

"I used to," he says, "but that was ages ago, when I was gullible and foolish."

"We both were, to some extent. But look how we turned out."

He checks his watch, and she does the same.

154

"We're both waiting for the same person," she says. "I guess I've been stood up."

"You? Never. That would be a crime punishable by hanging in these parts." He pushes his lapel out with both thumbs.

"Your accent is horrible, Partner." The sunlight catches a facet of her ring, and it flashes in her eye. "Maybe I should leave."

"No, please stay. Who knows when she'll show up, and she wanted to talk to you, right?"

"Well, I wanted to talk to her about the property."

"Is that where your cancer center will be built?" He grabs the paper, opening it to find the article.

She reaches for her coffee but decides it must be cold. Her phone buzzes with a text message from Mildred.

Sorry I'm so late. I can explain. Order me a BLT.

"She's on her way," says Maggie. "And she's hungry."

His phone buzzes with a text message from her, also.

I messed up. My granddaughter is at the diner waiting for me. I need to talk to her first.

He puts his phone in his briefcase.

"Problem?" she asks.

"I guess she wants to talk to us separately." He puts his paper in the briefcase and signals for the check. "I'll let her know I will be late."

"Why?" She catches herself. "Maybe it's best. She's not going to be happy with me."

He leans close enough for her to feel his warmth. "I'm kind of glad she was late, and I was early."

Maggie twirls the engagement ring as she watches him walk away. Outside, her grandmother's car pulls into the back lot. Let the games begin.

Mildred

Mildred enters the diner and scans the room for Maggie. Spotting her booth, she gives the room another once over. No David.

"If you're looking for David Parker, he left, but you can text him when we're done." Maggie leans across the table to give Mildred a peck on the cheek.

"I am so sorry I'm late. I almost ran over someone." Mildred settles into the bench seat and looks at the cup and teabag.

Maggie leans closer. "You were in an accident?"

"I wouldn't be here if I was," she says.

"What do you mean?"

"It's a long story." She looks at the menu. "Did you order a sandwich for me?"

"No," she says, and waves for the waitress. "I have to get back to the hospital, but I wanted to give you the news in person, rather than have you read it in the paper."

The waitress arrives, removes the empty cup and saucer, and takes Mildred's order.

"What is the news?" asks Mildred, not sure if she wants to hear it.

Maggie's voice cracks. "I know how you feel about keeping the property whole."

Mildred leans back. Oh, no. "You aren't thinking of letting Castleby destroy what has been in the family for two centuries, are you?"

"No, I don't want to see luxury estates any more than you, but I do want something else."

Mildred swallows what little saliva her mouth can produce and clenches her fists.

"It's about the children."

"I should have known," says Mildred, not really sure what she should have known, other than her granddaughter's commitment to the young cancer patients.

The waitress brings her BLT and unsweetened iced tea.

"Grandma." She reaches for her copy of the newspaper and then hesitates.

Mildred remembers the meeting. "That's why you ran off. You presented your idea to the hospital board, didn't you?"

"Don't get upset."

Mildred pushes her sandwich plate aside. "Show me the paper."

Maggie opens to the article and hands it to Mildred. After scanning the article, she studies the rendering.

"Where on our property are you planning to build this?"

"That's what I want to talk to you about," says Maggie.

"You want my help?"

"I need your help. I want you to want this, too. For me. And for Mom."

"Don't lay a guilt trip on me, Maggie." Mildred slams the paper on the table before Maggie and then raises a hand to her head.

"It will be an even bigger legacy than you could imagine." Maggie reaches for Mildred's hand. "You can even have your name on it."

"Do you think that's what I want, a legacy? " Mildred shakes her head and sighs. "Where did I go wrong?"

"You think I don't know how you've acted about the engagement?"

"I just want you to be happy."

"No you don't. You want you to be happy." Maggie folds the newspaper and stands.

"Where are you going?"

"I have to get back to my children, the ones who need a cancer center. They don't have time to waste."

Mildred reaches for her, but she slips out of reach and stomps away.

The waitress returns. "Do you not like your sandwich? Should I get you something else?"

Mildred looks at the food in front of her and shakes her head. "I'm suddenly not hungry."

Through the window, she watches Maggie walk back toward the hospital. She wants to run after her, but what would she say? Why are they fighting over something that Effie can take from them? She texts David and takes a sip of her iced tea.

As she puts it down, he walks through the door. She could tell it was him right away, remembering how Tilly would complain about his clothing choices when he went off to college and had to dress himself.

He was the same curly-haired kid with the two cutest dimples and blue eyes. Why couldn't Maggie have found him instead of Sam?

"I saw Maggie leave," he says, putting his briefcase on the seat across from where he had sat before. "She's quite a woman."

"Yes, she is," says Mildred.

"You didn't eat your lunch?"

The waitress returns and looks at David.

"I'll have one of those," he says, pointing to Mildred's sandwich.

"You can have mine," she says.

"Nonsense. You ordered it. We'll eat together." He turns back to the waitress. "Is that iced tea?"

"Yes. Unsweetened."

"I'll have one of those, too."

"I can see why you win so many cases," says Mildred.

"I may need help to tie a tie, but I know how to put myself in my client's shoes, so to speak."

Mildred isn't sure if she missed an inside joke, but she smiles just the same.

"My mom tells me my cousin is challenging you for your property. Don't you love families?"

The waitress brings his iced tea, and he smiles at her. She walks away, looking back at him and giggling.

"Did you two get along when you were growing up?"

"Mom became her foster parent when I was in high school, and then I went off to college, so we didn't spend much time together. She's really more like a stepsister than a cousin, but she got into the habit of calling Mom Auntie because her mother was still alive."

"Was?" Mildred sips her tea.

"She passed recently. I don't know the details, but it hit Effie hard. She had reconnected with her when she was in law school in Massachusetts but showed up back here at some point."

The waitress brings his BLT, and he reaches for it to take a bite. "It's good."

Mildred looks at her sandwich, and her stomach growls.

David chuckles. "You're a stubborn one. I can see where your granddaughter gets her determination and drive."

Mildred picks up the sandwich and takes a bite.

They share a few moments of silence while they eat. Mildred breaks the ice. "I wanted Maggie to inherit the property so it could stay in the family, and now she wants to use it to build a cancer center. Can I stop her from doing that?"

"Do you want to?"

Mildred puts her sandwich down on the plate. "I don't know, but neither of us will get what we want if Effie wins this case of hers."

"I checked with the court, and you don't have to appear tomorrow. I can do that for you. It's merely a formality."

She takes a sip of her tea. "What do you mean, a formality?"

"This is a hearing to see if there is a case to pursue here. Effie will make her case that the property was wrongfully inherited, and then I will counter on your behalf, demanding proof that Elcira killed Chester, which is at the heart of her claim."

"Doesn't the lock and key prove her point?" Mildred suddenly remembers the key on the floor of her car.

"It isn't proof. Even if the key Chester had on him fits the lock, which could be tough to prove given its age and degree of corrosion, they still don't have the mythical second key."

"It's not mythical," she says. "It exists."

"A key exists." He takes another bite and talks with his mouth full. He lowers his voice. "I wouldn't be too quick to give that up, though."

"It's in my car."

"Did you lock the car?"

"I think so," she says. She looks out the window, retracing her steps in her mind. "I'll go check."

"I'll go," he says. "Is your car in the back?" She hands him her key fob.

"Yes, the red Subaru Crosstrek. The key is in a plastic container."

He gets up and walks out the back door. After a few minutes, he returns through the front entrance, carrying the container in one hand and the cover in another.

"You will need to get your passenger window replaced. Who knew you had the key?"

"Just your mom."

"She has a hard time keeping a secret," he says.

"You think Effie broke into my car to steal the key?"

"Somebody did. Let's report this to the police. They can get access to the cameras. They are everywhere these days. They will find out who did it."

"What are you going to say was stolen?" she asks, thinking they can't mention the key that the police are looking for, or can they?

"That could be a problem, couldn't it?" He scratches his chin. "I can report it as a break-in. There have been a lot of those throughout the tri-state area."

"Do I need to stay here?"

"I'll stay with you. Finish your lunch." He pauses for a moment. "They will want our fingerprints to eliminate us as suspects, so we will have to stop at the station."

While David calls the police to report the crime, she waves for the waitress. If she's going to eat her fries, she needs mayonnaise. The waitress brings some packets of mayo in a small plate and places it before her.

"Mayo on fries? I thought I only did that," he says.

Mildred is starting to like him more.

"So, while we wait, tell me about Maggie," he says.

"What do you want to know? She's engaged."

He smiles. "That I know. But we hadn't seen each other since high school, you know."

Hadn't? Mildred wonders about his choice of words there.

Effie

Thursday

Effie looks out the window of Judge Philips's office at the diner across the street. A police car is blocking traffic with its lights flashing, causing cars to merge into one lane to pass. A flatbed tow truck beeps as it backs out onto the street, Mildred's red Subaru strapped in place behind the cab. A policeman waves the truck past the police car and then joins his partner standing at the entrance to the diner with Mildred and David. So, Cousin David's going to represent Mildred. This is going to be like stealing candy from a baby.

Effie feels a sore spot on her arm, a rash. She reaches into her purse and pulls out a tube of sunscreen, SPF 100. She applies it to both arms. She will need to limit her time in the sun. A rash and severe blistering are side effects of Bishop's Weed. It was a proven way to permanently darken one's skin, but it could be deadly. It causes the body to react drastically to UV light. The defense mechanism for the plant, to change its color and make it less attractive to animals, had the opposite effect on her, making her more attractive until the rashes started, that is. What's done is done. What started out as a way to get a permanent tan, may now pay off, if she can prove she deserves the inheritance her great-great-grandfather, Henry Townsend was denied.

"What's going on out there?" asks Judge Philips as he enters. The short, squat man, half bald, peels off his robe and hangs it on the lowest knob of the coat tree near the door.

"Looks like it might be another break-in," she says, stepping away from the window to divert his attention.

"At the diner, in broad daylight? They'll find that guy fast, I can guarantee it." Philips closes his door and walks around his desk, pulling out his leather chair, his back to the window.

Effie leans on the back of one of the chairs facing him. "I'm not dropping this, Judge. I have standing in this case."

"They taught you well, Effie," he says. "But as I told you, this would set an unusual precedent, declaring someone guilty without a trial after nearly two hundred years." He opens a folder and stares at a piece of paper.

"Unusual, yes. Dangerous, no." Effie pushes her chair aside and leans on the desk, facing him. She resists the urge to scratch her arm. More red bumps appear. Could stress bring this on?

"Well," he hesitates as he studies the paper in his hands. "Both, possibly."

"Lightfoot is publishing the story in tomorrow's paper, along with a photo of the key she used to lock herself in the shed. And the police found the lock itself."

"You have the key? Does it fit the lock?"

"I have the key, but the police have the lock." Effie opens her bag and pulls out a brass skeleton key. A tiny, tinted cube, the kind made of shatter-proof glass, falls on the chair. She takes out a tissue and picks it up as she hands the key to Philips.

"This isn't a modern case where we can rely on fingerprints and DNA evidence. We are flying blind here."

"But if the key fits the lock, doesn't that count as evidence?"

He wipes sweat from his bald head with a tissue, tosses it in the trash, and rests his chin on his clenched fists.

"What are you thinking?" Effie asks, taking her seat. She needs him on her side. She knows her case is weak, but if she can get him to send it to a jury trial, she knows she can win. Emotion counts just as much as evidence, if not more. "I believe we can get public opinion on our side. That will pressure Mildred into doing something."

"You mean to avoid a trial altogether?" he asks. "How would that help you? Not that I'm biased in any way, mind you. I am impartial here. We have to make that clear."

"Right," she says. "I need you to sign this," she says, handing him a paper. "It's an order for Mildred to delay the wedding until this issue is resolved."

He picks up the paper and reads it. "I can't sign this. On what authority could I do this?"

"Well," she says, leaning back in her chair and crossing her legs. "it becomes much more complicated if the property changes hands before I win this case. Can't you say that the ownership of the property is being challenged so it cannot be sold?"

"Come on, Effie, you're smarter than that." He leans back in his chair. "You aren't trying to halt a sale here. If the house was on the market, the press alone would make people cautious, and the value would drop. This is only a hearing. It may never get before a jury, so if you can work some magic to make it all go away, I will be very happy, but I have to stay impartial."

Effie swings her leg as she thinks, still leaning against the chair. Can she make it all go away? What will she settle for if not everything?

He hands back the paper. "I have scheduled the preliminary hearing for tomorrow at nine, so all parties can be present with counsel, and we can put this thing to bed by the weekend. I want this issue brought to a conclusion. Do you hear me?"

"I can have the press here and maybe some supporters, as well."

"Effie! Don't turn this into a circus." He leans forward so his feet can touch the floor.

"It's already the big top."

Effie reaches for the key, and something brushes against her arm, causing her to drop the key on the floor. She turns and looks at Philips, now standing at the window, watching the scene across the street. It wasn't him. She picks up the key and slips it into a zippered compartment in her purse. Her phone dings with a text message from the same unregistered number as before at the funeral, the one signed *Elcira*. This message is simply *LOL*

Maggie

The glass doors swoosh open as Maggie approaches, her white lab coat catching a breeze from the atrium, sending a cool sensation over her body, despite the scrubs. She has her thoughts on Gloria and Amy Grant, expecting to find them sitting on one of the stone benches with an IV tree on wheels hydrating Amy.

As she weaves her way around the planters and shaded seating areas, patients and family members offer a polite nod or smile, a momentary break from the reality they face with each visit, as well as the days between.

"Doctor Payton," a young male aide rushes to her side. "There is a gentleman waiting to talk to you. I told him you had a full schedule, but he is extremely persistent."

"Do you know who it is?"

"A Mr. Castleby?"

"Sam," she says with a sigh. "Tell him I—"

"He doesn't look well. I think you need to see him."

"Is he sick?" She spots Gloria and raises a hand to acknowledge her.

"No, but—"

"Where is he?" Maggie starts walking toward Gloria.

"In the waiting room. I told him to sit in the corner. He's a little out of it, if you know what I mean." He makes a gesture with his hand, cupping it and bringing it to his mouth.

"Great. Just what I need." She stops and turns toward the aide. "I'll be there in a few minutes."

He walks away, his head down and arms at his side, like a losing pitcher at a Little League playoff game.

Maggie bends and sits on her heels at Amy's side. "How is my super girl?"

Amy's eyes are red. Gloria's are as well.

"This was hard today," says Gloria. "Tell Doctor Payton what you told me, Amy."

"I feel my insides dying," she says, a crackle in her voice.

"That's the medicine working on the cancer, sweetie," says Maggie as she looks at the label on the bag draining into the port implanted in her chest. It is just saline for hydration. "This will help push that through your body and get every one of those nasty villains wherever they are hiding."

"It hurts."

"What hurts? This?" Maggie points to the bag.

"No," says Amy. "My belly hurts."

"You're feeling a little nauseous?" Maggie listens to her breathing and stomach through her stethoscope. "I'll have the nurse bring you something to chew that will make you feel better. It's like candy, but you just put it under your tongue and let it dissolve on its own."

Gloria wipes her eyes. "Thank you, Doctor."

Maggie touches Gloria's hand. "I need to talk with someone, but I will come back."

On her way to the waiting room, Maggie stops at the nurses' station and orders disintegrating tablets to ease the nausea.

The waiting room for the lab and cancer treatment area is small, with a long desk along one wall, divided into three private check-in stations, two of which are active as Maggie enters. Metal chairs line the other walls on both sides of the door to the lab where patients begin their protocol with blood samples. In the corner, under the overhead television screen, is Sam, his head in his hands in his lap.

The aide sitting next to him gets up as Maggie approaches. He gives her a look of compassion as he passes by.

"Sam." Maggie bends and touches his arm.

He moans and pushes back with his shoulder. She sits next to him. He smells of liquor and perspiration.

"Sam, can you get up? We need to go to my office."

He raises his head and looks at her, his squinted eyes bloodshot.

She waves for the aide to come back. All eyes in the room are on her and Sam.

"Bring me a wheelchair. I want to bring him to my office."

The aide grabs a wheelchair, opens it, and helps Maggie move Sam into the chair. He shows no resistance.

The aide pushes the button to open the doors. Maggie wheels Sam out and down the hall to her small office near the elevator.

She unlocks the door and pushes it open with the wheelchair, letting it close behind her. Putting him in the corner beside her desk, she locks the wheels and whispers into his ear.

"Sleep it off. I'll be back later."

On her way out, she looks back at him, wondering how he managed to get so drunk while waiting for her. He must have been drinking in the hospital. Like father, like son.

She locks the door and heads back to Gloria and Amy.

Mildred

THURSDAY

Wiping the ink off her fingers while waiting for David to be printed, Mildred replays in her head what she told the police. She shouldn't have mentioned the plastic container. The officer who questioned her spots her waiting for David and hurries over to her.

"I'm glad I caught you," he says, making her nervous.

"What's wrong?" she asks, her voice cracking.

"We're still waiting on the images from the cameras in the diner parking lot, but we have access to the street cameras, and they show several people entering the diner."

David joins them, cleaning his hands with a wipe. "What's up?"

"I was just explaining to Mrs. Cranberry that we were checking the CCTV footage and got a little confused because we were checking the wrong time. We saw you, Mr. Parker, enter the diner, stay a while and then leave, so we thought that was when you were with Mrs. Cranberry. We couldn't find anyone who went directly to the parking lot from the street, until we rolled the tape forward and saw the red Subaru arrive. Then we saw it."

"You saw who did it?"

"We saw a young man in a hoodie walk into the parking lot entrance and then come out shortly thereafter with his hands in his pockets. We were able to follow him from camera to camera until we lost him entering the courthouse."

"The courthouse?" David looks at Mildred. "What the-"

"Can you check to see who entered the courthouse before or after him?" asks Mildred.

He just looks at her. "It's a courthouse. Hundreds of people come and go each day."

She gives him a sheepish look.

"I'll see what I can do," he says.

David thanks him, and they head to his car to see his mom.

Clearing off her dining room table of magazines and unopened mail, Tilly puts them on a chair by the window to make room for them to continue their conversation.

"Who do you think broke into your car?" asks Tilly.

"Who do you think?" Mildred replies, emphasizing the word *you*. "She's staying with you, right? I want to be here when she arrives."

"Well, you may have a long wait," says Tilly.

David opens his briefcase and takes out a yellow pad and pen. "How did Effie know who had the key?" asks David. "Mom?"

"I didn't say anything about it," she says. "Not to her, anyway."

"Who did you talk to?" asks Mildred.

"Sylvie," she says, in a manner only Tilly can master. "We were having a nice conversation when Effie stopped by."

"I thought Sylvie passed," says David. "Are you saying you were talking to one of your spirits?"

"You know how they are, dear." Tilly motors to the kitchen. "Can I get you something? Bottled water? That's all I have unless you want me to make coffee. I just got a new machine from Amazon."

"Mom, you've got to stop ordering things. I told you. You need to manage your finances."

Mildred puts her head in her hands. "What are we going to do now?"

"It has those pods you put in to make one cup at a time. It came with samples so I've been making a lot of cups just to taste them. It will save me money in the long run, though, if I have a long run, that is." Tilly returns with two bottles of water and places them on the table. "But you can inherit it when I go."

"Mom, you were saying Effie heard you talking to Sylvie." David checks his watch and makes notes on his pad.

"Did you see Sylvie this time, or was it one of those birds?" Mildred scans the walls, looking for a mirror. Can she believe that what Tilly sees and hears is real?

"They are cardinals," says Tilly. "They let us know someone we care about is near. No, she was right there, where you're sitting, Millie. Oh, and she wanted me to thank you for her nails, whatever that means."

Mildred feels her body collapse into itself.

"Mom, I believe Effie had someone break into Mildred's car to steal the key." David makes another note on his pad.

"That's illegal," says Tilly. "Are you sure she has the key?"

Suddenly, the Venetian blinds on the window behind the chair rattle, and the pile of unopened mail falls to the floor.

"Ooh," says Tilly. "I guess she did."

Mildred turns to look at the window. "It's not open."

David opens the bottle of water and takes a swig. "I don't know what's happening here, but I must prepare our position for tomorrow."

"I thought you weren't too concerned," says Mildred, opening her bottle.

"Am I the only one here who thinks this is all a little too spooky?" he asks. "If Effie has the key and they found the lock, this could be a case of if the key fits you must convict."

Mildred takes out her phone and texts Maggie. "We need to all be on the same page with this nonsense. Maggie and I have different ideas about the future of this property, but while we are fighting with each other, we could lose everything."

"We won't lose everything," says David. "Mom, who in the garden club can we trust? I want a full courtroom tomorrow."

"Let me start texting, or I can do a Zoom call. That would be fun. Yes, I'll go do that from my bedroom." Tilly motors away, leaving David and Mildred looking at each other across the table.

"Mildred, think. Is there anything that could help us explain what the world was like on the Cranberry Farm back when Elcira and Chester lived?"

"The map," she says. "Oh, and maybe the book?"

"Map? Book? What are they? Where are they?"

"In the library at home."

"Mom, we have to go," yells David, "I will text you later."

Mildred stands and looks at the pile of mail on the floor and then back at the window. Can she accept the possibility that someone from beyond the grave is trying to help her? There has to be a practical explanation for all these strange occurrences. Maybe it's cataracts or floaters making her think there is someone there when there isn't? That could explain the figure in the mirror, but what about the woman she almost hit? Where did she go? She saved Mildred's life.

Jacqueline

Effie's mustard-yellow 2010 Honda Civic with the black hood and top blocks the circular drive, causing Harold to pull over into the curve. Jacqueline shakes her head while waiting for him to open her door.

"That girl needs to learn some manners," she says, stepping out of the car. "That beat-up old bumblebee of hers needs to be replaced with something more respectable if she is going to become one of the wealthiest residents of this old town."

Harold helps her stand and closes the door. "Shall I help her unload her things?" he asks.

Jacqueline's good eye focuses on the rear window of the car, covered with clothes and papers. "No, Harold. This is her mess, and I'm hoping it won't be my problem for long."

"It is nice of you to take her in," he says.

She stomps her walking stick on the gravel. "Let me make this perfectly clear, Harold. She will be here through this court situation and then on her own. I have no desire to take her in. We do quite well here on our own, thank you."

"Yes, ma'am."

"And by 'We,' I mean Preston and me, even though he is no longer here. Soon, this place will be the most sought-after property in Old Cranberry, a fitting legacy for us."

Harold leads her up the steps to the front door, which opens as they reach the landing.

Effie bolts from the doorway and runs down to her car, just barely avoiding hitting the two of them.

"Effie!" Jacqueline shouts and waves her walking stick. "While you're under my roof, you need to be respectful."

"I can't find it," she says, pulling clothes and bags out of her car's front seat and then working her way to the back.

"Can I help you, Ms. Devine?" asks Harold.

Jacqueline scrunches her lips and stares him down with both eyes almost working together.

Effie doesn't respond.

"Make sure you clean up that mess before you come in," says Jacqueline. "We need to discuss tomorrow."

Harold helps Jacqueline into the house and then heads back out to help Effie, ignoring Jacqueline's order.

"Men," she says. She stops in the foyer to admire the full-length portrait of herself over the marble fireplace at the base of the winding staircase. Late afternoon light from the rose window over the main entrance door bathes her likeness in an amber hue that paints blond highlights in her silver hair.

The wide-rimmed black and white polka dot sun hat with the pink bow is tipped to one side of her face, blocking the errant eye from view. The hat and matching gown were what she wore to the last Derby before moving to Old Cranberry. Preston was still alive then, and quite frisky with the ladies, having too much access to fertile youth. Moving here was supposed to be a way to keep him in the corral, not let him out to pasture.

That was forty years ago, coming up on half a lifetime, though it would be a shock should that fact be revealed at the garden club. There is no glamour in ranking the highest on the seniority scale.

Harold enters, his arms filled with wrinkled and bunched up clothing. He walks with both hands extended so the clothing isn't too close.

"Move quickly." Jacqueline points her walking stick in the direction of the laundry, and he bows his head, making a face of disgust at the pungent aroma that follows in his wake.

Effie enters in a frenzy, carrying nothing. "I don't know what happened to it."

"Calm down, dear," says Jacqueline, resting on her walking stick, the sunlight flickering as the wind outside blows the leaves on the sycamores. "What did you lose?"

"The blasted key!"

Jacqueline taps her steps aggressively to the doorway and looks at the car. Something black and shadowy inside the car moves. "Effie, I think I've found the culprits."

Effie runs out the door and heads toward her car, flailing her arms, "Shoo, shoo."

Two crows exit the vehicle and pass close to her head as they climb out of sight.

"They couldn't have," she says, "could they?"

Maggie

"Grandma? Are you home?" Maggie bursts through the doorway and flicks the switch to the chandelier, casting a prism of light through the crystals onto the walls and staircase. "Whose car is that in the drive?"

"We're in the library." Her grandmother's voice sounds almost cheerful.

"I can use some help out here." Maggie stops at the door to the library and stares at the tan suit and pink tie leaning over the desk. "David?"

"What do you need? I can help." He approaches, followed by Mildred.

"Uh," says Maggie. "I don't know. I think Grandma can help me." The last thing she wants right now is for David to judge her with those big, gorgeous color-blind eyes of his.

"Let's all go," says Mildred, looking puzzled as she passes Maggie.

David reaches the car first and looks in. "Oh."

Sam is stretched out in the back seat of Maggie's BMW. The smell of beer and urine waft from his clothes.

"It's Sam," says Maggie to her grandmother. "I didn't want to bring him home in this condition. I thought he'd be over it by now, but he's been out of it all day."

"He's been sick," says David, reaching for Sam's arms. "We're going to need to clean the car."

Maggie feels the blood rush to warm and redden her face. How embarrassing. This is the man she's going to marry?

"I checked him out at the hospital before we left. He just overdid it," says Maggie, reaching in from the other side to help push Sam out of the back seat. "I have a wheelchair in the trunk. It's a fold-up one."

"Good idea," says Mildred, walking gingerly toward the trunk.

"I'll get that, Mrs. Cranberry," says David. "It will make getting him out and up the walk easier."

Maggie pushes Sam into David's arms and then looks at her grandmother for support.

"You sure he's all right?" asks Mildred.

Maggie comes around and hands David some wipes from the package in her glove compartment.

"Where should I wheel him?" asks David, wiping his hands. "He needs to be washed up."

Maggie's head is throbbing. Why, Sam? She looks at the engagement ring on her finger, wanting to twirl it around so the diamond doesn't show.

"I can't ask you to do that," says Mildred. "Why don't we call his dad?"

"No," says Maggie. "I'll clean him up. He's my responsibility."

Sam opens his eyes slightly and squints to see who is around him. "Mags?"

"I'm here," she says. "You need to get cleaned up and then sleep it off." She wants to smack some sense into him, but she takes a deep breath only to choke on the smell.

David gets behind the wheelchair and pushes him toward the door.

"Whoa," says Sam. He leans forward and retches, but nothing comes out.

"Better hurry," says David.

Sam tilts his head back to look at David. He mumbles something, but Maggie doesn't catch it. Just keep calm, she tells herself. Try not to get emotional. Not now.

"I guess we'll put him in the downstairs guest bedroom. David, it's the green room down the hall from the library. It has an en suite." Maggie leads.

"Should I make some coffee?" asks Mildred.

"Please. I could use some," says Maggie.

"Me, too," says David. "We'll get him settled and get back to our research. I think we're onto something here."

Maggie enters the room and opens the door to the bathroom. "If you can get him on the toilet, I can take it from here."

"You can't manage this alone. He's too out of it."

"I feel so bad. Look, your suit is ruined."

"I can't tell," he says. "Colorblind."

She wants to smile, but she stays focused on Sam, stripping him of his shirt and signaling for David to hold him up by his arms so she can remove his pants.

"Can you stand, Sam?" asks Maggie.

He moans.

"I think it best to get him in the tub and then use the hand shower to rinse him off. His clothes caught most of the damage." David lifts Sam by propping him up, arms under Sam's armpits.

Maggie pulls the wheelchair out of the way and helps Sam's legs over the edge of the tub. She then grabs the hand shower to test the water's temperature before hosing Sam down.

After cleaning and drying him up, the two get him into bed. Maggie takes a decorative metal bowl from the bathroom counter and places it beside Sam in the bed.

While David heads back to the library, Maggie carries the laundry basket with Sam's clothes to the washer. How could he do this to her? Is this what life is going to be like with him? What set him off?

As she rinses off the clothes in the sink before loading them into the washer, she replays the events of the day. She was so worried about her grandmother seeing the newspaper before she had a chance to tell her, she totally forgot about Sam. Why didn't she think to tell him? She dries her hands and runs her fingers through her hair to push it back, away from her eyes. She must look a wreck. And now David has seen her at her worst. Why does that matter to her?

Grandma is sitting in an armchair in the library. Several books are open on the coffee table in front of her, along with two coffee cups and a small pitcher of milk.

David removes his suit jacket and places it on the coat rack.

"I'll get that cleaned," says Maggie.

"Don't worry about it. We have to go clean your car."

"I'll take care of that," says Mildred. "Why don't you fill Maggie in on what we discussed and discovered?"

Mildred leaves before Maggie can stop her. David lifts his shirt from his chest and sniffs. "Not toxic," he says.

She realizes he is trying to ease the discomfort she feels.

He leans forward and clinks his coffee cup against hers. "Cheers."

"What a day," she says. "I'm so sorry to drag you through this."

"Not an issue." He sips the coffee and smiles. "I've had my share of embarrassing moments."

"Not like that," she says, tilting her head toward the bedroom. Will she hear Sam if he gets up?

"No," he says. "Worse."

"Really?" This time, she lets a smile show through her defensive exterior. "You'll have to tell me sometime."

"Maybe I will."

He is being such a gentleman about this. But why wouldn't he? Why does it matter to her? David is just an old high school friend, right?

"So, what did you and Grandma discover?" Maggie puts her cup down and moves her chair closer to his.

"Well," he says, "you are part of a fascinating family with a secret history that no one knew much about."

"Which family? The Smith's, Payton's, or the Cranberry's?"

"We've only been scratching the surface, but the Cranberry's are ahead by a mile."

A breeze from the window blows across the table, flipping the pages of an open book and causing the library door to swing shut.

"And then there is that," says David.

"What?"

David turns toward her. "Your grandmother believes there are spirits in this house."

"My grandma? She doesn't even go to church." She sips her coffee and puts it down. "I'll admit I always seem busy on Sundays as well. It was Aunt Sylvie who made her way to town to listen to Pastor Tilton. I think he rambles on too much, myself."

Grandma returns with dirty towels. "I'll add these to the washer and start it."

Maggie turns back toward David to see him staring at her. She reaches for one of the books on the table.

"That is the one the spirit supposedly left open on the table over there for your grandmother to see." David opens it and shows Maggie Deborah's name.

"Who is that?"

David pulls the court papers he received from his briefcase. "According to Ephedra Devine, Effie, this Deborah Townsend was her ancestor."

"And she lived here?" Maggie looks at the cover of the book. "Was she a slave?"

"We don't know. We still have some work to do." David removes his laptop from his briefcase and looks at Maggie. "WiFi?"

She takes the laptop from him and types in the password. "What are you looking for?"

"I have a genealogy account. I've had it for years. Now, it can come in handy." He types in a name and starts a search.

"I doubt you will find a record of slaves by name," says Mildred, entering with her own cup of coffee.

"No," he says, "but I should find Deborah and Chester's son. I'd like to see how directly related Effie is to him."

"I had better make more coffee," says Mildred.

Sam

FRIDAY

S am struggles to remember. When did he go to the hospital? He remembers stopping a block away in the morning after leaving the house. Then he drove away. Where did he go?

He hasn't lost track of time like this in a long time. Now, here he is, sitting in the car while Maggie drives him back to where he must have parked his car. And she's not talking to him. She should talk to him. She owes him an explanation. Why didn't she tell him about her plans for the property?

She has no expression on her face. Her nose keeps twitching, most likely from the powerful antiseptic smell. He's surprised she isn't shoving his nose in it like a puppy who did his business on the kitchen floor.

Maggie's phone buzzes repeatedly, but she ignores it. Maybe it's that guy. Who was that? Sam remembers someone lifting him out of the car.

At the intersection ahead, blue and red lights flash, and two police cars block traffic, forcing it to take an alternate path.

"What's going on?" Maggie asks.

Is she asking him? "It looks like a parade or a protest." Sam tries to be helpful, but he feels she isn't paying attention.

She checks her phone and then brakes to make a U-turn.

Sam drops his head and stares at his pants. He remembers being sick and feeling wet. Then, in waves, the images locked away in the toxic cloud of his drunken memory start to roll in.

"I'm sorry," he says, looking at Maggie.

She doesn't respond. Did he expect her to? She has been cold all morning. If he keeps looking her way, she will eventually have to acknowledge his existence. Won't she? "You're not wearing your ring?" he asks.

"I forgot to put it on."

"I thought you never take it off." She wrinkles her brow and shakes her head. She has only had it a short time. Maybe he shouldn't have said that.

She cuts the wheel sharply to the left and pulls into the emergency ramp of the hospital. "You need to get out here to get your car. I have to report in and then meet Grandma at the courthouse at nine."

"I'll be there," he says, realizing he sounds like that puppy who dirtied the floor.

He gets out and stands in the doorway for a second before closing the door and walking down the ramp to the garage entrance. He wonders why she didn't park her car in the garage if she is going to check-in but then figures she will just leave her car at the entrance and run in and out.

As he pulls out of the garage, he sees her car headed back downtown. The clock on the dash reveals that it is not even eight o'clock. She must be meeting someone.

He follows at a distance for a while and then loses her with all the blocked roads and detours.

The parking lot of the building housing Castleby Development is almost full, which is most unusual for this time of day, for any time of day, for that matter. In addition to cars, there are media vans everywhere, and people walking around with cameras mounted on their shoulders. He avoids the crowd and heads for the elevator.

"What the hell is going on out there?" James meets him halfway down the hall. "And look at you. Where the hell have you been? You come to work dressed like that?"

"I love you, too, Dad," says Sam, walking into his office rather than toward his father. "It's a friggin' circus!"

Sam checks behind the door of his office and finds a suit and shirt covered in plastic from the cleaners. "Perfect," he says.

"Where did you rush off to yesterday?"

"You know, Dad, I can almost feel the love and concern in your voice. You should watch that." He isn't sure who he is angrier with, his father or himself.

"Don't be a wise ass," James says, following Sam into his office.

"You going to watch me change?" He removes his shirt and opens the plastic bag to unbutton the light blue Oxford.

James walks over to the window and looks out at the crowd. "They're blocking the streets from here to the courthouse." He opens the window. The sound of chanting and bullhorns compete with one another, making the whole thing incomprehensible.

James asks, "Who are they? Where did they come from?"

"Hell, if I know. But it's organized, that's for damn sure." He walks over to the window. "Look, they have banners and flags. There are even some BLM folks out there. I thought they were out of business."

"Mr. Castleby?" The secretary calls from the doorway. "CNN is on the phone. They want to ask you a few questions."

"About what?" asks James.

"Not you, Mr. Castleby. The other Mr. Castleby."

"Me?" Sam waves her off. "I'm not talking to CNN. What's this about, anyway?"

"Your wedding."

He holds up his pants.

"I can tell them you're indisposed." She turns and says, "The same for Fox News, too?"

"They're here as well?"

"They called earlier. And you may want to read this," she says, handing James the newspaper.

Sam glances over his father's shoulder at the headline as he puts on his pants. "What the-"

James tosses the paper on the desk. "We have to warn Maggie. Is she at the hospital?"

"No. She's on her way to the courthouse. Or I think she is." Sam zips up his pants and leans over the desk to read the paper. "There may not even be a wedding."

"What do you mean? What happened?" James reaches for Sam to grab his shoulders, but Sam pulls away. He wants to tell his father that this is all his fault. He should have talked to Maggie first, before planning his country estates. He could have been just as happy building her cancer center, but, no, he always knows better.

James reads aloud from the paper. "In a landmark ruling, Judge Philips has agreed to a hearing challenging the legality of the ancestral inheritance of the Cranberry Farm Estate. The recently identified descendants of Chester Cranberry and ex-slave Deborah Townsend have filed a petition claiming Elcira Cranberry should not have been able to inherit the property because she was responsible for her husband's death."

Sam grabs the paper. "This is perfect!"

James points to the crowd. "Now more of them are arriving. They're blocking traffic in all directions."

"I'm calling Maggie. If I call off the wedding, she won't inherit anything, and this will all go away."

"Don't be a fool, Sam. I don't think that would make any difference."

"Why not?" He knows he is speaking from pain and not reason, but he can't help it.

"They are challenging the original inheritance. And now they are turning this into a racial issue."

"What did you think she was going to do? Did you know this Effie person before she ran off and became a lawyer?"

"Yes, she worked for Kendal Lightfoot at the paper. I had many run-ins with him over the years."

"So, why not fight now? If you want to build something and save this business, you should be right there at Maggie's side. I know I'm going to be, even though she is probably fed up with me."

"What do you mean?"

"Fight fire with fire. Today, they have their circus, and tomorrow, we have ours."

James slaps both his hands on Sam's shoulders. "That's my boy."

"I'm not a boy," he responds and tucks his shirt in his pants. He shakes his head as he walks out of the office. Will Dad ever see him as a man? Will Maggie?

Kendal

FRIDAY

W hat on God's green earth did you do?" Kendal paces back and forth in his office, FaceTiming on the phone with Effie while holding another phone at arm's length. "I've got the Town trustees shouting at me on the other phone." He stands by the window, squinting to see through the dirty glass.

"It's your article that did this," Effie says, shouting to be heard over the din of the crowd. "There must be two thousand people here."

He has an idea who is behind all of this. He'd like to think Effie is being used, but she is headstrong, and this is the type of shenanigans she would pull. "You've got to make them go away!"

"No way!" She squeezes between a woman with her child strapped to her chest and a masked young man dressed in black, waving a rainbow flag. "Don't know what got him involved."

"What? Hold on." Kendal switches phones. "No, I didn't know that. I'm telling you, I didn't arrange this. I don't know anything about a permit. If a permit is required and they don't have one, then shut them down. That's the way it works, isn't it?"

"Your mother's whiskers!" he shouts to the space between the phones.

"Kendal? I need to hang up. They want to interview me."

"For God's sake, Effie. Effie?" She must have muted the phone, because he can still see her. He puts that phone down and returns to the other.

"I'm not yelling. Okay, yes I'm yelling, but I'm, not the cause of all this. Someone arranged this."

"Mr. Lightfoot, you have visitors." Kendal's secretary appears in the doorway, blocking the view of all but the heads of two police officers. "These gentlemen want to talk with you."

Of course they do. Kendal waves them in. "Look, I have to go. The police are here. I will straighten this all out and call you back."

"Mr. Lightfoot?" The two officers look like they have been cut from the same mold, though one is black and the other white. "We have a situation at the courthouse that seems to have manifested itself from your article."

The images on the phone on his desk show more people piling onto the steps.

"It did, did it? And how does a situation manifest itself? Does it pop out of a magician's hat or come down the chimney like Santa Claus?"

"Are you making fun of me, sir?" The Black officer steps forward.

"Me? Make fun of one of our finest? I'm the best friend you and your union have ever had here in Old Cranberry. So, why don't you go back down there are round up the rioters and their instigators?" He sees Effie being interviewed by regional news.

"I sense a tone in your voice," says the White officer.

"A tone? You call this a tone?" Kendal pushes hard against the arms of his chair causing its springs to groan as he lifts himself up. At full height, he is still at least one head shorter than they are, but his girth is enough to indicate his intent. "If you were down at the courthouse, you had to run into the instigator."

"If you mean Ms. Devine, she's the one who indicated that it was your newspaper that started this conflagration."

"Conflagration? Did someone give you a thesaurus for your birthday?"

"What do dinosaurs have to do with this?" the paler one responded.

"For your information, a conflagration is a fire. If you hurry down there, maybe you can stop this before the courthouse goes up in flames."

"Is that a threat?"

"I guess you don't watch Fox. No, it's not a threat. It's an anticipation of something far worse than is already happening." Kendal steps around his desk and starts walking toward them. They step back to make room in his tiny office.

"How are you going to straighten this out?" the other officer asks.

"I don't have a clue."

"But I heard you say…"

"You heard me buy some time. Now answer me this." He points to one and then the other. "How come you two can take time out from crowd control to visit me? Shouldn't you be out there clearing the streets?"

"We could take you in, sir."

"For what? For pointing out your responsibility to keep the peace?" Kendal puts his wrists together. "Go ahead, take me in. I welcome the thought. Maybe it will keep me from getting in any more trouble. Take me!" He knows they won't placate such a request. This is Kendal in his glory, right in the center of attention, and he knows how to play it well.

The Black officer turns to his partner and says, "I don't think we can just bring him in. What will we charge him with?"

"Get out!" Kendal uses his body to push them through the doorway. "I have to go to the bathroom."

"But we didn't solve the problem," says the officer.

Kendal walks past the secretary, grabs the key hanging from a hook near the door, and heads down the hall. "I don't give a—"

The bathroom door slams.

Effie

FRIDAY

This is what she wants more than anything else. This is the glory, the moment when the world notices her, this invisible, unwanted, and abandoned girl that no one took seriously. This is Effie's moment. What will she do when she wins? That's what they all want to know. Never before has a case like this been brought before the court. Sure, it is just a hearing, but that's not what the world sees. The world sees justice long deserved, finally being served against the ones who stole freedom from an entire race and kept it from them for generations, even after the laws said they couldn't.

The crowd flows out from the old courthouse steps to the sidewalk and onto the street below, where tall sycamore and oak trees create shade and invite curious birds to watch.

Standing on a makeshift platform made of wooden boxes, on the steps of the courthouse, Effie taps the microphone, causing feedback. A man hands her a megaphone, but she rejects it.

"Thank you for coming out today to help me right a serious wrong in this country."

Up in the tree, a crow waacs and caws, and the feedback returns, causing people to cover their ears.

"Elcira!" she shouts. "You've been sleeping comfortably too long. Time to wake you up and bring you to trial."

A breeze whips her braided hair extensions across her face.

A woman next to her starts chanting Elcira's name and the crowd joins in, "El-see-ra, El-see-ra."

"We have come a long way from the days of slavery in this country, but the vestiges of that era remain." Effie surveys the crowd, feeling the support growing as more curious onlookers arrive.

"Finally, we have reached a point of progress where support has grown for correcting the wrongs of the past. And you are that support."

The crowd roars. She looks out and spots the plants, those who were hired to stir up the crowd. Thank you, Jacqueline. Effie can see Mildred making her way through the crowd toward her.

"In this country, it's against the law to claim ownership of something that was stolen, even if you were not the one who stole it. I'm here to say that there is no statute of limitations on that law. An inheritance, falsely given, is stolen property."

"Effie!" Mildred makes her way through the crowd, followed by a dark, handsome gentleman Effie knows all too well, David Parker. "I believe you have something that belongs to me."

"Ms. Cranberry, you have it backwards. You have something that belongs to me. Uh, everything." She raises her hands and the crowd roars.

Mildred marches up the steps and pushes the newspaper in her face before grabbing the microphone. "The key belongs to me."

"I had a court order," Effie says.

"To dig up my property to find the key, but it wasn't there, was it?"

"I don't see what–"

"It wasn't there because you stole it from my car."

The crowd moans.

"I did no such thing!" Effie tries to speak, but the feedback returns. "Damn!"

David steps up to the microphone and addresses the crowd. "It appears that evidence obtained under false pretenses may not be admissible, so you don't have a case."

"We'll see-" The feedback grows louder.

Mildred holds out her hand. "The key!"

She doesn't have the key, but she will need it to make her case, so she isn't about to let Mildred know some damn birds stole it from her car. Effie reaches into her pocket but then hesitates and reveals her empty hand. "I don't have it."

Mildred grabs her hand and pulls so hard she rips Effie's shorts, causing a large tear revealing her leg.

"What the—?" Effie grabs Mildred's arm and pulls her down, causing Mildred to fall onto the steps.

David reaches for Mildred but gets pushed by someone in the crowd and falls down the steps.

"What's going on here?" A uniformed patrolman on a bicycle arrives, drops his bike and runs up the steps.

"I saw it all, Officer," a woman says, pointing to Mildred. "This white woman attacked the black woman and tore her clothes off."

"What?" Mildred nurses a scraped elbow as she tries to stand.

"That's true, Officer," says Effie, showing off her torn shorts.

"Okay, you'll have to come with me," he says, grabbing Mildred's arm.

"Are you arresting her?" asks David, trying to reach her but finding himself blocked by bodies and placards.

"I will need you to fill out a complaint, Miss," the officer says to Effie.

"Wait a minute," says David. "She didn't say she was filing a complaint."

"Well, I am," says Effie. "And I have witnesses."

"This doesn't look good, does it?" Mildred says as the officer calls for backup on his walkie-talkie.

"I will meet you at the station," says David. "I need to get some eye-witness accounts documented."

The officer marches Mildred down the steps, and the crowd parts to let her through.

"We're not leaving!" Effie says into the microphone. "This is proof that White Privilege is alive and thriving here in Old Cranberry."

The crowd roars as Effie shows off her exposed leg and watches Mildred being escorted through the crowd.

Mildred

The room where they are holding Mildred is one of those small interrogation rooms, like the ones shown on television, only this one has a coffee pot, small refrigerator and sink. more like a break room,

"I need to get out of here, David. I know you said you can handle the hearing yourself, but I have Sylvie's wake tomorrow." Mildred folds her hands in her lap. The metal chairs and table are the only real furniture in the small room. A stream of sunlight causes the dust particles in the air to twinkle like stars. The smell of burnt coffee causes Mildred to hold a tissue over her nose.

"Don't worry, I'll get you released. Just give them your statement and sign it. They can't hold you on this. They don't even have Effie here pressing charges."

"Are you sure?" Mildred wipes a tear from her eye. "Did you call Maggie?"

"Yes, on both counts."

He grabs his briefcase and puts it on his lap.

"You brought work?"

194

"We have a little time before the case. I'm hoping the police will clear the crowd from the courthouse by then." He pulls out a rolled-up map and gently opens it on his briefcase which he uses as a desk. "After looking over the map you have, I went to the Historical Society, and they dug this up."

"Is that my property?"

"Yes and no," he says. "This area here is the old cranberry farm, but this here is shown to belong to Colonel Townsend."

"Townsend? We heard that name before, right?"

"It's the name of the nanny according to the paper Effie filed." He pulls out that paper. "Deborah Townsend."

"Wait a minute," she says staring at the map. "That's where the carriage house is. That's Sylvie's property. Isn't that the old oak tree?" Mildred puts on her reading glasses to study the map more closely.

"I told you it was getting interesting."

The door opens with a creaking sound, and a police officer comes in. He dumps the coffee in the sink and refills it with water. "I'm going to make fresh. Do you want some?"

Mildred looks at her watch. "I'm hoping we are out of here before that is ready."

As he finishes setting up the coffee maker, the door opens again. This time it's Maggie. "Grandma? Are you all right?"

"Oh, Maggie," she says, standing to give her a hug. "I'm so sorry."

"It's not your fault that bitch caused all this trouble." Maggie looks at David and then at the map. "What's this?"

"It's a map of the Cranberry Farm property after the death of Chester."

"It's not right, though," says Mildred. "It shows the carriage house belonging to Colonel Townsend."

"If it was his, it should be what Effie is after. But it wound up in our family?"

Mildred tries to recall stories from her childhood. Her father used to talk about the history of the property, but she was never that interested. Another failure on her part.

"That's what we have to find out," says David. "This shows the property changed hands, maybe more than once. Deborah took the name Townsend, so she may have been the colonel's slave."

"Wait - What?" Maggie shakes her head

"But the book in the library has Deborah's name in it and it says Cranberry Farm, so she must have been living in the main house. Why would she do that if she owned the carriage house property?" asks Mildred. "We need to figure out when Elcira died, and who was living where." This is much more complicated than she had hoped. She should be home, grieving her aunt, trying to cope with all that she needs to do now. Sylvie's rose ring comes to mind. What did she do with it?

"Grandma, are you all right?" asks Maggie.

"I just want this all to be over so we can go back to our lives." As soon as she says it, she knows it won't be so. They can't go back, can they? She has to deal with this. Now. It won't wait.

"I'm confused about the split in the property. Do we know why it was given to Townsend?" asks Maggie, pulling up a chair beside David.

"The article claims Deborah's son, Henry, was Chester's son. That would make him an heir to the property," says David.

"When was he born?" asks Mildred.

"After Elcira and Chester's seven children, so he would not be first in line."

"But if she can prove that Elcira killed Chester?" asks Maggie.

"Then, the property should have gone to Elcira's firstborn son, right?" asks Mildred.

"Not necessarily. If Chester didn't list his son in the will, it would be up to the courts."

"So, it could be taken away from us, and then it won't matter what either of us want to do with it." Mildred sighs. What's the point of anything. "How can we not own what we own? What about all the generations of caring for that property and keeping it up? And the taxes paid." She is feeling her temperature rise.

David points to the map. "Don't jump to conclusions, Mildred. We know it was around the time Chester died, just before the property was divided at the row of bushes here that border the carriage house property today."

"Maybe it was payment for something Townsend did for him," says Maggie. "Or didn't do."

"What are you thinking?" asks David, shifting his focus from the map to her.

Mildred watches the two of them, how they look at one another, what their eyes are saying.

"If Deborah was living in the Townsend household, somewhere else in town, she must have been coming up to the farm regularly to watch the children. That could create an opportunity for Chester, right?" Maggie leans into David.

"Something's missing," says David. "We need to know when the property changed hands and when it changed back."

"Are you thinking Effie might be entitled to the Carriage House property?" asks Mildred. She can't have that. She will destroy Sylvie's garden.

"I didn't find a bill of sale, but I wasn't looking for that in the records," says David."We may learn more from Effie at the hearing." He looks at his watch. "We need to get you out of here."

David rolls up the map and puts it back in his briefcase. "Come, we have to get to the courthouse."

Mildred

The room in the old courthouse is too small for the crowd, who gathered outside hours before the doors opened. The police presence has improved considerably since Effie addressed the crowd, and now there was a path up the handicap ramp for people to wait in line to attend the hearing. Most of the women from the garden club manage to slip in and take seats behind Effie, except Tilly, who motors her way into one of the few handicapped spaces available upfront.

Jacqueline, however, has settled into a seat. Mildred can see her enormous hat blocking the view of several people behind her as she and David take their seats at the defendant's table. David bows his head to Effie, who is being interviewed by a television crew, but Mildred continues to scan the room, taking stock of who is present.

"This is going to be crazy," says Mildred.

"Grandma," says Maggie as she comes down the aisle to greet her with a strong show of support for the crowd.

"I love you," each says to the other.

"I don't care what happens today," says Maggie. "As long as we're together and not fighting anymore."

Mildred fights back tears. "Don't worry, I will not let Effie have the property."

"I don't care," she says.

Mildred places one hand on each of Maggie's shoulders and touches her forehead to Maggie's their eyes inches apart, and whispers, "This will be for the children with cancer."

"I have always thought it would be there, the garden, the pond, the open field where I used to play. I have great memories of Mom and Dad pushing me on the tire swing at the old tree and Grandpa holding me in his arms on the garden bench, reading me a story. They're all gone." She brushes away the tears. "We haven't really enjoyed it like we used to. Aunt Sylvie did. She had her garden and her tea parties."

"I know. It's just us, now."

"It has been for a while, Grandma. We could have spent more time together, but we have both been -"

"Preoccupied?" What was so important? Was everything for the garden club? Is that all she has become, an old garden club lady?

"I don't want to lose you, too."

Mildred kisses her on the cheek.

Sam makes his way through the crowd and sits in the back, several rows behind them and his parents. She watches him sit down and stare at his lap, as if sent to the corner for being a bad student.

"What's happening with you two?" asks Mildred.

Maggie looks back and shakes her head. She then looks past Mildred to David who is sorting through his papers. "I can't think about that now," she says.

Mildred holds Maggie's hands and notices the engagement ring is missing. She kisses her hands. "You should take a seat, or you'll have to stand."

"Bring it on," says David. "I'm feeling confident we have a good story to tell."

"I hope so," says Maggie.

"All rise." The bailiff is a tall black man with a near perfectly round head and a chest that entered the room before his nose. He has the look of a drill sergeant.

Judge Philips, on the other hand, looks like he slept in his robe. His monk-style hair, salt, and pepper around the rim and empty on the top, is accented by a two-day scruffy beard that shows more gray than black. He stands before his chair for longer than anyone finds comfortable, smiles a half-smile as though he is playing a game, and then says, "Be seated."

He takes his time adjusting his chair and looking over his notes before acknowledging the room's occupants. "This is a hearing, not a trial. Rarely do we have such a packed house for a preceding of this nature, so I am going to make the assumption here that this seemingly insignificant and exceedingly cold case is of paramount importance to the town and its community."

There is a murmur that quickly silences when the judge pauses.

Mildred looks at Effie sitting at the table to her right. She is looking for something among the papers and books on the table.

The judge opens a folder and lifts a paper to his nose, reading it as if he needs glasses but is too vain to admit it.

"As I was saying, this is a most interesting case we have before us today," he says, addressing himself in the plural. "We have a petition here to right a wrong that has had a detrimental impact on the very fabric of this community for over two hundred years, and that is not something that can easily be remedied."

Mildred grabs David's hand and squeezes as tight as she can.

"The petition presented by Ms. Devine asserts that the property known as the Cranberry Estate, formerly Cranberry Farms, was erroneously inherited and therefore has been in the possession of the wrong family for over five generations."

Mildred squeezes again, expecting David to object, but he keeps his focus on the judge instead.

"Now, let me offer a little bit of background here, in an effort to move this along," says Philips, spreading pages out before him.

"Your Honor, this is most unusual," says David. "I would think-"

"Mr. Parker, this is my courtroom, and I will decide what is unusual. Besides, unusual problems require unusual solutions, so if you think this is unusual, then I am sure you will accept an unusual resolution to this unique problem, don't you agree?"

"I would like to hear the petition before the court." says David.

"You would, would you? Maybe you would like to adjudicate this matter yourself?"

Effie laughs and Kendal Lightfoot pats her on the back, but Abigail punches him in the side and several of the ladies chuckle.

Mildred can hear Jacqueline commenting to Harold, who chose to stand at the door like a sentry. She glances around the room, noticing that her garden club members have successfully built a wall around Effie, preventing any of her fans and paid supporters from getting near her. Tilly, from her special spot up front, has an empty seat next to her. A woman tries to sit there, but Tilly waves her away, giving her a scowl. Mildred chuckles, wondering which spirit is keeping her company today.

Pastor Tilton is sitting near the back, on the aisle, possibly anticipating the need to suddenly rush off to administer last rites or perform a baptism.

Mildred closes her eyes, wishing it all away, but when she opens them again, it is no better than it was. At least, she rationalizes, the bulk of the protesters were not allowed in. Their chants form a steady din outside the window, which is left open due to the climbing summer heat, though some of that feeling may be self-generated by hormones.

A gentle touch on her shoulder causes Mildred to turn. Harriet squeezes her shoulder and smiles. "Don't worry."

"The petition before the court is unique and timely. Its precedent-setting nature, at a time in our nation's history when our collective consciousness has been raised to such matters of inequity and abuse of wealth, makes it all the more relevant and necessary."

"What the hell," says Maggie, sitting behind Mildred.

"Miss Devine, you claim that the property in question, a property which the Cranberry family has held for generations, was not passed down to the descendants of Chester H. Cranberry but to his murderer instead."

"I object, Your Honor," said David. "Elcira Cranberry was Chester's family. She was his wife, and her involvement in his murder has not been proven, and there is no way to-"

"Mr. Parker! Do you want me to eject you from this courtroom?"

"This is ridiculous," says Maggie.

"I believe I have a valid objection, Your Honor."

"You do not, Mr. Parker. All I said was Miss Devine alleges to be true. It is up to her to prove her case and for you to prove her wrong."

"I uh-"

"May I proceed, Mr. Parker?"

David gestures to the judge to continue, and the courtroom lets out a moan.

"Order!" The judge scowls, looks at Effie, and gives her a smile.

"I don't understand what this is all about," Tilly tells her imaginary neighbor.

Several women around her shush her.

"I am not going to say this again. You will respect my courtroom, or you will be asked to leave."

David shakes his head, turns to Mildred and bites his lip. She pats his arm and smiles.

"I'd like to get this over with if it's okay with everyone here," says Philips. "Both parties involved in this dispute have copies of the petition, so I will assume you have read it. As I said before this is not a trial, but a hearing, so we will proceed with hearing both sides of this argument, beginning with Ms. Devine."

"Thank you, Your Honor, sir."

"You are welcome," he responds with another smile.

"As you stated, the property in question is the Cranberry Estate. I have a map of the property that I would like to share." She walks over to a laptop and connects it to the cable that allows the audience to see her computer screen on a large flat-screen television.

As soon as the map appears, Mildred looks at David who nods. The map is out-dated.

"As you can see, there are two buildings on the property. Here and here," she says, pointing to a large rectangular building on the upper corner of the map and a smaller one below, more centrally located. "This small house here is where the carriage house stands today, and between the two houses, in this area is where the garden and old oak tree are. It is believed that this area is where the potting shed was located, and the barn where Chester Cranberry was murdered is this structure here," she says, pointing to a square building and two round silos off to the right.

"Miss Devine, please get to the point. I don't have all day.'

"Of course," she says. "Chester Cranberry was murdered in the barn, stabbed in the groin with a pitchfork, a second pitch-fork through the chest and stomach, and then left on a pile of manure."

The audience groans.

"His wife, Elcira Cranberry, was the primary suspect, because she was nowhere to be found when a neighbor, Sam Green arrived and discovered the body. He informed Constable Tucker who found Mrs. Cranberry locked in the potting shed. A brass skeleton key to the shed was in Chester's pocket, so the police assumed he locked her in it before he was murdered, thereby eliminating her as a suspect."

"Bravo," says Tilly to the empty chair.

The judge shushes her.

"With the discovery of a second key in the garden, here, by Mrs. Sylvie Rose, we have opportunity, because I believe this is where the outhouse was located."

She turns to the judge and smiles. Mildred tries to follow her logic. She has heard the old wives tale before about a second key that Elcira could have used to lock herself in the shed, but no such key was found on her.

"Elcira Cranberry murdered her husband, placed one key in his pocket and used the other to lock herself in the shed. The constable found Elcira locked in the shed. After being released, Elcira used the outhouse where she deposited the key."

Mildred leans close enough to David to whisper, "Where was Deborah?"

"Objection, Your Honor. This is pure speculation on her part." David stands and points at Effie.

"This is a hearing, Mr. Parker. We should hear her out first, and then you will have a chance to argue your opposing points."

"Brother," David says under his breath.

"Do you have a problem with that, Mr. Parker?"

"No, Your Honor." David sits and averts his eyes.

"Now, Miss Devine, do you have this extra key in your possession?"

"Not at this time, Your Honor." Effie looks to the back of the courtroom. "I expect to have it soon."

Mildred looks at David and raises her hands in a questioning gesture.

"And you can prove that it is the same key?"

"Yes, Your Honor. And a lock was found on the site. The key that Chester had, which I believe you have as evidence was determined to be a possible match for that lock."

"Possible or actual?"

"The lock is quite corroded. Further analysis is required to determine an exact match."

"Is that all?"

"No, Your Honor. I wish to present this document as evidence that Chester Cranberry was the father of the son of his hired nanny, Deborah Townsend. The son's name was Henry Townsend, born a free black man to a woman who had been a slave. Upon Chester's death, the property was inherited by his wife, but under the circumstances, since she killed him, it should have gone to his son, Henry instead."

"Objection."

"On what grounds, Mr. Parker?"

"Elcira's guilt is not proven. And there were other children of Chester."

"I will accept it for now," he says, turning to Effie. "Anything else, Miss Devine?"

"Not at this time, Your Honor."

"Well, I don't think we can move forward until that key turns up and is proven to be a match for the one Chester had on his person."

He reaches for his gavel. "We will adjourn this hearing and resume on Monday morning at nine a.m.. That should be enough time for you, right, Miss Devine?"

"Your Honor -" David stands.

"Mr. Parker, I am making your job easier. You don't need to offer anything at this point."

David opens his mouth, but the judge slams his gavel and rises.

The audience applauds Effie as she grabs her laptop and makes her way out of the courtroom.

"This is a total screw-up," says David to Mildred.

"I thought she had the key."

"She did, too."

Jacqueline

This is definitely not going as planned. How could she lose that key? As Jacqueline descends the court steps, Harold is ready with the door open for her, but she stops when she reaches him and pushes her face up to his. "Where is that little minx?"

"I'm not sure I know what you are referring to, Ms. Hudson."

"Effie," she says, "where is she?"

She spots her in the center of a crowd of protesters across the street, gathered outside the diner.

Kendal Lightfoot uses a cane to navigate the steps. He stops a few feet from Harold and Jacqueline and leans on his cane. "Well, that went better than I expected. Don't you agree?"

"It was a total disgrace," says Jacqueline, tapping her walking stick on his belly. "You and Effie made a mockery of this case, and now it looks like she was not prepared at all."

"What do you mean?" He chuckles. "I had the whole damn county yelling at me this morning, fearful a riot was about to start and turn into a real fiasco, and look, the place is clearing out. People think she's won."

"Hrumpf." Jacqueline turns to Harold. "She doesn't have a snowflake's chance in West Texas of finding that blasted key. You need to track it down, Harold."

"I beg your pardon?" He steps away from the car door. "How do you propose that I do that? We tore her car apart and found nothing. I tell you, those birds took the key."

"What?" Kendal leans forward on his cane. "What did you say?"

"I know crows are smart, but what would possess them to grab a key out of Effie's car?" asks Jacqueline. "Harold, I think you are intentionally holding back. Cecil never would have disobeyed me like this."

"Miss Hudson, I am not Cecil, and I didn't disobey you. Why is this battle so important to you anyway?"

"Pardon me?" She raises her walking stick but the open door between them prevents her from prodding him. "I'm doing this for your people."

"My people? Which people would that be, madam? The Browns of Bridgeport, or the Kennedys of Massachusetts? Maybe the Sopranos of New Jersey?"

"Don't make fun of me. You know what I mean."

He turns to Kendal and stares at him and then looks at her. "You mean black people like me as if we are all the same. Right? Well I am not looking for payment for something that happened centuries ago by an ignorant people who didn't know any better. You need to let this go. You are only encouraging Ms. Devine to incite violence in what used to be a peaceful town."

"What do you know about this peaceful town?" It wasn't her idea to come here. Kentucky is her home. This is no substitute, even after all she has done to make it her town. This was supposed to be Preston's chance to change his ways. It had cost way too much in money and reputation to fend off those floozies who chased him and trapped him in their boudoirs back home. And who did he have eyes for but Mildred Cranberry Smith, the pretty young wife of a milk toast accountant?

"Now, Jac-lene, please calm down. You're attracting a crowd."

Several people take a wide path around them as they leave the courthouse.

"Where is the key?" I need that key to unseat that queen from her throne.

"I would guess that question is for the birds."

"Oh, that's a good one," says Kendal, taking out his pad and pencil.

"Why do you think I have it? If I did, though, I would give it back to the one who found it." Harold is treading on thin ice.

"She's dead and going to be cremated." Jacqueline gasps. "You didn't. Take me to the funeral home! Now!" It wasn't birds. It was Harold. He put the key in the casket.

"You are crazy! Why are you doing this?"

"I have a good mind to fire you right now."

"Then how would you get home? Uber? Lyft?" He laughs. "For someone of your standing, Ms. Hudson, you don't pay a lot of mind, as you would say to what others think of you, and that's a mistake."

"I declare," she says, leaning on her accent for support.

Kendal takes out his phone and starts recording. Several people have now gathered and are doing the same.

"This is fun for you, isn't it? The Cranberry property is the one thing your husband wasn't able to lay his hands on, so you want to bring it down. I believed you when you said you wanted to bring justice and equity to all who didn't get a fair shake, but triggering a reparations movement is not what you are after, is it?"

"Take me to the funeral home, Harold."

"I'm taking you home."

"How dare you disobey an order." She gets in the car and slams the door shut.

He does the same and turns to her. "Where to, ma'am?"

They remain silent for the entire trip. As they head over the tracks and into the poorer part of town, she presses her face against the window and stares.

At the funeral home, he opens her door and extends a hand, but she refuses it, taps her walking stick on the ground, and ambles angrily toward the door. How dare he? She can't lose control. Not now.

"May I help you?" asks the young man making adjustments to the room after an earlier viewing had taken place.

"I'm Jac-lene Hudson, a friend of Sylvie Rose. Has she been cremated yet?"

"Sylvie Rose?" He scratches his head. "Oh, that's tomorrow's wake. No, she won't be cremated until after the service. They decided on an open casket."

"Can I see her?" Jacqueline ponders her options. "You didn't happen to recover anything from the body or the coffin, did you?"

"You mean like her jewelry? Some people want us to leave it with the deceased. When jewelry is exposed to those temperatures it melts, so the crematory scoops that out and recycles it. Ms. Cranberry is stopping by to pick it up after the showing, so, no, we haven't removed anything yet. Do you need to talk to her? I think she is coming for a meeting with my dad."

"No. No. No. Just curious, dearie. And where is this cremato-rium, by the way?"

"Normally we use Barker's in town, but they have a backlog. It has been a busy time."

"I'm sure," she says, wanting to hear more.

"For Ms. Rose we are using Gentle Touch in Stamford."

"Do they remove the metal before cremation?"

"We have only used them a few times and I don't believe we had any metal other than replacement parts, hips, knees and the like." He smiles. "You are interested in this, aren't you?"

"Well, when the time comes…"

"Ah," he says. "Well we would be glad to sit with you and plan what you would like so you will have peace of mind that everything will be handled the way you wish."

"Thank you, that would be nice. Can I have your card?"

"Sure. Let me just go to the office and get you one."

"Damn you, Harold," Jacqueline mumbles as she taps her walking stick and ponders her next move. "You're going to make this right!"

"Jacqueline," says Mildred as she catches her in the act. "Nice to see you here. Planning your funeral?"

Jacqueline straightens up and rests her weight on her walking stick, turning to face Mildred.

"Er, yes and no. Just planning ahead."

"It's always good to have a plan." Mildred smiles. "Sylvie had everything planned long before she needed it. She thought of everything."

"Yes. You never would think that when you met her. Always talking about her roses and squirrels. Simple things make some people so happy."

"Oh, Ms. Cranberry," says Vince Maguire, returning with a business card in hand. "You got your wish, Ms. Hudson. Here's my card."

"How nice," she says, turning toward the door, but waiting to hear what Mildred was up to. Perhaps she has the key and is going to plant it in the casket so no one would find it.

"Vince, is your father around?"

"He's in his office."

"Before I go see him, here is Aunt Sylvie's rose ring. Could you put it on her for me?" She hands him a small box from her purse. Jacqueline is itching to see if it holds the key.

"Sure will, Mrs. Cranberry."

Cranberry. She's a Smith, a plain, old Smith. How disrespectful not to acknowledge her husband that way.

"Did you want me for something, Jac-lene?"

Jacqueline shakes her head.

"Well, then I will leave you and go see what he needs. I leave you to your goodbyes."

As Mildred leaves, Vince says, "I guess you changed your mind about talking to Ms. Cranberry?"

Jacqueline taps the business card on her walking stick and smiles.

"So?" Harold asks as he holds the door for her upon her arrival.

"Get me out of here. This area is disgusting."

"Really?" He turns and talks to her through the glass partition. "I am so close to home, I will pass by and show you on our way."

Jacqueline turns her head, her lips scrunching up to keep her from saying what she's thinking.

Sam

Friday

S am could typically walk from the diner across from the court-house to his office in less than ten minutes, but today, he has a lot on his mind. Every shop he passes reminds him of what he is about to lose, as if his life with Maggie has already played out and is about to be erased from his future memories.

He imagines one day when he and Maggie will be shopping for a mattress and sheets at Dolton's, baby clothes at GG's, and even toothpaste and diapers at the Old Cranberry Drug Store. Can that future still exist?

Maybe his father is right. Perhaps he's just a boy trying to act like a man.

As the elevator doors close and he ascends to the third floor, he remembers the 'For Sale' sign on his front lawn. Dad needs this project, and it's not going to happen. Even if Mildred and Maggie win the case and keep the property, Maggie wants to give most of it to the hospital. It's a lost cause.

The doors open, and he starts down the hall to the Castleby Development offices. How long will we be able to hold onto this? We should move now to someplace cheaper, smaller. We could re-brand ourselves as a boutique outfit. Maybe it's too late.

Back in his office, he hangs his jacket on the back of the door and spots his clothes on the chair. She's not wearing her ring. She knew David in high school. Sam, you've been such a fool. You practically wrapped him in a ribbon and gave him to her.

Fight fire with fire, Sam. How?

He loosens his tie and logs into his computer. He scans through the folders for the CAD files used to create the 3D model of the Cranberry property. He makes a copy and clears off all the proposed buildings of his father's dream, the Cranberry Estates. With an empty canvas before him, he reaches into the wastebasket for the newspaper and opens it to the Children's Cancer Center rendering. He picks up his phone and calls home.

"Mom?" His voice cracks.

"Sam, where are you? I've been so worried." Her voice is shaky.

"I'm at the office. I'm okay. Don't worry, but I could use your help."

"Is your father there?"

"I don't know. I just got here." He pulls out a blank sheet of paper and a mechanical pencil. "I'm going to put you on the speaker and ask you some questions about the cancer center. Do you have time?"

He lays out the paper beside his keyboard and places the phone on a stand before him.

"I know you don't work at the hospital, but just volunteer, but you spend time with all the patients. What do they want and need?"

"Oh, Sam. I'm not qualified to say."

"Please, Mom," he says. "It's important."

"Let me think." She hums and mumbles to herself.

"I've been to the atrium, more than once," he says, remembering his last visit when he saw her there with the children but didn't go in. He should have. "It is usually filled with old people. Kids don't have a place to play while their siblings are being treated."

"Yes, yes! A bigger atrium with fresh air in the summertime and a soft play area." His mom's voice is more animated, alive.

"Like a playground?" He scratches several quick drawings on the paper.

"Maybe, but indoor. And maybe a big fish tank with tropical fish."

"A fish tank, huh?" He nods as he draws, imagining the children sitting around it. "Maybe we can make a wall of fish. Do they need a television screen?"

"I don't think so. But maybe a reading corner, like in preschools, and a separate reading nook for older kids." She is definitely sounding more excited.

They spend several more minutes chatting about possibilities, each one adding more to the enthusiasm Sam is feeling. This is what he should have been doing with Maggie from the start. She had told him it was her dream. Why didn't he listen? Why does it take almost losing someone to discover how much you depend on them, love them?

It was him, wasn't it? The minute he spoke in the courtroom, Sam knew. He knew that voice, the voice that talked to him in the car, and in the bathroom. He is the reason Maggie isn't wearing her ring.

"I can't think of anything else right now, Sam," says his mom.

"That's perfect, Mom," he says, "I'll start with this and call you back. Let me know if you think of anything else."

"What's going on?" James pushes open the door and walks in.

"Hi, hon," says Harriet over the phone. "I'll see you both later."

Sam points to a chair, and James pulls it up to the desk.

"Did I interrupt something? I'm glad you were talking to your mother. She has been worried sick about you."

Sam shares his sketch with his father. "This is an idea for Maggie's Children's Cancer Center."

"Did she ask you to do that?" He leans over the drawings on his desk.

"No. I'm starting a fire."

"So, this is what you meant?" Sam notices something different in his father's eyes. It made him feel warm and close. He didn't want to lose that moment.

"Can I help?" James reaches for Sam's shoulder.

"Pull the chair around. Maybe you can build the model after I lay it out. I think I would like to be able to open the roof and look inside, so we can show Maggie what the kids will experience."

"I like it," says James. "Let's go into the conference room. I can take apart the model and reuse that."

"Are you sure?" asks Sam. "You are so proud of that model."

"You created the spark. Now, we need to fuel the fire."

Sam drank up the smile his father sent his way. Maybe they can work together.

Mildred

FRIDAY

When Mildred arrives on her street, cars are lined up on the Carriage House driveway and along the street up to the drive to the main house.

She pulls over and gets out. Two more cars arrive, David's and Maggie's.

"What's going on?" asks Maggie as she exits her vehicle.

Mildred walks up to the open front door and peers in. "Oh my God!"

"What's wrong?" asks David, hustling to reach her.

Mildred enters and continues through to the garden room, where the French doors are open to the patio. The grass is covered with plastic tarps, and members of the garden club are ferrying plants and wheelbarrows of soil from place to place.

"Millie!" shouts Tilly, motoring across the patio toward her. "I can't get down and dirty with the ladies, so I am supervising."

"You're putting Sylvie's garden back together?" Mildred's eyes fill up.

"Grandma, look," says Maggie, pointing to a cardinal sitting on the garden bench while the women plant and move dirt nearby. "It's just sitting there."

"Sylvie. She's the real supervisor," says Tilly. "Oh, and I have something for you."

Tilly reaches into the pouch of her wheelchair and pulls out the brass skeleton key. "A little birdie dropped this off for you."

"What?" Mildred grabs the key.

"Actually it was two big birdies, but you know what I mean."

"I don't understand," says David. "How did you find the key?"

"I didn't," says Tilly.

Abigail runs toward them, covered with dirt, her hair radiating from her head like a static electricity experiment. "They were here a minute ago. They just swooped down and dropped the key on the bench."

"A bit melodramatic if you ask me," says Tilly. "Leave it to Elcira to make a big splash, so to speak."

"I am so confused," says Maggie.

"Yes, Tilly," says Mildred. "You can't drop this bird business on us and go on as if nothing unusual is taking place here." Mildred rubs her fingers over the key. "No wonder Effie couldn't produce it."

"Are you saying that someone broke into Grandma's car, stole the key and two birds fetched it and brought it back, like hunting dogs? That's bizarre." Maggie shakes her head as if trying to rearrange the marbles.

"It's not really so strange, Maggie. A spirit wouldn't be able to pick up anything on its own. It needs a host. In this case, two hosts, so, obviously, two spirits. I think they may be sisters. Oh, well," she says motoring away.

Out in the yard, ladies are kneeling on cushions, holding trowels with gloved hands, accompanied by music from a wireless speaker. One or two women could be heard singing off key, as usual.

Mildred kisses Maggie. "I'm going to change, and then tell me how I can help."

"I'll go get some sandwiches," says Maggie.

"I'll go with you," says David. "I want to talk about your plans for the hospital. We may be able to sway public opinion on Monday."

By the time David and Maggie return with sandwiches, the ladies are finishing up with their restoration of Sylvie's garden.

Mildred calls the women together to thank them. "You have done Sylvie proud, ladies. The garden looks even better than before. Sorry Auntie."

The ladies laugh.

"She is here with us," says Tilly.

"Yes, Tilly, and she always will be." Mildred takes Maggie by the hand. "We had a trying day today, and we want to thank you all for being there supporting us. You know we don't want to tear this community apart. And I believe the true story of Old Cranberry will come out, showing the world that we are a loving and supportive community. Hatred and privilege are not labels we want to define us."

The ladies applaud.

"Now, let's all wash up, and then have some sandwiches and tea in honor of Aunt Sylvie," says Maggie, pointing to the table on the patio.

After they eat, one by one, the ladies gather their trowels and gloves and head to their cars. When they are all gone, Maggie escorts David to his car, and Mildred takes a cup of tea out to the garden bench. The cardinal is no longer hanging around, but that doesn't stop Mildred from talking to her aunt.

"I had mine already, but here is a cup for you, Auntie. Did you see that I left The Times crossword on the table with your erasable red pen?" A tear forms and she lets it drop onto her cheek without wiping it away.

"I miss doing them with you," she says, clearing her throat. "Yes, I know, you did them and I just talked to you while you did. Occasionally I would come up with the answer, though. Give me that."

A light breeze rustles the leaves in the tree. She looks to see if a bird or butterfly had joined them.

"I like to think you are still here with me, that you will always be here. Funny, I didn't feel like this when Audrey passed. It was different, then. Raw anger was all I had. I never even thought to sit out here and talk to her like this. Is she with you?"

"I guess I have Tilly to thank for that." She chuckles. "I always thought she was just a crazy old woman. Maybe she is. What does that make us, huh?"

"What's it like where you are?" Mildred looks up. "Maybe you don't know yet if you are still here. Tilly says the cardinal is a sign that you are."

Mildred shakes her head. "I am going crazy."

She stands and brushes the wrinkles from her house dress, walks to the patio and turns to take in the view of the entire backyard from the pond off to the right to the iron gate that leads to the main house on the left.

"I may need your help, Auntie. Maybe you can gather the family together and support us through this battle. I just have this feeling that there is something we aren't seeing, something important that will prove we belong here."

She picks up the teacup and tests the temperature with her pinkie. "I left it too long, Auntie. Iced tea now."

"I have a feeling that our family tree has roots we didn't know about."

"Grandma, who are you talking to?" Maggie enters the patio area from the house. "David said he'll call you if he comes up with anything else."

They hug and exchange kisses.

"I am getting to know you more and more each day, Margaret Payton. I figure I better call you that one more time before you become a Castleby."

"Maybe, maybe not."

"You're not changing your mind are you? I feel it is my fault." Mildred holds Maggie's hands in hers. "I was wrong to force my vision of your future on you. That's for you to decide."

"I don't see it that way, Grandma." She lifts Mildred's hands to her lips and kisses them. "You planned to give up everything for me. You don't need to do that. I know you and Grandpa promised Mom, but she's not holding you to that."

"How do you know?"

"I know. I've been a bitch about this whole thing, keeping my plan for the hospital a secret from you, rather than talking about it. I may have lost Sam, but I don't want to lose you."

Tears flood Mildred's eyes. As she wipes them, she sees Maggie doing the same.

"Bitchiness is in our genes, dear."

"You bet your ass it is."

Mildred watches as Maggie crosses the patio to the carriage house. She turns to glance back at the garden bench, remembering all the times she sat with Maggie, telling her stories of her own childhood and those of her mother.

"I can't let this go," she says turning the key over and over in her hand inside her dress pocket. She walks over to the rose bush near the gate and kneels on the grass. "Sylvie, is this where you found it?"

She pauses, half hoping a bird will land and identify the exact spot, but it doesn't happen. Instead, her phone rings.

"Mildred, it's David. Sorry to bother you again, but I have been reviewing the genealogy you and Maggie put together for Sylvie's family, and I found something interesting."

Mildred lets the key drop into her pocket and sits on the bench. "What did you find?"

"There was a first son before Felix. Felix was Chester and Elcira's firstborn, but not Chester's firstborn."

"He had a son with the nanny. Oh, but that was later, right?"

"He had a son before that with someone else, his first wife. This is how we have two Cranberry families."

"What? What does that do to our case?"

"Well, if Elcira is somehow found guilty, the property wouldn't go to the nanny's son or any of the illegitimate children. It would go to his first son, Garfield."

"Garfield? Like the cat?"

"Yep. And Garfield is Sylvie's great-great-grandfather."

"Really?"

"I told you it gets interesting."

"Does that mean Effie can't win?"

"Unless something totally screwed up happens, she is S-O-L."

"S-O-L?"

"Sorry. Let's just say she is out of luck."

"Thank you, David. This is great news."

"Have a great day, Mildred. See you at the wake. We can talk more then."

Mildred jumps up but lands wrong and feels a sharp pain in her ankle. "Damn it!"

Effie

FRIDAY

Kendal rocks in his desk chair as Effie paces back and forth between his desk and the chair on which Jacqueline is perched, her walking stick in her gloved hand.

"They aren't going to do anything until Monday, right? So we have time to figure out how to get that key," says Effie.

"You shouldn't have let it out of your sight, Effie," says Jacqueline, tapping her foot and walking stick in a non-melodic way.

"Jac-lene, why do you think it is in the coffin?" Kendal pops a handful of popcorn into his mouth and sips a Coke.

"It's the most logical place for it."

"It is?" asks Kendal.

"It's where I would put it to make sure it disappears forever," says Effie.

"Effie, would you stop pacing? You're making me dizzy," says Kendal.

She stops at the window and rubs the glass with a tissue. "You can't see a thing out this window, Lightfoot. Don't you ever clean anything?"

"There is nothing to see," he says. He reaches into the bag to load up on more popcorn.

"Has the crowd dispersed?" asks Jacqueline.

"How much did that cost you?" asks Kendal. "Whatever it was, I think it did the job."

"Do you think we need them again on Monday?" asks Effie.

Jacqueline shoots her a look of disapproval, but she ignores it.

"We've got two days to build up support," says Kendal. "If we play our cards right, you won't need to spend any more money."

"That's what I want to hear," says Jacqueline. "But we still need that key, don't we?"

"What do you suggest?" asks Kendal.

"Whatever it is, it has to be done during the wake," says Effie. "Maybe you can get Harold to check out the coffin.

"Harold?" Jacqueline shakes her head.

"Well, I can't do it," says Effie. "They won't let me anywhere near her."

"Unless you go early." Kendal munches more popcorn and mumbles something.

"I don't have standing here. Only a Cranberry can get in to be with the body before people arrive."

"You're a Cranberry, aren't you?" Jacqueline points to Effie. "Isn't that your whole argument?"

"Yes, but-"

"No buts about it," she says, nodding her head. "You have standing here. I didn't give you all that money to have you fail, Miss Reparations. This is a game-changer. Isn't that what you said?"

"She's right, Effie." He picks at his teeth with his pen.

"Look, girl," says Jacqueline. "and I don't say that because you're Black. I say that because you're young. Feisty, yes, but still young and a bit ignorant of the goings on in this town. I was raised on a horse farm with all kinds of folk, from holier-than-thou, Bible-thumpin' types to land-rich, pocket-money poor folk who never went to school, and everyone in between. You have to take what you can get when you can get it. That's why I have what I have."

Effie rolls her eyes, tired of being talked down to. That's the whole point, isn't it? Finally, she can have standing, respect.

"Now Jacqueline," says Lightfoot, choking on his popcorn. "That's a bit much."

"She sleeps in her car, Kendal!"

"Effie?" he says. "Is that true? I thought your aunt put you up."

"Tilly?" Jacqueline laughs. "You should see her place."

"Come on," says Effie, "that's not fair."

"She's a hoarder. Isn't that why you don't stay there?"

"She took me in when I had no place to go, Jac-lene. She's been like a mom to me, my foster mom."

"Then why do you call her your aunt?" asks Jacqueline.

"Very funny. You know the story. Stop pretending you're above everyone else, Jac-lene."

"Then, go stay with her. You can clear out your things from my home and free up my laundry."

"Jacqueline, aren't you pushing a little too hard?" asks Kendal, leaning forward in his chair.

"Preston left me a tidy sum, but I can't take care of everyone." Jacqueline pumps her leg while she talks. "You don't see Mildred opening her doors to anyone, do you? It's high time she gets knocked off that high horse of hers."

"You really have it in for her, don't you?" Kendal opens his wallet and counts out some money. "Here, Effie, go get a room. There's a cheap motel near the train station. You can't sleep in your car."

"But we need the key to show Judge Philips our story is believable, don't we?" asks Effie.

"Believable, yes, but not one you can prove beyond a doubt. Judge Philips is obviously taking your claim seriously. He didn't even let the other side present. Maybe you don't need to prove it completely."

"What?" Jacqueline shoots him a look that would cause a horse to gallop. "We don't need to prove that Elcira orchestrated the whole thing, making her guilty of murder?"

"Listen. Without the key, we may not need to even have a trial." Lightfoot shifts his weight in his chair, causing it to groan. "This is all about righting a wrong, right? So, what if we point out how wrong it was to ignore the stepchildren?"

"You mean the illegitimate children." Effie crosses her arms. "I don't see how we can do that."

"We don't have to do that," says Lightfoot. "The community will do it. Young black descendant of Chester Cranberry has to sleep in her car because the Cranberry family won't give her a fair share of her inheritance. That makes great story. This may be the era of social media, but this community still reads the daily newspaper, and I happen to be the publisher."

"I see what you are doing," says Jacqueline. "You're starting a revolution."

"No," he says. "You and Effie started that at the courthouse. I just need to craft a story that gets everyone to join the party. 'Staid New England Town Rights A Centuries Old Wrong.'"

"I don't know about this," says Effie. She imagines all the ways this could backfire, leaving her with nothing. Maybe she shouldn't have gone to them, neither of them. Everyone has an agenda.

"What do you mean, child? This is your baby here. You birthed it, you raise it." Jacqueline raises her fist. "This will make amends for generations of abuse."

Effie looks at Jacqueline and wonders if she is talking about Old Cranberry or her own history. The idea of settling for some of the inheritance and not all of it should bother Jacqueline, but for some reason, it doesn't. Is she to be trusted?

"The headline will get people talking. Most folks don't read more than that, and they are usually quick to post their own content to support their view on this, but we will need an interesting story for those who will take the time to read it."

"Effie, dear, do you have any information about this ancestor of yours, Townsend?" asks Jacqueline.

"Only what I presented in the courtroom."

"Go back down to the Historical Society and see if they have anything on folks living at the time. We don't need to link stuff exactly to Townsend. If there's a good story about another nanny who inherited property or was abused, we can use that too." Lightfoot grabbed a handful of popcorn. "If someone, like Parker, your brother, checks our facts and calls us out, we can always publish a retraction somewhere in the next issue. This is too important to waste time getting it perfect."

"Now, this is the fun I was hoping to have in this town," says Jacqueline. "Preston, eat your heart out unless the worms did that already."

Effie takes the money from Kendal and puts it in her purse. Jacqueline's eyes seem to be on her and Kendal at the same time. It is hard to know what she is up to, and Effie is starting to feel she is getting in over her head.

As she follows Jacqueline to her car, she notices Harold staring at her, like a disapproving father. She never felt like this before, almost ashamed. He holds the door open for her, and she feels a hand brush against her arm. She thinks it is him, but his hands are no where near her.

Mildred

Mildred places the key on the table alongside the open books and maps she and David had been studying. Why would the crows steal the key and bring it to her?

A cool breeze lifts the curtain at the window facing the garden. Mildred moves the leather armchair to see across the library and out that window. Her phone buzzes with a text from David.

We're at the Historical Society. Effie's car is here. I need to find out what she's looking for. I'll check in later.

We? Is Maggie with him?

Mildred can't shake the feeling that there are clues here among the books and news clippings Alfred and her dad saved, not to mention all the Cranberry men who came before them. Why didn't she pay more attention? She is sure any one of them could tell her what she needs to know, whatever secret is hidden here among the ghosts of Cranberry Farm.

A warm presence surrounds her, but it is calm and cooler today. The open windows and French Doors have kept the house comfortable, even here in the library, which has been left to its own devices for years.

As she stares at the old oak and the garden bench beside it, the image becomes wavy, as though the air is being disturbed by a heat source. When the radiators come on in the Fall, the temperature change has that effect, or is it her eyes?

Maybe there is a logical explanation for all these unusual events.

She picks up the book that had captured her interest before, the one with the writing in the margin. Deborah Townsend.

She is certain Effie is looking for information on her. But who was this woman, and why did she write in this book? Could she have been leaving a clue?

What happened in 1865? The Civil War? Did she move out? How long was she living here?

Mildred flips through the papers, searching for a family tree. There has to be one somewhere. Or perhaps a journal or diary. That's where she needs to look.

Standing, she kicks off her shoes and pulls the bookcase ladder across the brass rail at the top of the case so she can climb safely to the top shelf. Would the oldest books be here?

One by one, she pulls the books from their resting place and checks the inside cover for a name or label indicating whose book it had been. Would the boys have written about the family, or would one of the girls be a better choice?

For hours, as the sun's light grows dim, Mildred's search drags on, resulting in a pile of books on the table and desk, far too many for her to read.

When Maggie and David arrive, she is sitting in the leather chair, one book on her lap and another in her hands.

"My God," says Maggie. "What are you doing?"

"I've been going crazy," says Mildred. "All these years we have lived among these memories and treasures, and we've ignored them completely."

"We found something interesting about this property that may help us sort through all this," says David.

"Does it have to do with the Underground Railroad?" asks Mildred.

"Yes!" Maggie shouts.

"How did you know?" asks David.

"Deborah Townsend," says Mildred. "She got me thinking and I found something I wasn't expecting." Mildred puts her book down and reaches for a stack of small, thin books across the table. "These."

Maggie grabs one, and David takes another.

"I had books like this. Mom used to read to me at night," says Maggie.

"This one is written in, all over the margins," says David. "This must be how the children were taught to read and write."

"That's what I thought at first but look at this one." Mildred picks up a similar book and hands it to David.

He flips through it and looks at her.

"Read what it says on the inside cover," says Mildred.

"Wow," he says. "This book belongs to, and then in handwriting that is actually pretty clear, William Freeman."

"Free man," says Mildred. "I believe Deborah was teaching freed slaves how to read and write so they could get jobs."

"You could be right," says David.

"There's more," says Mildred. She walks back to the bookcase and climbs the ladder. On the second shelf she pulls out a small leather-bound book, its cover falling off and the pages loose. She comes down and hands it to David. "Look at the cover."

"J.J.J." he says.

"Look at the first page," she says. "Careful, it is brittle."

"Josiah's Journal, June 14, 1833." He looks up. "It is poorly written, as if he is just learning to write." David flips gingerly through the pages. "His handwriting is getting better. This is priceless."

"There are many more up there," says Mildred. "Enough to start our own historical society."

"Let me see," says Maggie.

Mildred goes over to the desk and picks up the map with the smudge mark. "I thought the mark on this map was pointing to the outhouse, but I think it might have been the potting shed."

"Why?" asks Maggie, coming around to look closely at it.

"The key was found near the oak tree, but the outhouse was further away. The lilacs covered the smell. It bothered me that the potting shed would be on Townsend's property, but it makes sense if it was used for hiding runaway slaves."

"Oh my God!" says Maggie.

"So, Effie's ancestor, the nanny of Elcira and Chester's children, used this place as a school?"

"It's possible."

"Then the children must have helped," says David.

"And Elcira, too. Until she passed away." Mildred is suddenly very warm.

David puts the books down. "We found a tax record from 1833, the year after Chester was killed." He hands a photocopy to Mildred.

"It lists twenty-five freed slaves working on the farm, along with ten immigrants, all considered white," says Maggie.

"Slaves were not taxed as high as Whites," says David. "Eventually, they weren't taxed at all, so they were not counted in the census, but this could be evidence of your theory."

"Who would have thought Old Cranberry would have such a rich history?" asks Mildred.

"Yeah, it's not the kind of riches we think about today."

"Does Effie know about this?" asks Mildred.

"We didn't tell her," says Maggie.

David turns to Maggie. "She will find out soon enough. We've got some work to do before Monday."

"I'm hungry," says Mildred. "Let's go get something to eat."

Mildred

Mildred puts a rose on her daughter's grave and puts a smooth stone on the headstone. "This is for your brother," she says. I know you never met while you were alive, but I am sure you have run into each other since."

A black sedan pulls up and stops not far from where she stands.

"Time for the showdown," she says as she corners the mausoleum and leans on the wrought iron fence. "Hello, Jac-lene."

"Millie," she says, walking toward her, a tap of her walking stick with each step. "It sounded urgent on the phone, so I asked Harold to drive me right over."

"I appreciate that," she says. "Shall we sit?"

They convene at what looks like a new plastic-coated metal bench. As Mildred sits, she notices the dedication plaque, "In Memory of Preston Chennelsworth Hudson IV".

"A new addition, I see," Mildred says. "Nice. I have often come, and there is no place to sit."

"I am getting too old to stand for too long, so I donated it. But you can sit there if you like."

"I already have."

"You probably know I went to the Garden Club after that hideous display at the courthouse."

"The Garden Club. Why didn't I think of that? Oh, that's right. They were all there, so I guess you didn't have to go far."

"I formally requested to have you removed from the board."

"Thank you," she says. "Saves me the trouble. You do know I have been asked to run for Town Council more than once, and the last time was after the hearing."

"You think you are so important in this town, don't you?"

"Another thing I have you to thank for, Jac-lene."

"Don't mock me, Mildred."

"It must be hard to live in the shadow of greatness."

"Bah," she says.

"Humbug." Mildred smiles. "I was talking about your beloved husband." Mildred taps the plaque on the bench. "He certainly had his hands in a lot of things."

Jacqueline plants her palms on the top of her walking stick. "Well, I never."

"That may have been the problem, Jackie."

"Jac-lene to you."

"Nothing to me, I'm afraid."

Jacqueline puckers her lips as if having sucked a lemon. "Did you call me just to insult me, or is there something you wanted to tell me?"

"I want to end this silly feud so we can all go back to our own lives and stop messing around in the affairs of others."

"Are you accusing me of messing with your affairs?"

"That's funny."

"What's so funny about it?" Jacqueline lifts her walking stick with both hands.

"There is something you need to know about that husband of yours," Mildred says.

Jacqueline leans forward as if preparing to run. "I don't know if I want to hear it."

"After all the trouble you have gone through to destroy my life?" Mildred slaps her hand on Jacqueline's knee.

"So you admit it?"

"Admit what?" Mildred bites her lower lip.

"You know what," says Jacqueline. "I saw the way you chased after Preston."

"Excuse me?" Mildred reaches for her purse, wondering if she should show Jacqueline what she found among the papers and envelopes in the library. "If I tell you the truth, will you stop this nonsense?"

She taps her stick several times and turns her head away.

"You are such a bitch."

"Me? You're the one who slept with my husband."

"Ha!" Mildred stands, putting weight on her sore ankle and feeling a shooting pain up her leg. "One of these days the truth will come out and slap you right in the face." Mildred looks down at her.

Jacqueline removes her glove and slaps Mildred in the face. "I will see you in hell."

Mildred raises her hand to her cheek. "You may have a hard time finding me."

As she walks away, she hears Jacqueline yelling something unintelligible. Mildred flips the bird. As the car drives away, Mildred drops back down on the bench.

"That was quite a showdown," says Pastor Tilton, heading toward her from the circular drive in the front of the church.

"I didn't see you when I arrived," says Mildred.

"May I join you?" He doesn't wait for an answer and sits on the bench. "I don't think I would have put this here. It is hardly ever in the shade. Not very comforting."

Mildred chuckles.

"What?"

"You have a deceptively gentle way about you, Pastor."

"What do you mean?" he asks, wiping his brow with a colorful handkerchief.

"I think you know a lot more than you let on."

"I'm new here, remember?" He smiles and returns his handkerchief to his jacket pocket.

"You are, but this church isn't," she says. "When I was a girl, I would ride my bicycle down here at noon to hear the church bells up close. I could hear them from home, but before this monstrosity of a mausoleum was here, you could see for miles."

"The town has really built up a lot since then," he says. "Oh, no offense."

"I know I'm old, Douglas. You could be my grandson."

He holds his hand in front of his face. "I don't think so," he says. "Then again, we never know, do we, unless we do DNA testing. I wonder how many people are learning that their ancestors were African, or Asian, or South American."

"That's what started this whole thing," says Mildred.

Tilton turns to face her, as much as possible on the bench. "Is that what started it, or was it something else?"

Mildred looks at her purse.

"I heard you tell your daughter that she had a brother."

"You were standing there a long time," she says.

"Is he buried here?"

"No."

Tilton remains quiet, waiting for her to continue.

She pulls out a piece of paper from her purse and hands it to him. He unfolds it carefully.

"This is quite old," he says.

"He would be forty-eight this week," she says.

"Audrey's older brother? But your husband's name is missing."

"Yeah," she says. "I thought he never knew, but I found this in his desk, folded in an envelope addressed to me."

"Oh," he says. "And you wanted to share this with Jacqueline?"

"Alfred died thinking I had an affair with Preston, and I am sure Jacqueline feels the same way, but the truth is—"

"It was non-consensual?"

Mildred's eyes spill over. Her throat tightens. "Preston was always the life of the party, and a good number of those parties were ones that he and Jacqueline hosted. I didn't know it at the time, but that was his way of getting women drunk and then having his way with them."

"You were one of those women?"

She bows her head. "He was handsome and debonair, with that Southern charm and accent. Every woman wanted to be near him, but not that close. I wanted to tell Alfred, but he thought the baby was his, so I didn't say anything, and Preston went on doing what Preston always did."

"If he raped you-"

"I shouldn't have been that drunk," she says, wiping her eyes.

"But according to this note, Alfred knew the baby wasn't his."

"I thought the baby being stillborn would end it all, and life could go on. I should have known he would find out the truth."

Tilton folds the note and gives it back to her. "He didn't know the truth, that you didn't have an affair with Preston. Who is this from? It isn't signed."

"Jacqueline. I'd recognize that chicken scratch handwriting of hers anytime, even after so many years." Mildred takes the note and puts it in her purse. "She must have slipped it to him in church and left it open so he would read it."

"But he never confronted you?"

"No. That's how Alfred was. He was such a good man, and I let him down."

Pastor Tilton takes her hand in his. "He knows now. You can let go of it."

"How could I let him go to his grave thinking that?"

"You had no idea he knew, did you?"

"No. He took care of everything, including getting this certificate, taking care of the cremation, and he even went to try to obtain permission for a burial site on our property."

"Do you think at the time, he thought the child was his?"

"I thought so, but Preston bragged that he and I—" She chokes.

"Your Alfred was quite a man." Tilton takes out his handkerchief and wipes his brow again. "What did you do with the ashes? Are they buried on your property?"

"No, but they could have been. Apparently, we already have a burial site on the property, though the graves are not marked. I would like to find it. I think slaves were buried there."

"Did you know I studied as an archaeologist before going to seminary?" Tilton smiles.

"Do you think finding a burial site could help keep the property from being developed?"

"What are you thinking?"

"That could hurt Maggie's plans."

"We can start by doing a little research." He pats her hands, smiles and walks away.

Elcira

Elcira arranges lilacs in the large vase on the floor in the corner of the room, while Sylvie stands over her body at the casket. She knows most of them won't be able to see or smell them, but a few will, the few she wants to know she is here.

"What do you think, Sylvie?" asks Elcira, fluffing up the flowers on the branches.

"I look dead," she says.

"You are dead."

"They could have made me smile, just a little. I guess we never like what we see, do we?" Elcira drifts over to Sylvie and slips her gloved hands into the casket all around the body.

"What are you doing?" asks Sylvie, wearing the same dress she is being buried in.

Elcira convinces herself that the key is not here. "I never got to see myself laid out like that."

"Why?" Sylvie touches her hair, but it doesn't move.

"We didn't do these things the same way in my day. A plain box. A few prayers and back to work."

"That's terrible," says Sylvie, blowing at the hair she feels is out of place on her face in the casket.

"They called it the White Plague back then, and it killed a lot of people in the industrial towns. Cranberry was mostly rural, but my dad worked in the mills. I went to visit him when he got sick, and that was the end of me."

"Really?" Sylvie keeps trying to adjust the errant wisp of hair on the face before her.

"Oh, Wally thought it was pneumonia and I would get better. They brought me home. I guess I could have improved if I didn't insist on going to the funeral. Deborah was with me, and my sisters, Lila and Dana."

"What about your children?" Sylvie continues pushing the air to move the hair.

"It's a long story. We'll have time for me to share it with you later."

Sylvie crosses her arms and sighs.

"What's wrong?"

"It hangs down a bit too close to my eye."

Elcira moves in close and sends a puff of air toward the strand of hair, bringing it back in place. "I have figured a few things out in my time here. A breeze is the easiest thing to master. Everything else takes more work."

"Will I get to do that?"

"You won't be here long enough for that. But if you are sent to bring someone home, you might have enough time. We come for family."

"You knew I was dying when you came?" Sylvie recalls the day she found the key. "I thought the key brought you here."

"I didn't know who I came for."

"I saw you take Gertrude away. She wasn't family."

"Are you sure?" Elcira isn't sure how Gertrude is connected, but she must be in some way. "You are one of my descendants, so I stayed to bring you home when it was time for you to go."

"I decided that," she says. "I didn't want to make Millie suffer. She let me go home, and I had everyone around me. Did you come before when Audrey died?"

Elcira floats in and out of the sprays of roses and other flowers people had sent. "I don't remember Audrey, but I could have come for her. Everything sometimes gets so cloudy in my head. I believe we are shown what we need to know. I needed to ask who Mildred was when I arrived." She tries to remember Audrey in the hospital. "I knew about the pandemic. Many came home then, some of your relatives, too. You will meet them."

"How come Tilly can see you? Is it a gift or can anyone learn to do it?"

"I don't know for certain. I do know that others have seen me, though I wanted them to."

"Can I make Millie see me?"

Elcira is not sure how to answer her. If she says she can, who knows what she will do. It is bad enough that Tilly will arrive soon, and she can see her. "Maybe."

"Ooh!" Sylvie sniffs the roses. "When are they coming?"

"We have time. That's one thing we have plenty of. Time flows differently for us. You'll see."

"I was hoping to see the wedding," she says, moving over to the window. "It will be so beautiful in my garden."

"I have no control over when we leave, Sylvie," she lies.

Sylvie stares at her for a moment before asking, "Did you do it?"

"Do what?"

"You know. Kill Chester and lock yourself in the shed."

Should she tell her that she was locked in the shed by Deborah when Chester was stabbed the first time? "I don't know."

"How could you not know? You were there. You have to know."

"Right now, for you, everything seems clear, but do you know who was in the room with you when you passed?"

Sylvie remains silent.

"You know some people, but do you remember the aides who cleaned and comforted you? Some things just aren't as clear for us in this state we are in. Do you remember talking to me?"

"I think so. Millie was there, too, right?"

"Yes."

"I so wanted her to understand me, but she seemed lost. I wanted her to know I saw you."

"She knows now."

Sylvie stares out the window at a cardinal.

"Go ahead," Elcira tells her. "They are good carriers for us. Tell it who you would like to visit and go with him."

In an instant, Sylvie is gone. Elcira reaches down and touches Sylvie's painted face. Drawing her gloved finger along her cheek to her hairline, she manages to push the wave of hair further up her forehead. "Now that looks better."

She reaches all around the casket again, looking for the key. Maybe Mildred isn't going to bury it. Then, she may lose the property, and all the spirits Elcira and Deborah laid to rest will be disturbed. What might that bring upon them? She will do what she can to keep Josiah, his father, Cyrus, and all the others from being unearthed. That would not be good.

Mildred

SATURDAY

As Mildred readies herself for Aunt Sylvie's wake, she imagines the house filled with students, young and old, learning how to read and write. After a long day in the field, they would come to the main house and wash up, have something to eat, and then what?

Would they break off into separate rooms? What about the garden club meetings that were held here? Would the place be magically transformed after a meeting or event? After Chester was gone, did the men stop coming to discuss politics and feed prices? How did the people in town treat the widow they suspected of killing her husband? Did Deborah watch the children while Elcira ran the farm? Could she do that alone? She must have kept it going. It was still going after she passed, so someone had to take over. One of her sons, maybe? Perhaps her father helped her, while he was alive.

Turning the home into a school for slaves seems like too radical and dangerous an idea, certainly not something the men would have thought to do.

But Deborah might have.

What would it have been like to live here in those days? She will have to read the journals. What was his name? Josiah. What was his story?

She stands at the mirror in her closet and stares at the flap of loose skin under her chin. "You look like a rooster," she says, patting it with the back of her hand.

Seeing herself all in black makes her feel older. Maybe it's a memory from her childhood. Come to think of it, her whole life has been marked by funerals.

She opens the small drawer in the center of her dressing table and removes the metal box, now tarnished, almost black. She places the cremains on the table and inspects the wax seal that has withstood the passing of decades. Not daring to open it, Mildred offers a silent prayer to her son.

"I'm so sorry," she says and bends to kiss the box.

"Grandma," says Maggie, calling from the bedroom. "Are you in here?"

"In the closet," she says, putting the box back in the drawer and closing it.

"I brought two roses from Aunt Sylvie's garden." She enters and hands one to Mildred. "I have pins. Here."

Mildred stays seated while Maggie pins the rose onto her blouse.

"I thought a bit of color would be okay."

"It's perfect," says Mildred. "You look lovely."

Maggie's dress is a round neck crepe black dress of midi length, lightweight but fit. She has black heels and a clutch bag, her lipstick matching the color of the rose.

"I don't have many dressy dresses," she says. "This was one of Mom's. I had it cleaned."

"It fits you so well," says Mildred. "I am so glad you helped pick out Aunt Sylvie's dress. I couldn't have done that on my own."

"It was easy. She had a note pinned to it saying 'Pick Me' like Alice and the looking glass."

Mildred offers a partial smile.

"I was thinking about what we learned today. What happened here is so amazing," says Maggie.

"I know," says Mildred, standing to slip on her shoes. "I have to organize all that stuff downstairs for Monday."

"David and I will help with that," she says.

"You two have spent much time together," says Mildred. She steps gingerly into what hasn't been said.

"We're working on the case, all three of us." Maggie looks down at her shoes. "I'll admit, he is charming."

Mildred looks at Maggie's hand but remains silent.

"I told Vince at the funeral home that I would arrive early, but you can come later."

"I'll go with you," says Maggie. "One car is better than two."

"I just need to transfer the contents of my purse. I think I left it downstairs."

"I'll get it." Maggie rushes off and quickly returns, holding the purse in one hand and the key in the other.

"Oh, yeah." Mildred takes the key. "Where should I put this?"

"Why don't we put it back where Aunt Sylvie found it?" asks Maggie. "It's nothing but trouble."

"I don't want to put it where anyone can find it."

"I'll take it then," says Maggie. "If we make it go away, they can't prove their case, right?"

"But then this nonsense will never end. Someone else can come along and start it all over again." Mildred reaches for the key and purse.

Maggie hands her the purse but keeps the key. "Let's go. You can switch purses in the car. I want to do this before anyone gets there." Maggie turns and walks away.

"What are you going to do?"

"You'll see," she yells. "Come on!"

On the way to the funeral home, Mildred plays scenario after scenario in her head.

Will Jacqueline create a scene? Should she let Maggie get rid of the key? Maybe she should talk to David. What is going on with David and Maggie? What about Sam? Is the wedding still on? Mildred was the one who wanted to stop the wedding, and now she is worried it won't happen. What will constitute a win on Monday?

Her stomach is building up acid, and yet she hasn't eaten anything.

The car bumps its way over the train tracks and down the sloping street, a sign that they are getting close. Tilly is going up the ramp in her motorized chair.

"Looks like we're not the first, Grandma."

"Yeah, I see that. Pull around back, and let's try to head her off."

Inside, they are greeted by Vince and his father.

"The doors are closed until you give us the okay to open them, but you can go right in," says Vince.

"Thank you," says Mildred. Maggie opens the door, and the two slip in, closing the door behind them.

The aroma of fresh-cut flowers is almost choking, but one fragrance stands out. Lilacs.

"Where is that coming from?" asks Mildred, limping her way to the casket.

"Your ankle is still bothering you?" asks Maggie.

"I'll survive," says Mildred.

Several large sprays of roses, petunias and daisies line the walls, each with a ribbon or card identifying who sent it. But in the corner, by the window, a large vase on the floor is nearly falling over with branches of lilacs of a variety of colors.

"Who sent that?" asks Maggie, rushing over to it. "There's no card."

"I'll ask Vince where they came from," says Mildred. "After I check on Aunt Sylvie."

Standing over the casket, Mildred finds it hard to catch her breath. "She looks beautiful. So peaceful."

Maggie comes and stands beside her. She unpins the rose from her dress and pins it on Sylvie's floral print blouse.

Mildred touches Sylvie's hands and caresses her fingers. Her lips are barely tinted, and the edges of her mouth tip slightly as though Sylvie is about to crack a joke.

"You did good, Grandma."

"I want to pick her up and take her home." A tear escapes and starts its trek across her cheek.

Maggie reaches in her purse for a tissue, and the key pops out into her hand.

"Hide that," says Mildred.

Maggie steps close to block the view, even though they are alone. She takes the key and slides it under Sylvie, puffing up the lining to cover any trace of her action.

"Are you sure?" asks Mildred.

"It's done."

As they turn to leave, Maggie pulls on Mildred's sleeve. "What if they start digging up the yard again?"

Mildred pauses, turns, and pauses again.

The door opens, and Vince enters, followed by Tilly in her vehicle.

"Damn," says Maggie.

"Sorry," says Vince. "I peeked in, and it looked like you were done. Is everything in order?"

"Where did those lilacs come from?" asks Mildred.

"What lilacs?" he asks.

Mildred turns and points to the corner where the vase is.

"Oh, that's an empty vase. We just put it there, so people don't hang out in the corner." Vince says.

"But it's not empty," says Maggie.

Vince gives her a strange look.

Tilly motors over to the vase and leans forward, sniffing. "They smell so nice."

"Whatever," says Vince.

Effie

The Soundview Hotel is not the cheapest place to get a room in town, but that is only because the Vanguard Motel near the highway hasn't been torn down yet. Despite its reputation as a one-night to one-hour stopover, getting a room there is almost impossible so Lightfoot reserved a room for Effie at the Soundview. Its name suggests it has a view of the water, but only if you climb on the roof in the winter when the trees are bare.

Effie dumps the pillowcase on one of the two twin beds and starts sorting her clothes. The laundromat near the train station is boarded up pending demolition and development of a new station plaza, so she had spent the better part of the day witnessing her blouses, jeans, tees, and delicates wrestle each other in an Eco-friendly washing machine that uses less water and takes three times as long to wash and spin dry. Now, frustrated and tired, she pulls wrinkled sleeves from pant legs and discovers that nothing is as dry as she would like.

"She throws everything onto the bed and drops into the one chair in the room, an old armchair that looks like it has never been cleaned or vacuumed. "What a stupid thing to do," she says, cursing herself for not holding onto the key.

She grabs her wallet from the nightstand and rifles through the singles. Eight dollars, not enough to get dinner. She puts the cash and some change she has left in her pocket and heads down the outside walkway to the snack machines. When she arrives, a young girl, maybe five or younger, stands in front of the machine. Effie stands beside her at the beverage machine, inserts two dollars, and selects a sparkling soda.

"Could you help me?" the girl asks. "I want chips. How much do I need?"

Effie looks at the change in the girl's hand and smiles at her. "I don't think you have enough. Where is your mommy?"

"Er- she's in the room, asleep." The girl's clothes are stained and torn. Her face could use a washcloth as well.

Effie puts one dollar in the slot. "Okay. Just put in two quarters and make your selection," she says.

The girl puts in the coins and studies the choices, holding her finger to her chin. "I can't decide."

"Let me help you," she says, bending to get closer. "Do you like these?" She points to a bag of Cheetos. "Or these?" The next choice is Lays Original Potato Chips.

"Those," she says, waiting for Effie to press the buttons.

"Thank you," the girl says, grabbing the bag from the drawer.

"Have you had dinner?" Effie asks, taking a guess, and the girl shakes her head, "No."

Effie reaches for her hand and says, "Come, I will take you to your room. Can you show me where it is?"

The girl nods and smiles, clutching her hand tightly.

When they arrive at the room, Effie notices the door is ajar, held open by a shoe. "Did you do this?"

"Yes, so I can get back in. I don't have a key."

On the bed, Effie sees a young woman, possibly in her late twenties or early thirties. She is totally covered by the blanket and yet is shaking, her teeth chattering.

"Mommy got sick," the girl says. "I wanted to get her something to eat."

Effie puts her hand to the woman's head. It is too hot for Effie to leave her. "I think we should get a doctor for your mommy, okay?"

"Okay," she says. She jumps on the bed and curls up beside her mother.

"How long has she been like this?"

"I don't know." The girl starts to cry. Effie kneels next to the bed, strokes the girl's hair, and rests her head on her shoulder.

"I'm going to get her help. Your mommy will be all right," she says, hoping she is telling the truth. She wipes the tears from the girl's face, pulls out a tissue to clean the smudges and then walks into the bathroom, closing the door behind her.

"Kendal," Effie says into her phone. "I need your help."

"What now?" He sounds annoyed.

"Don't give me a hard time. It is not about me. I'm at the hotel you set up for me, and a young girl is here. Her mom is running a fever and isn't responding. I'm going to call an ambulance. Can you meet me at the hospital?"

"Do you know who she is?"

"Does it matter? Just do it."

She calls for an ambulance and then goes back into the room with a washcloth soaked in cold water. There is a small refrigerator in the room, but it isn't working. An ice machine is down the hall, but she doesn't want to leave the girl. She places the washcloth on the woman's head and pulls the chair close to the bed.

"Your mom is not hungry right now. You sit here and enjoy the chips and soda. I will take care of her."

"Thank you," she says, more tears beginning to drop onto her cheeks.

"I'm Effie. What's your name?"

"Mommy told me not to tell anyone my name," she says.

"Okay. So what if I call you Angel?" Effie smiles.

"I like angels," she says. She pops a chip in her mouth and crunches it.

"I do, too." Effie holds the mother's wrist but is not sure where to find a pulse. "Did you and your mommy just get here?"

The girl nods and then looks at her mother, who continues to shake. "Is she gonna die?"

"No," says Effie, hoping it's true. "We will get her to the doctor, and she will be fine."

In the distance, sirens get louder and louder.

Sam

The overhead lights in the conference room go out, indicating a lack of movement. Sam's head drops as one of his elbows slips from the table and throws him off balance. The sensors detect the movement, and the lights come back on, piercing his eyes and causing him to squint to adjust.

He takes a deep breath, thankful his head didn't damage the model of the proposed children's cancer center. He pushes his chair back and looks over the project with bleary eyes.

"Sam?" His mother's voice echoes in the hallway as her heels tap out an anxious rhythm with her approach. "Are you coming with me?"

Sam checks his watch. The wake.

"I'm in the conference room."

Harriet walks past the glass walls and stares in at the model. "What is that?"

"Come, look," he says. "Dad built this from my design. I didn't know he was that good."

Harriet steps closer, her mouth open. She walks around the table, bending to look in the windows and doors, or through the clear walls. "How long did you two work on this?"

250

"We started yesterday afternoon."

"Where is your father?" She looks around. "Did you sleep here?"

"He said he was going home to take a nap, and I was going to follow him, but I got caught up inspecting the model for necessary corrections and improvements."

Sam wipes his face and yawns.

"You can't go to the wake like this. Are you okay to drive?"

Sam leans back in his chair. "You go, Mom."

"Why? Maggie will be disappointed if you don't show up." She comes close and rubs his hair.

He pulls away. "She's got her mind on other things."

"And you?" She points to the model. "I imagine you did this for her. So, you need to be there for her."

"Leave it, Mom." He stands and walks around the table toward the door.

Harriet takes another look at the model. "I can see inside. How did you do that?"

"It opens. The top comes off, and you can see each floor, including the atria."

Harriet grabs him forcefully and gives him a hug. "When are you going to show this to her?"

"It's not done. I want to add a residence for the families." He points to an empty space on the board.

"You did all this for her."

He steps back and looks into her eyes. "I did it for you and Dad, Mom."

She leans on the table with one hand to steady herself.

"We're going to lose everything. We need this project. Dad's dream project will never happen, but this one will. Maggie wants this more than anything else." He bites his lower lip.

"What about the wedding?" Harriet gives him that Mother-always-knows look.

He starts for the door. "I'll meet you at the funeral home. I have to shower and change at home."

As he heads down the hall, he expects to hear his mother's heels following him, but there is only silence.

Sitting in his car, he replays all that has happened the last few days. It is as though all his hopes and dreams have been flushed down the toilet, and here he is, alone, rejected, and insecure, just like always. As he starts the engine, it occurs to him that his mother just came from home and didn't know where his father was.

He rushes home and pulls into the driveway behind his father's car. The front door is open. He steps in uncertain what he will find. "Dad?"

Silence.

He tries the den. Empty. Then the kitchen.

"Dad, you left the door open."

James is sitting on a stool at the counter, a glass with melting ice before him. "Come here, boy! Celebrate with me! Come on, I'll pour you one. That design of yours is a winner."

Sam pulls up a stool and sits down.

He knows he should leave his father to his own devices and wash up, dress, and go to the wake. But he can't bring himself to do that. Why? Why does he always give up on his dreams to put up with their nightmares? His father pours him a double whiskey, adds fresh crushed ice from the fridge door and slaps Sam on the back.

Dream over.

Jacqueline

SATURDAY

Several of the streetlights are out or blinking, making the approach to the funeral home look even more ominous than normal, given its austere, nineteenth-century regional bank facade. Jacqueline clutches her walking stick with both gloved hands, leaning forward as far as the glass between her and Harold will allow.

"I should have had you drive me here earlier. Now we are in this hideous neighborhood in the dark, and God knows what types of spooks roam these streets," says Jacqueline.

"I beg your pardon, madam," says Harold, stepping on the brake hard enough to jolt the car.

"Watch where you're going, Harold. I don't want us to get stuck in this dreadful place." She taps her walking stick on the glass. "Walk me in. I am not going there alone."

"You really don't hear yourself, do you?" he says, loud enough for her to hear.

"Don't be disrespectful, Harold."

He opens her door and reaches for her hand, but she uses her stick to help her stand, ignoring his offer of assistance.

"It was more an observation, madam." He smiles at her and then turns around to lead the way in.

At the door, she reaches for his sleeve and stops him. "Don't forget to check the casket."

"But you told me not to be disrespectful," he says.

"Don't push it." She pulls him closer. "I want that key."

He straightens his back and pulls his sleeve free of her grasp. Then, without saying a word, he opens the door for her and follows her in.

Around the small wooden podium with the guest book is a traffic jam of walkers and rollators, blocking one of the entrances to the room.

Many of the folding chairs are occupied by far more women than men, an indicator of their age. They have outlived their hard-working spouses, who left most of them well cared for. With one eye roving, Jacqueline manages to take in a stereoscopic view of the room, which normally would cause her head to ache, but sometimes, like now, it is an advantage. She can keep one eye on Mildred and the other on Maggie.

Behind her, a buzz like a motorboat grows louder, eventually cutting in front of her, blocking her approach to the casket.

"Hello, Tilly."

"Jacqueline, I can't see anything down here. Could you point out where Pastor Tilton is? I want to chat with him about something," says Tilly.

While not wanting to respond, she happens to see the target in question off in the corner. "He's by the big, empty vase," she says.

"Oh, you think it's empty, too," says Tilly. She laughs and motors down the aisle to turn before those standing in line to offer prayers for Sylvie.

"Crazy woman," says Jacqueline. She looks at Harold in the back and motions for him to get in line.

A light flashes in her left eye, and she turns to see Abigail holding her cell phone directly in front of her face, only her nearly bald head showing. "Did you see Sylvie, yet? I took a picture of her. She looks so much better than Gertrude did. I think we should definitely post this on social media."

"Get away from me, you idiot," shouts Jacqueline, arousing the interest of several rows of mourners.

"Someone got up on the wrong side of the bed this evening," says Abigail as she walks away and poses for a selfie in front of one of the sprays of roses.

"You know, the club is getting smaller and smaller, Jacqueline. If you plan to take it over, you should at least pretend to care about these women." Mildred's voice is much calmer and more friendly than the last time they met. What is she up to?

"I can't stay too long, Mildred, dear," says Jacqueline. "Prior commitments and that sort of thing."

"Oh, I understand." Mildred steps around her and starts walking away. "The demands of popularity cannot be ignored, can they?"

"Bitch."

Harold has made his way to the line and will soon be at the casket.

Several garden club members stop to talk to Jacqueline, but she quickly brushes them off. A few leave in a huff, but she cannot be bothered by them. There is business to attend to. And where is Light-foot? He is supposed to be here for the big reveal.

Jacqueline takes her place in line two people behind Harold. As the person in front of him leaves, she taps the young man in front of her on the shoulder, not knowing it is David.

"Oh, hello, Ms. Hudson." He smiles at her. "I'm glad you could come. My mother talks about you so often."

Jacqueline wants to escape, but she needs to keep him preoccupied so Harold can search for the key. "Tilly does talk to everyone, doesn't she."

"Well, she has always had pleasant things to say about you."

"She has?" She finds that hard to believe. What is his game?

Suddenly, a light flashes. Abigail is taking another selfie, standing next to Harold, whose hands are inside the casket.

David turns around and bumps into Harold, who gets flustered and runs away empty-handed.

"Oh," says Abigail, "did I do that?"

Jacqueline looks at Mildred, who gives Maggie a high five.

Maggie

Maggie waits for Tilly and the others to move away from them and then takes Mildred aside near the vase of lilacs. "How did you know?" Maggie asks.

"I didn't," says Mildred.

"But you removed the key before they came. Why?" Maggie tries to keep her words to a whisper.

"I thought about what you said. This nonsense will never stop if the key is lost forever." Mildred pats her purse. "We need to put this to bed. It is what Sylvie was trying to do."

"You think so?" Maggie looks at the crowd gathered around the casket, all Sylvie's friends.

"She wanted the club to get involved. Maybe she thought they could solve the puzzle of who killed Chester and put the legend of the key to rest."

Maggie surveys the room. "They're all here."

"Yes," says Mildred. "I think we should invite them all to the house tomorrow and share what we learned."

"Jacqueline, too?"

"I'll think about that." Mildred pats Maggie on the arm and heads off to mingle with the crowd.

Maggie spots Harriet at the guest book and goes to meet her.

"Oh, Maggie, I'm so sorry," she says, hugging Maggie tightly. "I wanted to get here earlier, but things just didn't work out."

"Is Sam with you?" she asks, looking toward the door.

"No," says Harriet, focusing on writing in the book. "I expect him to be here soon. Hopefully, it won't be too late."

A few people file past nodding to her as they make their way to the door. Maggie isn't sure if the women are garden club members. She looks back to see her grandmother working the crowd.

Harriet picks up one of the prayer cards and puts it in her purse. "The funeral is on Monday?"

"No," says Maggie. "She is going to be cremated. "Grandma has prepared a spot for Aunt Sylvie in her garden."

"Oh?" She looks shocked. "Have you decided against donating the property to the hospital?"

"You read the article in the paper," she says, stepping away to allow Harriet to enter the room. "We haven't worked out the details yet."

"Sam was pretty upset that he didn't know your plans."

Maggie catches Harriet glancing at her ring finger, which is still ringless. "He was, was he?"

Harriet touches Maggie on the arm and smiles, "But he is fully behind you. I probably shouldn't let the cat out of the bag, but he has even been working on something for you. That's why he's late."

"Oh?" The garden club ladies are starting to leave, each wanting Maggie's attention. "I'm sorry, Harriet."

"No problem," she says, heading off to Sylvie.

"I will see you tomorrow, Maggie," says Tilly, pushing through the crowd. "It will be so good to have a club meeting back where it all began. I'm sure Abigail will take plenty of pictures."

"Great. See you then."

What is Sam working on, and why isn't he here? Sometimes, his priorities get all mixed up. Why couldn't he be more like David. There, she said it, or thought it. It is all she's been thinking about. You would think Sam would realize they are slipping apart and work hard

257

to keep them together. Is that what he thinks he is doing working while she is at Aunt Sylvie's wake?

"Oh, Maggie, I'm so sorry for your loss." A gray-haired woman she doesn't know gives her a peck on the cheek.

One by one, they leave until only Pastor Tilton, Grandma, and Harriet are left. Harriet talks to Pastor Tilton as Maggie reaches Mildred's side at the casket.

"Well?" asks Maggie.

Mildred pats her purse and then pats Maggie's hand. "If I change my mind, I can still get it here tomorrow."

Pastor Tilton stands between them, putting his arms around them. Harriet walks by and continues toward the door.

"I expected to see Sam," says Tilton.

"So did I," says Maggie. So did everyone else.

"Well, maybe we can all chat after church tomorrow."

"Sure," says Maggie, not wanting to discuss it further.

"Remember," says Mildred, "we have that meeting at noon."

"Plenty of time," he says. "Our service ends at eleven. We can have a quick chat with you, Sam, and I, and then you can head off to your meeting. I want to make sure to block out your wedding on my calendar so there is no conflict."

Maggie smiles. Mildred's eyes widen and then she turns to kneel at Sylvie's side, giving a cue to Tilton that this conversation is over.

"Until tomorrow," he says and then leaves.

Vince walks over and stands at the head of the casket. "Do you want to take any of the flowers?"

"Oh," says Mildred. "Can I get them tomorrow?"

"Of course," he says. "Oh, except for the lilacs you mentioned. It looks like someone already took those."

Effie

Effie and Angel follow the ambulance to the hospital, where Angel's mom is admitted to Emergency as Cynthia Roberts, according to the driver's license Effie found in her purse. Angel sits quietly in a metal chair near the glass door. She holds the edge of a curtain that drapes across half the room to separate one side from the other so two patients could be in the room simultaneously.

"And you are?" asks the nurse's aide, who is hooking Cynthia up to the heart monitor, oxygen and taping an oxygen monitor to her finger.

"Ephedra Devine."

"Are you related?"

"Yes," she lies. "We are cousins."

Angel looks at her and Effie holds her finger up to her lips. "Call me Auntie Eff, okay?"

"Are we playing a game?" she asks.

"Yes," says Effie. "Pretend you are invisible and no one can see you. See if you can make funny faces that make me notice you. If you do, you win and I lose."

"Oh, fun!" she says, sticking her tongue out and pulling her ears.

"She is running a high fever. You should put on masks just in case. I will go get the nurse and let the doctor know."

"Do I have to?" asks Angel.

"No," says Effie.

"Ha! I won!"

Effie laughs and gives her a high five. "You outsmarted me, you little pixie."

"What's a pixie?"

"An elf."

"I'm an elf," she shouts. "And you are Auntie Elf."

Her mother stirs a bit, the first sign of life since Effie entered her room.

"I understand you are Ms. Roberts' cousin?" says the doctor, a short man in a long white jacket and a white N95 face mask. He is donning blue gloves as he approaches the bed.

As he bends over Cynthia, Angel points to his head. "What kind of hat is that?"

"Hello, child," he says. "Some people call it a skull cap."

"Can I get one?" she asks.

"Usually girls don't wear those," says Effie, giving the doctor an eyebrow raise and shoulder shrug.

"I think I can find one for you," he says. He removes the stethoscope from around his neck and listens to Cynthia's heart and lungs. "I am going to have the nurse give her some antibiotics for the fever and take some blood for tests. Do you know if she has a history of congestive heart failure?"

Effie's eyes open wide and she looks at Angel, who is playing with the curtain. "I don't know."

"Well, I want to rule everything out. This could just be a virus, but I would rather be cautious."

"I understand."

"She will need to be admitted in either case. Someone from admissions will come by. I assume you can sign for her. Do you know if she has a health care proxy?"

"Is Mommy gonna die?" asks Angel, her lower lip starting to quiver.

"Come, Angel," says Effie, grabbing her hand. "Let's let the doctor help Mommy and we'll go see if we can find someplace to sit."

Effie grabs her phone and calls Kendal. "Are you coming?"

"I'm here. I'm in the waiting room at Emergency."

"Heading there now."

With Angel in tow, Effie makes her way back to where she entered. Kendal stands to free up a chair for Angel.

"Angel, this is Mr. Lightfoot," Effie says.

Angel giggles, looking at Kendal's feet.

"Yes," says Kendal, "not light, am I? Have a seat, Angel, while I talk to Ms. Devine."

"Auntie Elf," she says.

"Huh?"

"Never mind," says Effie.

He guides Effie away by her elbow. "What's going on?"

"She hasn't eaten. I don't know for how long, but I found her at the snack machine with a small amount of change, looking to get some food."

"And you don't have any money either, right?" He gives her a fatherly look. "I think the cafeteria is open until eight o'clock, so we can go get something there, but what about her mom?"

"Cynthia Roberts. Not good, but I don't know how bad."

"Sounds serious." He looks at Angel who is studying an old man who is snoring in the corner.

"With my luck, it is." She goes over to Angel and takes her hand. "You go to the cafeteria with Mr. Lightfoot. I'll give the nurse my cell number in case they need us to come back."

"Come, let's get something to eat," says Kendal.

"What about Mommy?"

"The doctor will make sure Mommy gets something. Don't worry," says Effie, caressing the girl's face.

"You sure you haven't done this before?" Kendal asks.

"Shut up!"

Effie heads back to the check-in desk and asks if she can see Mrs. Roberts again. She is given a visitor's pass, and the doors buzz open.

Walking back to the room, Effie steps aside several times to make room for passing gurneys and doctors holding iPads, talking with nurses as they walk almost blindly from one patient to another. So long as the hospital thinks Effie is related, they won't call Child Welfare Services. She will not let Angel, or whatever her name is, be treated the way she was when her mom went away.

Priority one, though, is to find members of Cynthia's family, a husband, parents or siblings. Someone must exist who can take care of Angel. She needs to come up with a plausible story. Think.

"Excuse me," she says, approaching a nurse standing near Cynthia's room. "I brought Mrs. Roberts in. She's in this room here."

"Yes, Doctor Miller ordered some tests for her."

"Miller? Oh, I thought it was a different name. He's the short one with the skull cap?"

"Yes, that's him," the nurse says, turning her attention back to her iPad. "He is having her admitted. Can you wait here? The admissions person will be right with you."

Effie is about to object when the woman walks away. She enters and stands over the bed, looking at the monitor of Cynthia's vital signs above her head.

A hand grabs Effie's arm. Cynthia's eyes are open wide and there is a look of terror on her face. "Jessie? Where's my baby?" Her voice is scratchy and hard to hear.

Effie leans closer. "She's fine. She is having some dinner. She is very worried about you."

"Who are you?" The whites of her eyes stand out against her dark skin.

"A friend," she says.

"I don't have friends. Bring me my child!"

The monitor sends out a loud alarm, and Cynthia starts shaking wildly.

Suddenly, nurses and orderlies rush in, pushing Effie out of the way. "You need to leave," one says.

An orderly pushes her out and pulls the curtain. Effie can hear them shuffling around and talking to Cynthia. The alarm continues, getting louder.

Jacqueline

SUNDAY

The limestone wall of the mausoleum feels cool to the touch. The wall, a bright white in direct sunlight, has a rich orange glow as the sun sets. "You always loved the sunsets, didn't you, dear. That's why I put the door on the other side, facing East, so you can be reminded of each new day that you are not here."

She taps her walking stick against the stone, walks a few steps, and stumbles.

In an instant, Harold is by her side, holding her up with one hand while propping himself against the wall with the other. "You all right, Ms. Hudson?"

"You leave me be," she says, twisting her body to get away from him.

"Look, Ms. Hudson," he says, releasing her. "I don't take from anybody, and I'm tired of putting up with your false airs and here one day gone the next accent. I swear you ain't from Kentucky, are you?" Harold leans against the wall and puts one leg on the wrought iron fence surrounding it.

"Why are you talking to me like that, Harold?"

"Because you are one stubborn, annoying bitch, that's why. Look what you did to this community. People hate their neighbors, all over an idea that no one is going to support."

"You should not be talking to me like this. Cecil-"

"Cecil is not here, and I can see why he left. In fact," he says, tapping the wall. "I can see why this guy left you too. You are one holy nightmare!"

"I will not take this from you," she says, raising her walking stick.

"Go ahead," he says. "You want a court case? You'll have one if you strike this Black man." He points to his chest.

Jacqueline feels her legs starting to shake. "Take me home."

Harold doesn't move or say anything.

"I want to go home. Now!" Her voice cracks.

He walks up to her and grabs her arm to steady her.

"That hurts," she says.

"I don't want you to fall, not on my watch." He looks her in the eyes. "Where is your family? I know you had kids. Where are they? Why are you living alone in that big house?"

"It's none of your business," she says, trying to loosen herself from his grip. "I don't have to answer to you or anyone."

"Oh, but you do, Ms. Hudson." He lets go of her arm and leans on the wall beside her. "You had me try to steal that stupid key and organize that mob at the courthouse, and for what? The whole town is now at each other's throats. This is not about you wanting to help us with reparations, is it?"

She turns away, refusing to look directly at him.

"This is personal."

Her good eye rolls toward her husband's mausoleum. She starts to turn to walk to the car.

"Ms. Hudson."

Jacqueline stops but still does not look at him. "Leave me alone." She keeps walking, using her walking stick to help her keep her balance. "Damn you, Preston," she says.

Looking back, she sees Harold. He is peering through the bars of the mausoleum at Preston's tomb. When he gets to the car, Jacqueline sits quietly in the back, facing away from him.

"Take me home," she says.

"Your husband was not a good man, was he?"

"How dare you," she says. "First, you insult me, and now you insult Preston?"

"Your inscription calls him a small man who loved too much. To me, that sounds like someone who got around."

"No one asked you," she says. "Let's go home."

As they join the line of cars leaving the church parking lot after the ten o'clock service, Jacqueline spots Pastor Tilton leaning into the driver's side window of Mildred's red Subaru.

"Pull over," she says to Harold.

"Change your mind?" He pulls out of the line and idles the car near the exit.

"Something's going on," she says. "Go over there and find out what it is."

Harold turns and gives her a puzzled look.

"Go on," she says, waving her gloved hand at him, acting as if they had not just had words.

She watches him walk over to Pastor Tilton, wait for him to finish his conversation with Mildred, and then chat briefly before returning.

"Well?" she asks. "What is going on?"

"Nothing," he says. He gets behind the wheel and closes the door.

"Follow that car," she says.

"Really?"

As they pull up onto the street leading to Mildred's property, they can see several familiar cars lining the driveway. A wheelchair van makes its way back down the lane toward them and then passes by.

"That bitch," she says. "She's having a garden club meeting without me."

"How do you know?" asks Harold.

"That was Tilly's ride and I would know these cars anywhere." She grabs her walking stick and puts it on her lap.

"Do you want me to drive up there?" he asks.

She thinks about it momentarily, letting her curiosity argue with her pride. Her pride wins. "No. Go home."

"Your wish is my command," he says.

She wants to smack him, but that would be wrong on so many counts.

Mildred

As the women file into the foyer of the main house, Tilly greets them in her wheelchair and directs them through the house to the great room. Mildred stands near the French doors leading to the patio and hedgerow that leads to the carriage house and garden. Folding chairs form a semi-circle in the room where Maggie stands, handing each woman a piece of paper. In front of Mildred is a table with books, maps, and letters laid out.

"Thank you all for coming here on such short notice," says Mildred. "The paper Maggie gave you is the family tree we will be talking about at tomorrow's court appearance. We thought you would all want a copy so you can follow along. We appreciate all you have done to restore Sylvie's garden and seeing you all last night was so special for us."

Everyone settles in and offers each other positive comments or nods.

"I see a few new faces. Welcome. If you are a friend or relative of a garden club member, you may know something about us, but I think what we have to share will surprise even the long-standing members."

The murmur picks up and Mildred can see curiosity blooming in many of the faces.

Abigail's flash captures something, and as always, causes heads to turn toward her.

"As you know, we head back to court to make our case for rightful ownership of our own property, and while that statement is enough to make blood boil, I am coming to realize we have been living with this unanswered question for too long."

"You tell them, Millie," says Tilly.

Several people cheer, though Mildred is certain they may not have even heard what she had said.

David enters and leans against the far wall beside the oval mirror. Mildred can see her reflection, making it look like she is standing next to him.

"Because of the court hearing, Maggie and I have been working closely with David Parker, back there, researching the history of the farm and ancestry of the Cranberry line. What we found is startling, to say the least."

Several people "Ooh and aah."

"David will give you a preview of what we will be presenting tomorrow with regard to our ancestors, going all the way back to Elcira and Chester. But I want to share what I have on this table."

Mildred starts with the book signed by Deborah Townsend and tells how the property came to be an important stop in the Underground Railway.

Maggie takes the book and passes it around. "We never realized what a storehouse of historical information we have right here in this house, or more accurately, in the house that stood here for over sixty years before this one was built."

"Isn't this the person mentioned in the court case?" asks one of the women.

"Yes, Agnes," says Mildred. "She is the ex-slave who is an ancestor of Effie Devine."

"And she lived in this house?"

David steps forward. "We're not sure if she was living here or in the carriage house, but she was a resident of the farm."

"So, that confirms what Effie was saying?" asks Tilly.

Mildred spots a dark figure standing just outside the room, in the foyer. It's Harold. She looks at David and then at Maggie. "Yes."

Before she could say anything else, the papers catch a breeze and blow off the table. In the mirror across the room, Mildred sees the wispy figure of a woman appear behind her. She turns to look, but no one is there. Turning back, the woman's features become clearer. She knows it isn't Elcira. The woman is Black.

"Grandma?" Maggie's voice breaks through the silence. "Are you okay?"

David steps forward and turns around. "We believe Deborah and Elcira, and possibly the entire Ladies Garden Club, were running a school here on the farm."

"A school?" One of the women cups her ear. "Did you say a school?"

"It was a school for runaway and freed slaves. We found these books that lead us to believe they were being taught to read and write and then hired to work the farm." David picks up the primers and passes them around.

"Abigail, take some pictures," yells Tilly. "This is just what we need to generate interest in the club."

Maggie walks over to Mildred who remains focused on the mirror. "Did you see someone?"

"Yes," she says. "Deborah."

Mildred takes a deep breath and closes her eyes to compose herself before proceeding.

"There's more," she says, walking toward the patio to avoid looking in the mirror.

"These primers are written in, using pencil, and you can still read what's written," one of the women says before passing them along.

Mildred picks up several of the leather-bound journals. "Here are just a few of a slave boy's journals. His name was Josiah Jeremiah Johnson, a name he chose for himself. I haven't had a chance to read much of what he wrote, but it is clear that his writing and vocabulary improved a great deal while he was living and working here."

"He was a slave?" asks Harold.

"Yes, Harold," says Mildred. "He and his father escaped being captured when his mom was taken, and they wound up here. This was a stop on the Underground Railroad, and that potting shed with the double lock was where Elcira hid them."

Harold opens a folding chair and sits down.

Tilly motors to the center of the circle and turns to face the group. "It seems our illustrious garden club was a group of hell-raising women. What do you think about that?"

Everyone cheers.

"I could really use your help. Let's put this story together for court tomorrow." Mildred goes over to the cabinet and pulls out a bottle of whiskey. "Any takers?"

Effie

"A untie, I need your help," says Effie to her Aunt Tilly. "Can you see me? I'm Face-timing you."

"Who?" Tilly asks, her ear blocking the camera. "Sylvie, is that you?"

"No, Auntie, it's me, Effie." She can hear a faint buzzing sound in the background.

"Oh, Effie, I can hardly hear you. I'm outside at Millie's. We had a meeting. I think they might be trimming the trees or something. Or maybe it's one of those leaf blowers. You know it's not even autumn. There are no leaves falling this time of year. I thought they had outlawed those noisy things. Or maybe it was just the gas ones. You know-"

"Auntie!" Effie shouts at the phone. "I need to find someone to take care of a young girl."

"Oh, dearie, you can take care of yourself. You're a smart woman. Look how you got the whole town excited about repairing things that are broken."

"Reparations, Auntie, but I'm not the one who needs care. It's Angel, or maybe it's Jessie. That's the name her mother cried out when she woke up."

"Is it one or two people?"

"One. Her mom is very sick and may die."

There is muffled silence for a moment and then Tilly returns. "I think they stopped with the blower or whatever it was. Can you hear me now?"

"I could hear you before."

"Before what?"

"Auntie, turn the phone around and look into it."

"Oh, hey, that's you, and me too. I'm over here. How did you do that?"

"It's Face-time, Auntie."

"Who's that next to you, it's a girl, right? Can't be too sure these days, even with the long braided hair. Could be a boy, or whatever else."

"It's Angel."

"Oh, I never saw a Black angel before. She's so cute." She studies the image closely, bringing her eye to the phone. "How did she die?"

"She didn't die, Auntie. She was looking for food."

"You didn't kidnap her, did you? I can't have a kidnapper in my family. Did you?"

"No, Auntie. I told you her mom is sick." Effie holds the phone away from Angel and whispers. "Auntie, her mom is really sick."

"Oh, I thought for a moment she was yours and that's why you decided to be black, because you gave birth to a little black girl."

"What? Auntie, she's four years old."

"When did you have her and where has she been?"

"Auntie, you aren't listening to me." Effie holds the phone up to her face. "She and her mom were in a room near mine at the hotel. She was looking for food when I found her. Her mom is sick, so I called an ambulance. I had to tell them I was related so they would let me see her and take care of her, but they are looking for her father. If he doesn't show up, they are going to take her away."

"Oh."

"You got all that?"

"You sure do get yourself into things, dearie."

"Can I bring her to you?"

"You can't just take her, can you?" Tilly's ride pulls up.

"They have my number."

"What do I have to do?" asks Tilly. She motors up to the van.

"Just watch her for a few hours."

"I guess. I raised you, didn't I?"

"Yes, but you were a lot younger then, and you could get around better."

"I'm not dead, Effie. Not yet anyway, and I can always call for help. I am never really alone, you know."

"It won't be for long. As soon as I find her father or other family members, I can bring her back to the hospital."

"Auntie Eff? When can we see Mommy?"

"She calls you Auntie, like you do with me?"

"You heard that? How come you don't hear me?

"I hear you. Sometimes."

"I told her how you became my Auntie when my mom had to go away." Effie pauses. "We'll be right over. She's tired, so she will probably sleep the whole way."

"Is her mother going to survive?"

"I don't know."

"Why don't you call Maggie? She's a doctor there. She can help."

"No."

"Okay. we'll meet at home." Tilly ends the call.

"Where are we going, Auntie Elf?" asks Angel.

"I know someone who can help us, but I need you to look sad." Effie cups her hands on Angel's cheeks.

Angel pouts. "Like this?"

"That's perfect."

Maggie

Maggie carries the last of the folding chairs into the storage closet next to the library as Mildred gathers up the books and papers that are scattered about the room. David is on the phone, waving at Maggie to get her attention as she returns.

"What's up?" she asks.

He rolls his eyes and ends the call. "It's my mom. Something has happened with Effie at the hospital. She's outside."

"Effie?"

"No, my mom." He puts his phone away. "Just come with me and help me understand what happened."

"Grandma, I'll be right back," she says, following David out the door.

Tilly and her ride are blocking the drive, causing some of the members to sit on their horns. David runs to the van driver and has him pull out to let the people go. One of the cars at the bottom of the hill catches Maggie's eye. It belongs to Jacqueline. Harold enters and drives away.

Tilly motors to the walkway and waves her phone in the air at David.

"What's wrong?" asks Maggie of Tilly.

"She kidnapped an angel and wants me to keep her hidden in my home." Tilly is shaking, her face a blank stare, as if she is having a stroke.

"Mom, calm down," says David.

As the last of the cars rolls by, the van returns and the driver opens the side door to lower the elevated platform for Tilly's wheelchair.

"Where is Effie?"

"At the hospital."

"Is she staying there?" asks Maggie, dialing a number on her phone.

"No. Yes. No. I don't know," says Tilly.

While David talks to his mother, Maggie checks with the hospital. There is no record of Effie, but several women and children have been brought into the emergency room.

"What is the girl's name?" asks Maggie, holding her phone away from her ear.

"Angel," says Tilly. "Or maybe Jessie?"

Maggie asks but neither name matches admissions or the emergency room records.

"Tilly," says Maggie. "you go home. David and I will go to the hospital. If Effie shows up, call us, and we'll do the same."

David helps Tilly get on the platform and the driver clicks her in before pushing the button to raise her up.

"I'll get my car and meet you at the bottom of the driveway," David says and runs off.

Maggie watches the van pull away and looks back toward the house, waiting for David, when another car pulls into the drive. It is Sam.

"I'm glad I caught you," he says, jumping out of the car like a little kid with a new toy to show off. "I want you to see what I've been working on for you."

Before she can say anything, he opens his hatchback and points inside. "Look!"

"I don't really have time right now, Sam," says Maggie, walking around his car with a quick glance at a model made of white display boards.

"It's your children's cancer center."

"What?" Maggie looks more closely at the structures with clear plastic doors, windows, and paper cut-out trees. What is she supposed to say or do? She looks at Sam, and she feels her entire body deflate. Now? Are we going to do this now? "Sam, can we do this later? I have an emergency here."

David pulls up in his car. "Hi, Sam," he says. "Sorry, man. We have to go."

Maggie runs around to the passenger side of the car. "We'll talk later," she says and then jumps in.

"Did I interrupt something?" asks David as they pull away.

Maggie looks back at Sam, standing behind his car. "Timing sucks."

"I'm sorry you have to get involved in this. Between my mom and Effie, I never know what the hell is going on."

"I hear you," she says. "Hopefully, this is a false alarm. So many of them are."

David nods and then says, "But so many aren't."

Dana

Sunday

Whose idea was it for us to appear as crows, anyway? Dana hopes she looks better than her sister, but how much different can crows look? Now, a raven would have been better, with its curved beak and larger body. They could probably fly right into one of these courthouse windows and smash it, if they were ravens.

"The windows are all closed, Dana," says Lila, perched next to her on a branch of a nearby tree.

"We can try the other floors. Maybe a bathroom window is open."

"And how will you get out of the bathroom?" Dana shakes her head and watches her beak move from side to side. "You have to admit, we can get around better than when we were on horseback."

"That's because you don't know how to ride."

"Let's not start that again," says Dana.

"Why did we let Elcira talk us into this, Lila?" says Dana, the self-professed more elegant of the two, fluffing her feathers and picking at them with her beak. "Did you take an ant bath today? I think you're covered with parasites."

"I'm stronger than you, Lila."

"You were the one who said we had nothing to do."

Dana flies over to the nearest window sill and hovers to look inside. "When was that?"

"I don't know. You know how time works for us. It's all relative."

"I think this is the judge's office."

"It's called chambers," says Lila.

"What is?"

"The office. It's the judge's chambers."

"I don't think so," says Dana.

"Well, what do you think, smarty?" asks Lila.

"A judge can have an office where he does his paperwork, and he conducts official business in chambers."

"Listen to you. How do you know that?"

"Netflix," she says, and the two caw out loud.

"We should be quiet," says Lila.

"Why? It's Sunday. No one is in the building. All we need to do is find an open window, and we're in."

"So, I thought we already got the key, why are we here for the key again?"

"There are two keys, the one we got and the one that was in the archives for nearly two hundred years. The judge has that one. Elcira wants both so that the chain of custody can be broken, and the case is thrown out."

"Netflix, again?"

"Law and Order," says Dana.

"When do you have time? Never mind," says Lila. "You have always been one to slip out and leave me covering for you."

"It pays to have a look-alike sister, or at least it used to when we were alive."

"Yeah, remember when we went to Hartford, when Elcira was sick?"

"Back to work."

"Okay, so we have to find his office, see if he left the key lying around, steal it, and find our way out of there. Bum, bum, bum-bum. Bum, bum, bum-bum."

"That's Mission Impossible, not Law and Order. Ca-Chung!" Dana caws and taps her feet. "There has to be an open window somewhere in the building. Once we get in, we can go into any office because there are transoms that they keep open for the heat."

"Why does she want the key, anyway? I thought they had the key," says Lila.

"I told you. There are two keys, dummy," says Dana. "The one the judge has is the one Chester had on him."

"Oh, I didn't like him. Luckily, he liked you more than he liked me."

"Lucky for you," says Dana. "If we take that key, they won't have any evidence from the murder."

"What about the pitchforks? Do they have those in evidence?"

"I don't know."

"The pitchforks are what killed him, not the key."

"Don't confuse the situation. We need the key."

Dana lifts off first, and as she passes the window to Judge Philips' chambers, she spots someone and circles back. "There's someone in that office. Maybe we can get his attention."

"And then what? You think he will open the window and let us in?"

"We can at least listen in." She perches on a branch with a clear view of the office. "Look, someone just entered."

Philips looks at Effie from behind his desk. "Who is this?" he asks, smiling at Angel. "Hello, dear."

Dana moves closer.

"Hello, sir."

"Oh, so polite." He points to Effie. "Is this your Mommy?"

"No, my mommy is sick." To Effie, "Auntie Eff, who is this man? And why are you mad at him?"

"Astute little girl, isn't she, Auntie," he says, stretching the word.

"I'm not mad at him."

"Auntie Eff, what about my mom?" asks Angel, tugging on Effie's shorts. "I want to go see her."

"Wait, Angel. We need Judge Philips to help us with something first." She brings Angel over to a chair by the door and sits her down. "Wait here while I talk to him privately."

She goes over to the judge and leans into him, her hands on the arms of his chair, so her face is inches from his. "First, I want the key from the hearing."

He pats the folder on his desk and says, "No can do, Effie. It's evidence."

"But -"

"Careful, Effie. What else do you want? You didn't drag me here on a Sunday to ask for a key."

She whispers, "Her mother is sick, real sick. I need to find her family. I have asked her about relatives, but she says she has none. She may have been too young to remember a father or grandparents."

"What is her mother's name?"

"Cynthia Roberts."

He shakes his head.

"What? You won't help me?"

"You should talk to the police."

"Come on," Effie says, standing before him.

Dana turns to Lila and says, "Let's give this guy a scare. You know some people think crows are a sign of death coming for you."

"Oh, you are devious," says Lila.

"Two of a kind, sis. Let's find an open window on one of the other floors. A window that isn't in a bathroom.."

On the first floor, a janitor is emptying trash into a dumpster. He left the door propped open, so Lila and Dana make their way in and up the staircase to the second floor.

"Auntie!" Angel yells and points to the open door. "Birds!"

A big black crow flies into the office and flutters its wings, creating a breeze that blows the papers on the judge's desk.

"What the-?" Philips grabs one of the papers as a second crow enters and swoops down to clutch the folder and spill the contents onto the floor. The brass key bounces before Angel and Effie rush to grab it.

281

"Follow her," says Dana and heads for the hallway.

Effie yells at Angel, "Run! I'm right behind you."

Angel runs down the hall toward the lobby while Effie waves her hands to fend off Lila's dips and swoops.

Philips runs after Effie while Lila swoops and pecks at his collar.

"Oh oh," says Lila.

"I got you," says Philips, getting ready to take a swing. Dana lets out a loud screech behind him throwing him off guard. Dana drops onto his head, causing him to lose his balance and he tumbles down a flight of stairs.

"Oops,"says Lila. "I think we did it that time."

"Let's get out of here," says Dana.

"Oh, Elcira is not going to be happy with us," says Lila.

"Is she ever?"

Mildred

Expecting Maggie to return, Mildred walks out the front door and heads down the drive toward the street. As she rounds the curve, she spots Sam's car, its hatchback open. There is no sign of Sam, at least not at first.

She finds him sitting on the back bumper of his car, his head in his hands. She thinks he's been crying.

"Sam?"

He sits upright and wipes his eyes.

"Are you okay?" she asks, reaching for his shoulder. Looking past him, she sees the model on the folded back seats. It is significant, occupying most of the space, with the model's buildings extending upward over a foot high. "What is this?"

"Oh. Mrs. Cranberry," he says, his voice shaky. "My dad helped me with this. I designed it for Maggie's cancer center."

Mildred steps back and moves over to the other side of the car to get a closer look.

"I shouldn't have come by," he says.

"Why? Didn't Maggie like it?" Mildred sees that Sam feels sorry for himself, which he does very well.

"She ran off with him."

"David?" Mildred pushes him over and sits next to him on the truck opening. "He's working for me on this stupid court case. We just had a garden club meeting, and his mom called with an emergency. It was something about Effie."

"It's always something," he says.

Mildred turns toward him and, with her hands on his shoulders, turns his body toward hers. "Sam, I'm talking to you as if you are my son. Do you love Maggie?"

"Of course I do," he says, "I asked her to marry me."

"But do you love her?"

"Why are you asking me this?"

"Because you aren't acting like you do. You're acting like you're afraid of losing her."

"I am!" he says. "I don't want to lose her."

"What do you love about her?" Mildred knows she is cutting hard. "Do you love that she is tough as nails and stubborn as an ox? Or that she doesn't listen, but goes off on her own without checking with anyone else? Or that she places those dying kids above everyone, including herself?"

He tries to speak but can't.

"Listen to me, Sam," says Mildred. "Nobody knows how deep her words can cut and make you bleed more than I do. She blamed me for her mother dying alone, even though I couldn't get to her with COVID. How do you think that feels?"

"I didn't think of that," he says. "But you know she loves you. She worries about you all the time."

"What does that tell you?"

"She loves you?"

"And what about you? What do you want from a relationship?"

"I don't know," he says, bowing his head.

"You have known her for a year. In all that time, what have you learned about her? Does she like to be surprised with models of her dream as seen through your eyes? Or would she rather have worked on it with you?"

David sniffles and looks up. "I screwed up again, didn't I?"

"Did you ask her who created the rendering she showed the board?"

"No," he says.

"Or did you feel hurt that she didn't ask you?"

He wipes his nose with a tissue. "Why didn't she tell me about it?"

"Did you ask her that?"

"I just assumed-"

"That she wanted to keep your father out of it? Or that she wanted to hurt you?"

"I screwed up."

"It's not too late to fix this, but you need to know what you want first."

His lips tighten.

"I am old enough to be your grandmother, and I am learning every day. I thought the most important thing was to keep this property as I received it, to preserve the legacy for all time, but that's not up to me. Maggie saw the potential to do something which will have a lasting impact on this community, just like her ancestors did. So, who screwed up, Sam?"

Sam slowly stands and turns to kiss her on the cheek. "Thank you."

"Go home, Sam."

"But I want to be there for her."

"Then be at the courthouse tomorrow."

"What do I do with this?" he asks, pointing to his model.

She smiles and pats him on the arm. "See you tomorrow, Sam."

Mildred watches him leave and decides to give Maggie a call.

"Where are you?" Mildred could hear activity in the background.

"We're at the hospital," says Maggie, "it's crazy here. The police arrested Effie, and David is going down there to bail her out."

"Why did she get arrested?" asks Mildred, trying to do what she always has to do, read between the lines.

"The police accused Effie of kidnapping the girl. It makes no sense. She was trying to help."

"You sound like you are on her side." Mildred immediately realizes that didn't come out the way she intended.

"What side, Grandma? She was trying to do the right thing."

Mildred hears that echo in her thoughts. Trying to do the right thing. Isn't that what she has been trying to do? "Do you need me to come get you?"

Mildred hears Maggie talking with someone. "Sorry, that was Kendal Lightfoot. He knows more about this than he's telling. I wouldn't be surprised if he's the one who called the police. If she had just stayed in the hospital, they wouldn't have a case against her. There's something weird about this whole situation. I think the mother is the one who kidnapped her daughter."

"The mom?"

"She is in serious shape. I'm going to stay here for a while. Someone needs to sit with the daughter until her family comes. They can't seem to figure out her family situation."

"No father?" asks Mildred.

"I don't know." Maggie pauses.

"Let me know what you need me to do," says Mildred.

"Just get ready for tomorrow," she says. "It's going to be another circus. I can guarantee you that."

"We have a good case, but I hoped to prepare with David tonight."

"Looks like he's going to be too busy." Maggie responds to someone's call. "Gotta go. Love you."

The line drops.

"Love you, too," says Mildred. She puts the phone down and walks into the library, intent on preparing for the hearing.

The pile of books from the garden club meeting and a stack of disorganized papers are on the desk. Mildred works on sorting through them, arranging them in two piles, one for books and papers related to the training of slaves and the other for everything else. She picks up the book signed with Deborah's name and sits in the leather desk chair. It is a small book written by freed slave James Mars.

After reading, she puts the book down on the desk and stares at the bookcase. Did Deborah know James? Like Josiah, he escaped slavery as a boy, but he went on to become a leader in Hartford, the same place where Elcira's father died. Did James teach her how to read and write, and that's why her name is in the book? How was Cranberry Farm involved in the Underground Railroad? Was it part of a network of abolitionists that helped slaves avoid being returned to their owners in the South?

What must it have been like for the children?

She grabs her phone and car keys.

Maggie

Maggie can tell a patient's status by the activity or lack thereof in the room. Weekends are always quiet, and Sunday evenings are almost spooky, with dimmed lights and the sounds of monitors, the only signs that anything is happening at all.

The emergency room, though, is different. Squirreled away at street level or lower, with bright lights eliminating nearly all shadows and directed overhead lights focused on each bed, patients rarely sleep unless sedated or unconscious. While more emergency room deaths occur on weekends, primarily because of the increased weekend patient traffic. Maggie can usually expect to find one of her Audrey's Angel volunteers available on standby on the weekend, but a quick call to the hot-line tells her all volunteers are busy. So, once again, she steps in, this time for Cynthia Roberts, the woman with the mysterious ailment whose condition keeps worsening.

A nurse comes to the open door and looks in, but Maggie shows her badge. They nod to each other, and no words are needed. What Cynthia needs more than a doctor's care, is a loving family to support her. A child would be ideal, but that's hard on the child.

"Cynthia, I'm Maggie. I want you to know your daughter is fine. She's in good hands, and she loves you so much." Maggie is not sure where the police have Cynthia's daughter, but she need her to stay calm.

Cynthia shows no response.

"The doctor tells me your daughter's name is Angel. That's a pretty name," says Maggie, stroking her hand. She looks at the plastic I.D. band and notices a bruise. It is an old one. She finds others on her arms and legs.

A shadow passes over her. A uniformed officer is standing in the doorway.

"I assume you aren't family?" he asks, stepping into the light. He looks like he owns a Cross Fit on the side. Black tattoos form an abstract pattern on his hands which are just a few shades lighter. The effect is mesmerizing, and Maggie imagines the tats tell an interesting story when he is not in uniform.

"No," she says, staring at his clean-shaven face. "I'm Doctor Payton, but I'm here as an Audrey's Angels volunteer."

"What's that?" he says, standing at ease, as if in the military.

"When a patient needs someone by her side, we come and keep them company."

"And you have time for that?" His questions are professional, direct and without emotion.

"No." She turns back to look at Cynthia. "I just happen to be here. I'm waiting for her daughter to come back."

"Oh," he says, bending closer. "That's not happening."

"What?"

"We were trying to reach Jessie's grandfather, but I just got word that Mr. Roberts, Jessie's father, is going to pick her up at the station."

With that, Cynthia's arms thrash wildly, hitting Maggie in the face. "No!" she shouts, her eyes bulging.

The monitor alarms go off triggering a buzz of activity in the hall.

"Jessie!" shouts Cynthia.

A nurse's aide comes in and grabs her arms, with the officer giving assistance. Another aide and a nurse rush in.

The officer pulls Maggie aside and leads her into the hallway while they attend to Cynthia.

Maggie grabs his arm and pulls him down close. "Someone has been beating her," she says.

"Are you sure?" he asks.

"You saw how she reacted. She used every ounce of strength she had to do that. It may kill her. You need to go and check on that girl, wherever the hell you have her."

As Maggie and the officer step through the double doors from the Emergency Room to the waiting area, Mildred appears.

"They wouldn't let me in," says Mildred. "He wouldn't let me in." She points to the officer.

"This is my grandma," says Maggie.

"You two are dangerous," he says.

"We'll follow you," says Maggie.

At the police station, the cop with the tattoos motions for them to wait while he talks to his supervisor.

David rushes over to greet them. "They don't want to release Effie."

"Why?" asks Mildred.

"They think she kidnapped the girl, when she brought her to your mom's house, right?" asks Maggie.

"Yes, but it's more than that," says David. "She threatened the policewoman who took the girl away from her."

"Of course she did," says Mildred. "She's been trouble her whole life, don't you remember? You should just leave her here."

"I can't do that," he says. "Besides, we need her to attend court tomorrow, or the whole thing will be postponed."

"That wouldn't be a bad thing." Mildred walks over to a chair and sits down.

Maggie takes David aside to fill him in on the incident with Cynthia.

"You think her husband abused her?"

"I'm not sure he is her husband, but he's the girl's father, and Child Protective Services wants to give her back to him."

"That's actually good news for Effie. I can use that to explain her actions."

"You think they'll buy it?"

"It's worth a try." He takes her hand and looks at Mildred. "Take your grandmother home. I've got this."

"Are you sure?" Maggie feels she should pull her hand away, but she waits for him to release it instead. She wants to tell him that he is playing both sides of this, helping Effie and her grandma. But he knows that.

"Grandma, let's go home."

Mildred walks over to David. "What about tomorrow?"

"Meet me at the coffee shop across the plaza near the courthouse, not the diner. We can talk there, away from the crowd." David gives Mildred a kiss on the cheek.

Maggie looks at Mildred and wrinkles her brow.

As they get to the car, Maggie's phone chimes with a text.

"It's from Sam," she says.

"Do you want to call him?" asks Mildred.

"No," she says, putting her phone away.

"But you do need to talk with him," she says.

"I know," says Maggie, rubbing the finger on her left hand where the ring should be. One thing at a time.

Mildred

Mildred arrives at the coffee shop an hour early for her meeting with David and is surprised to see he is already seated in the corner, his briefcase open on the seat beside him. The plaza in front of the courthouse is empty, save for a few pigeons, the only ones Mildred has seen in Old Cranberry.

"Where is everyone?" Mildred asks. "I was expecting that crowd to be back, even bigger than last week."

"Maybe they're sleeping late," says David.

The music at the coffee bar is a bit loud, but here in the corner, not far from the restroom, it is a little quieter. Mildred sits facing David and the window. From here, she can see the steps of the courthouse.

"Did you sleep all right last night, or did today's proceedings keep you up?" he asks. He takes the cover off his latte and sips, leaving a white mustache on his upper lip.

"I kept thinking about that poor little girl, Jessie or Angel, whatever her name is." Mildred sips her tea and finds it too hot. She removes the cover and blows on it. "What's going to happen to her?"

He puts both hands on the table and leans forward. "I have to hand it to the police. They really did a good job putting the pieces together. They tracked down both the father and the grandfather of the girl, the mother's father. Their stories were totally different, so they had a child psychologist talk to Jessie, that's her name."

Mildred leans closer to try to hear over the music. "All this happened last night?"

David sips his latte. "After I left you, I got a call from Effie. They had agreed to drop the charge of kidnapping. They credit her with saving the woman's life, and she convinced them she was afraid whoever abused the mom would go after the child."

"They confirmed she was abused?"

"Yes, and the girl's grandfather confirmed that he was afraid the father would hurt them both."

"Is the mom going to make it?" asks Mildred.

"It doesn't look good, so the grandfather is taking the girl home."

"And the father?"

"They are holding him for now."

"Will Effie make it this morning?" Mildred has mixed feelings about this. She almost feels sorry for Effie, and that bothers her.

"Yes. She has been charged with assault of a police officer, but that's all."

"That's all?" Mildred shakes her head.

"Maybe she'll drop the assault charge against you, then."

"Fat chance," says Mildred. "David, I just want this to be over."

"At any cost?" he asks.

She is about to say something but decides against it.

"What was that?" he asks.

"What was what?"

"I asked you a question, and you started to respond but chose not to run with it."

"I just decided what I was going to say was not relevant at the time, I guess."

"Normally, in court, we tell our clients to answer the question as simply and directly as possible. But that won't work with this judge. We need him to question himself."

"I think I understand," says Mildred. "You want me to answer the question and then look like I am going to say something else, but don't?"

"Exactly."

Mildred undoes her pocketbook clasp and fishes inside with an unseen hand. "What do we do about the key?"

"You're going to have to turn it in." David rubs his chin. "He will ask for it so they can match it to the one he has on file. If the lock works, he wants to test them both."

Mildred pulls out the key and looks at it. "Wait a minute," she says. "The keys don't prove Elcira did it. They only provide evidence that she could do it, right?"

"Where are you going with this?"

"But so did Deborah."

"You're right," he says. "That introduces doubt."

"We know the two women worked together to form an apparently secret school for slaves."

"Maybe they worked together on Chester as well?"

While they finish their coffee and tea, people gather on the plaza.

"Looks like the crowd is coming back," says Mildred.

"Why don't we take advantage of that?" says David, closing his briefcase. "Come on."

As they cross the plaza, the crowd thickens around them, anticipating a speech. David runs up to the top of the steps, puts his briefcase down, and raises his hands above his head. "Can we have your attention for a moment?"

The chatter quiets down. More people arrive and join, some carrying hand-written placards.

"You were promised a show on Friday, and you didn't really get one. Today, though, if you come into the courthouse and take a seat, you will get one."

The crowd cheers.

He waves his hands to quiet them again. "But it may not be the show you're expecting. We have done a fair amount of research into this town's history, and we discovered something that surprised us. I'm sure it will also surprise you and make you proud of our heritage here."

The chatter grows louder.

"Calm down. When the doors open, come in and take your seats. I promise you will be glad you did."

As he finishes, Effie arrives and tries to get through the crowd. Mildred spots her and smiles.

"What's going on?" asks Effie.

"We're just warming up the audience." Mildred turns and heads up the steps.

Mildred

Monday

The seats in the courtroom fill quickly. David looks at Mildred and pats her hand. She soaks in the room's aura, imagining what it might have been like in Elcira's day. Surely the courtroom would have been smaller and less formal. Instead of smooth wooden panels stained dark and adorned with moldings, the walls would have been cut from local trees, covered in pitch and soaked in the cigar smoke of years of official use.

Breaking into Mildred's thoughts, the bailiff announces the arrival of the judge.

"All rise! The Honorable Judge Mason Amogerone, presiding." A tall, curly-haired, deeply tanned man appears and walks to the bench, standing before the leather chair. The nameplate in front of him reads "Judge Nelson Philips".

David looks at Mildred who notices that Effie is wide-eyed and slack jawed.

The judge smiles and then immediately becomes serious. "Judge Philips was supposed to be here today, but he has had an unfortunate accident, so I will be presiding over this hearing. Please be seated." He is handed a folder which he places in front of him but he doesn't open it. "I have been fully briefed, having read through the minutes of last Friday's preliminary hearing, and frankly, I find the whole case a bit confusing, so I would like to start with a few questions for both parties involved. If counsels would approach the bench, please."

David and Effie meet at the bench. Judge Amogerone leans forward and talks to the two briefly and both nod in agreement. They walk back to their respective tables.

"Give me the key," says David.

Mildred pulls it out and hands it to him.

"Bailiff," says the judge, "would you kindly bring me the key that Mr. Parker has and then go get the one Ms. Devine has?"

Mildred looks at Effie, confused. How did she get a key?

"Excuse me, Your Honor," says David. "Where is the key that was in evidence, the one from the crime scene in 1832?"

Judge Amogerone opens a folder, pulls out a pen and uses the point of it to skim the page. The bailiff puts Mildred's key on the bench to the right of the Judge and then gets Effie's key to place on the left side of the bench.

"Mr. Parker, I was told by Judge Philips that Ms. Devine is in possession of that key. Most unusual, I admit, but we will get to the bottom of this forthwith."

"Thank you, Your Honor," says David. He pokes Mildred and whispers, "We've got this."

"Ah, here we are. Mr. Parker, I see you did not have a chance to present your case on Friday, is that right?"

"Yes, Your Honor."

"In your opinion, Mr. Parker, was that because there was no time to do so?" He looks at David.

"No, Your Honor. It was because Miss Devine could not produce any evidence."

"Objection, Your Honor," says Effie.

"Oh?" The judge turns his attention to Effie. "Did Mr. Parker misrepresent the situation? What do you feel was the reason?"

"Yes and no, Your Honor," she says, "it was because of the key."

"This key?" He holds up the key that she provided.

"No, Your Honor, the other one that Mr. Parker gave you."

"So, where did this key that I'm holding come from?"

Effie coughs and clears her throat. "It was the key that was in evidence."

"And how did you get it?"

"I got it from Judge Philips, Your Honor."

"He gave it to you?"

"Not exactly," she says, her hands shaking.

"How exactly, then did you get it?"

"There was a commotion in his office when the birds attacked, and it fell. I picked it up and ran from the birds."

The audience laughs and chatters. The judge pounds his gavel to quiet the room.

"You realize, Ms. Devine, that the chain has been broken here. By removing the key from the court's control, we no longer have an unbroken chain of custody, rendering the key that was in evidence inadmissible."

"I am sorry, Your Honor. It was not intentional," Effie says.

"Your Honor," says David, standing. "We would like an opportunity to present our case, even if the evidence in question is inadmissible."

"And why is that, Mr. Parker?" Judge Amogerone asks.

"On Friday, the town was pitted against itself over the issue of rightful inheritance, and even if Ms. Devine's assertion that her ancestor should have been the rightful heir is valid, we have evidence that casts doubt on that ancestor's innocence in the crime."

The audience groans.

"I object, Your Honor," says Effie.

"What are you objecting to, Ms. Devine?"

"How can he prove my ancestor is guilty?"

Mildred pokes David in the side.

The Judge turns to Mildred. "Did you want to say something, Mrs. Cranberry?"

"No, Your Honor."

"Sit down, Mr. Parker and Ms. Devine. I agree to entertain this request for a short while. If we can put this case to rest after two centuries, I'm all for it. I certainly don't want to revisit this issue in the future."

"Thank you, Your Honor," says David.

"So, Ms. Devine, tell me what is so important about this key."

"It is the key to the potting shed that Elcira Cranberry was locked in."

"This key that I am holding? The one you had in your custody?"

"It is that key, Your Honor."

"Now, Mr. Parker, what is this other key that you provided?"

"Your Honor, that key was found in the garden of the Cranberry carriage house."

"Ms. Devine, what makes this key so important to this case? Do you believe it has some magical power to turn Mrs. Cranberry's property into your inheritance?"

A rumble rolls through the room.

"You see, Ms. Devine, I have read the transcript, and I'm curious about your claim. Please elaborate."

"The key is evidence, Your Honor."

"Evidence? Do we have a crime here?"

"Yes," she says.

"And what is the alleged crime, Ms. Devine? Has someone been locked out of their home and the key will keep them from taking possession?"

"I beg your pardon, Your Honor," she says. "I'm that person."

"Oh. Where is your home and who locked you out?"

Effie remains silent.

"I understand why you are reluctant to speak, Ms. Devine. This is an unusual case and you know that trying to explain why you feel you have a claim to this property will sound, let me say politely, ridiculous!"

The room is suddenly silent.

"Your Honor," says Mildred. "Ms. Devine has had a chance to explain her perspective on Friday, and we did not, but I think I can bring this to an end right here and now."

"By all means, Mrs. Cranberry. You have the floor."

"Objection," yells Effie. "I know what she's going to say, and it's all lies."

"Ms. Devine," says Judge Amogerone. "I can hold you in contempt for an outburst like that. You will have a chance to speak after Mrs. Cranberry, and you can ask any questions you like as counsel for yourself."

"Sorry, Your Honor," she says, dropping back into her seat and folding her hands.

Mildred stands. "First, Your Honor, I would like to say that Ms. Devine is correct."

Effie opens her mouth but then closes it again.

"Her ancestor is Deborah Townsend, the nanny to the seven Cranberry children. She and Elcira Cranberry were the two women near the barn at the time when Chester was murdered. We have two women, two keys, two pitchforks and one dead two-timing man. Today, we would call him a rapist."

The crowd roars, and Judge Amogerone pounds his gavel repeatedly to quiet the room.

"Are you saying, Mrs. Cranberry, that either of these women, or both, for that matter, had both motive and opportunity to kill Chester Cranberry?"

"Yes, Your Honor," she says.

"But," says Effie. The judge looks at her.

"Now, Ms. Devine," the judge says, "I believe I understand the situation here. You believe Mrs. Elcira Cranberry killed her husband and Ms. Deborah Townsend, your ancestor, found the body while Mrs. Elcira Cranberry was locked in the potting shed. Is that correct?"

"Yes, Your Honor. She had a key and could lock herself in."

"That is what you believe, and we have two keys here to prove that one could have been in the shed while the other was in Mr. Cranberry's pants pocket."

"Correct." Effie nods her head.

"But Mrs. Cranberry here offers another possibility. Or is it two possibilities?"

"It is two, Your Honor," says Mildred. "Either Deborah locked Elcira in the shed and killed Chester, or they both killed him, hence the two pitchforks."

"No!" shouts Effie.

"Ms. Devine, I warned you."

"I'm sorry, Your Honor, but she has no proof."

"That seems to be the problem here, doesn't it?" Judge Amogerone puts his hands together and rests his chin on them.

"Your Honor," says Mildred. "May I address the court?"

"Yes, Mrs. Cranberry."

Mildred gets up and turns to face the audience in the courtroom. Looking around, she can see Sam sitting with his mother and father, all the members of the garden club, including Tilly in her special spot, and Jacqueline. Lining the back and side walls are the people with their posters and placards on the floor behind them.

"This two-hundred-year-old cold case has been the source of too much speculation, rumor, and legend in this town. It has brought us to the verge of splitting apart over the belief that a gross miscarriage of justice has occurred. Mr. Parker, my granddaughter, Maggie, and I have you all to thank for the education we received this past weekend. Because Ms. Devine made this a racial injustice issue, we went back to the books and letters and we discovered something we didn't expect."

Effie's eyebrows roll forward as she listens.

"Your Honor, do you have the lock in question?"

The bailiff retrieves it and hands it to Mildred.

"Look closely at this lock, which we believe was on the potting shed. Why would such a lock be needed? Normally the inside would be a nob that you turn to get out, and the outside would be where the key would go. What would be the reason to lock oneself in a shed and not have someone on the outside be able to get in?"

Mildred looks at Effie and goes over to the table. David hands her a book from his briefcase.

"This book is almost as old as this lock. It was written by a former slave who was involved in helping other slaves get their freedom." Mildred opens the book to the page with Deborah's name written on it and holds it up for all to see. "This writing here says Deborah Townsend Cranberry Farm 1865. That's four years after Elcira Cranberry passed away. Deborah was living on the farm with Elcira after her job as nanny was over. Why? Because the two women, and we believe some of the men formed a Ladies Garden Club to hide the fact that they were teaching former slaves how to read and write."

The chatter grows to a roar.

"Wait," she says, "there's more."

David gives her a thumb up.

"We believe the potting shed was where they hid slaves when their former owners sent people North looking for them. And there were also some locals who made a tidy sum by capturing freed slaves and selling them back to former owners and others."

Jacqueline stands and taps her walking stick with each step as she leaves the room.

"So, thank you all for giving us a reason to reset our historical record. Not everything is clear cut, black and white."

Some people applaud while others remain silent.

"Ms. Devine," says Judge Amogerone, "would you like to add something?"

"Deborah Townsend was my ancestor. She had a child, Henry, with Chester Cranberry. That child should inherit the property."

"Mrs. Cranberry?"

"He did," Mildred says. "Chester gave the property that is now where the carriage house stands to Colonel Townsend, and Henry inherited that property when the colonel and Deborah both passed. Deborah lived on the farm and was buried where the gazebo now stands."

The audience reacts.

"Colonel Townsend was one of the most prestigious members of the church community. He had no sons, but he had a daughter, Penelope, who married Garfield Cranberry, Chester's son by a prior marriage. After Colonel Townsend's death, Garfield bought the property from Henry Townsend. Garfield was Sylvie's great-great-grandfather. That is how the carriage house and surrounding parcel wound up in her family. When Aunt Sylvie couldn't manage it anymore, my father offered to repurchase it and let her continue to live on it."

Mildred walks over to the table to take a sip of water.

Judge Amogerone says, "This is a lot to grasp all at once. You said the colonel left the property to Henry, but he had a daughter?"

"Yes, Your Honor. Because Deborah's mom was Colonel Townsend's slave, Deborah was born into slavery but, by law, was made a free woman when she reached adulthood. She was the last slave to be freed in Cranberry in 1826. She took Townsend's name, and he gave her the small parcel of property to live on until he died. Townsend left the property to Henry, possibly because he knew the whole story."

Mildred turns to the judge and then sits down.

"Thank you, Mrs. Cranberry," says the judge. "This hearing was formed for the purpose of resolving an issue of ownership, and I believe, if I understand the facts and the ancestral records, that we have ended up where we began."

"Your Honor," says Effie. "we have not resolved the ownership at all."

"May I, Your Honor?" asks David.

"Please."

David pulls out copies of a family tree and hands one to the judge and one to Effie. "Your Honor, what we can prove is that even if Elcira killed her husband, the property would have been inherited by her descendants."

"Explain."

"The property's current owner is Mildred Cranberry, but there was another Mildred Cranberry who was a descendant of Garfield Cranberry. She married August Cranberry, a distant cousin. August was Felix Cranberry's son, Chester Cranberry's grandson, and our Mildred Cranberry's great-grandfather. So, even if one could prove that Elcira should not inherit the property because she killed her husband, it would have gone to Garfield, the first son, and it all would wind up exactly where it wound up."

The courtroom explodes in applause.

"Order," says Judge Amogerone, pounding his gavel. "No wonder this property was fought over for so many generations. It has quite a history, and if what you say is true, it may qualify as a historical landmark." The judge turns to Effie. "I believe we have reached a reasonable resolution of this issue, don't you agree, Ms. Devine?"

"I don't agree with any of this," shouts Effie. She slams her papers on the table.

The room erupts in a cacophony of noise, drowning out Judge Amogerone's gavel.

"I need a moment of silence here to address one open item, Ms. Devine. It concerns the matter of the key. Your tampering with evidence cannot be tolerated. See me in my chambers. Court dismissed."

Mildred and David make their way out of the courtroom.

Jacqueline approaches, having watched the proceedings from the hallway. "Touché," she says.

"I'm glad you're touched," says Mildred, stepping around her walking stick and avoiding her wandering eye. "That is what it means, you know."

"This isn't over, Millie," she says tapping her stick on the floor.

"It's Mildred to you," she says.

Jacqueline turns her head and walks toward the door.

Mildred's phone rings and she answers it. "Okay. Thanks." She turns to David. "I have to go. Sylvie's ashes are being delivered to the church for burial."

Sylvie

MONDAY

Pastor Tilton is standing at the entrance to the cemetery when Mildred arrives, Sylvie and Elcira in tow. "Thanks for coming right over," he says. "You actually got here before the funeral home."

"Oh? I thought the crematory was delivering the ashes."

"That would be my ashes, Millie," says Sylvie. "Handle with care, dearie."

"Protocol. The funeral home subcontracts to the crematory, so the ashes are delivered back to them, and they bring them to us." He smiles as though he is talking about planning an event. "Although, I could have told them to deliver them to you."

"You mean we could have an interment at home?" Mildred smiles.

Sylvie wraps herself around Mildred, trying to give her a hug. "I would love that, Millie."

Elcira looks at Sylvie.

"When could we do it?" asks Mildred of Pastor Tilton.

"My question as well," says Elcira.

Sylvie says, "Elcira, dear, I assume you're with me on this. I know you're supposed to take me home, wherever that is, and I hope it isn't where I think it is. I should have visited church more often, but Pastor Tilton can vouch for me. He knows I am a good person. Or I was."

"We could do it any time," he says. "I assume you wouldn't want a large crowd."

"No," says Mildred.

"Oh, yes, dear," says Sylvie. "Have a crowd. It will be fun to see everyone there."

"You just saw them all at your wake and when they repaired your garden," says Elcira.

Pastor Tilton walks over to the new bench. "Why don't we sit while we wait?"

Mildred takes a seat beside him and the two spirits hover nearby.

"Did you win your case?" he asks.

"I think we finally put this whole inheritance issue to bed."

"So, who killed Chester Cranberry?" he asks, folding his hands like a small boy waiting for his ice cream cone.

"We don't know," she says.

Sylvie looks at Elcira who is pretending not to be listening.

"So how did you end the controversy?"

"It's a long story," she says. "Let's just say that we showed the court that it doesn't matter who killed him. The property would wind up where it is."

"She is definitely cut from the same cloth as me, Sylvie," says Elcira. "I am glad I got to know her."

"Can we have the interment tomorrow?" asks Mildred.

"She is special," says Sylvie. "So, can I stay for the interment?"

"We'll see," says Elcira. "I do need to get the keys back where they belong, though."

"Keys? Why does it matter?" Sylvie asks.

"I think the keys keep calling me back here," she says. "One key and the lock were buried but one was held in evidence. I sent my sisters to get that one so both could be buried and they failed. Now I have to find a way to do it myself."

"But don't you want to come back again?" asks Sylvie.

"Tomorrow could work," says Pastor Tilton. "And maybe we could do the same for the baby."

"The baby?" asks Sylvie. "Oh my God, after all this time?"

"Yes. I have his ashes at home. I would like that," says Mildred.

"Why didn't you bury him here?"

"I didn't want to hurt anyone," she says.

He turns toward the mausoleum and nods his head. "I understand."

"What does he understand?" asks Sylvie. "Does he know what happened? I want to know."

"Sylvie, you can know everything from now on," says Elcira.

"Really?" Sylvie puts a finger on her cheek and sticks her tongue out between her lips.

"What are you doing?" Elcira asks.

"I'm thinking of what I want to know. Oh, I know. Can I do crossword puzzles where we are going?"

"I need to get all these things behind me." Mildred turns and rubs her fingers across the plaque on the bench. She then pats it and smiles.

"How old would the child be? Close to fifty, I guess?"

"Forty-eight! I was young at the time."

Tilton gets up and walks over to the headstones behind the mausoleum. Mildred follows him.

"That would mean he was your firstborn?"

"Yes."

"Before you were married to your husband?"

"No."

"So, what is his name?"

"It could have been Preston after his father, but I was going to name him Alfred for my husband."

"Holy Mary, Mother of God!" says Sylvie.

"You want to go home faster?" asks Elcira.

"Sorry, I was raised a Catholic," says Sylvie. "Do you have many of those up there? I assume it is up there and not down there."

Pastor Tilton's phone buzzes and he answers the call. "Yes, we're here at the cemetery. Pull around back, and we will meet you in the parking lot. "They're here."

Tilton starts walking and then stops when he realizes Mildred is not moving.

"You okay?"

"Yeah," she says. "I have kept it a secret for so long. It's just hard. I so wanted Jacqueline to know what he did to me. I couldn't bring myself to say it. You would think I wouldn't care about hurting her after all she has done to me."

"She carries a different version of history than the one you carry."

"That's what all this has been about, isn't it? We don't know what we don't know, but it eats away at us anyway."

Sylvie tries to hug her. "Oh, dear. I keep forgetting I can't do that anymore."

"Go ahead and get close anyway, Sylvie. She may feel your presence."

Sylvie expands as she gets closer to Mildred, until she has enveloped her. Sylvie can feel Mildred's body tremble.

"I'm here for you, dearie. Let it go."

Mildred turns to face Tilton. "So, how many times am I supposed to forgive? Seven times? Isn't that what Peter asked?"

"I have a hard time with that one myself. Seventy-seven times. Once is hard enough. Can you do that?" Tilton waves to the driver of the black Escalade from the funeral home.

"She must have heard me," says Sylvie.

"While you have her attention," says Elcira. "Tell her we need to get those keys back from the judge."

Maggie

Monday

From the upstairs guest bedroom, Maggie watches her grandmother remove her shoes and stamp her footprints in the grass. Maggie stares as though expecting the blades of grass to gather the strength to right themselves. She follows them to the source at the edge of the garden, where the bowed heads of several roses continue to pay tribute to Aunt Sylvie.

Mildred stands in the thorny bushes and reaches to push the iron gate. It doesn't budge, rusted open and entwined with ivy. The only pathway from the carriage house to the main house will remain defiantly unwilling to fade into the past.

Touching a droopy rose head, it drops a petal.

Maggie opens the window and takes a deep breath. She imagines what it would be like to be married and living here in the carriage house. But looking at her grandmother deadheading roses with one hand and placing the heads on the bench to retrieve later, she wonders if she should live here. And what about Sam?

She turns toward the gazebo, imagining what it was like in those early days, with slaves working the yard as freedmen and learning to read and write along with the children. Did the women do all the teaching? How it must have been a bustling little community in this secret garden.

Off to the left, near the gate, a small metal table holds all of Sylvie's gardening tools. Mildred bends to grab a trowel and picks the gloves from among the pots and bags of soil and fertilizer. She holds the gloves, rubbing her fingers along the empty digits, and then brings them to her heart.

She's saying goodbye to her dearest friend. Maggie wipes her eyes and pulls a tissue from the box on the nightstand.

Maggie ties the waist ties of her sundress and grabs the cloth bag David gave her at the courthouse after Mildred left. She heads for the doorway and down the stairs.

As Maggie approaches, she hears her grandmother talking to the gloves.

"You never did wear these, did you, Auntie?" she says, rubbing the fingers of the gloves. "You could never keep the dirt from under those nails of yours, and now?"

She looks up with watery eyes, then tosses the gloves back on the table.

Mildred stops at the iron gate. With the trowel in one hand, she grabs the iron handle and lifts it, using it as a lever to close the gate. After several attempts, she abandons it. She takes a step and brushes against a rosebush, catching her dress.

"Grandma?" Maggie reaches down and unhooks the dress from the bush. "I guess Aunt Sylvie wants you to stay."

Mildred holds onto Maggie's arm and lets herself be guided to the bench. "I've neglected her garden," she says.

"We all have," says Maggie. She sits Mildred down and walks back to the patio where a small wooden cube painted black soaks up the midday sun. She lifts it, expecting it to be much heavier than it is, and carries it like a child to the bench. She looks into Mildred's eyes and gives her a half smile.

"I know she wants to be here," Mildred says, placing a hand behind her neck and rubbing it gently. "This part of the property will stay in the family. It will be yours."

"Let's not discuss that now, Grandma." She walks over to the table, removes the unused garden gloves, and returns. Reaching for the trowel, she plants herself between the bench and the oak tree in the garden's center. "Here?"

Mildred reaches out to hold Maggie's gloved hands in hers. She hugs them for a moment and then nods.

Maggie works the hole, using the trowel first as a spade and then as a scoop to remove the dirt, piling it beside the box that holds Aunt Sylvie's ashes.

Mildred's head hangs so low that Maggie holds up her hand to catch her.

"I'm okay," says Mildred. "Is it deep enough?"

Maggie stands the trowel beside the box and places it in the hole. "A little more," she says.

Beads of sweat drip from Maggie's forehead, and she wipes them away with her wrist and the edge of her glove. "I can see why Aunt Sylvie didn't like these things," she says, removing the gloves. "They make you sweat."

A cool breeze brushes against Maggie's forehead, causing the curl of her hair to flip.

"Did you feel that?" Maggie asks. She turns to see Mildred using her hands to fan herself. "Guess not."

She tests the depth of the hole again. "Should we say a few words?"

Mildred places her hands on her knees and rocks to gather the momentum to push herself up. "I asked Pastor Tilton to say a few words tomorrow."

"God, no," she says. "I'm sure Aunt Sylvie would rather a tweet than a tome."

"I guess it's up to the team of Smith and Payton," says Mildred.

"You mean Cranberry, don't you?"

"I guess we will always be that." She covers her mouth. "The name is going to disappear from here. In a way, it already has, and no one will know."

Maggie looks up. A bright yellow and green butterfly hovers overhead and then lands on the black box.

"Yeah, it's just us." Maggie opens the cloth bag and produces the keys and lock. She places them in the hole.

"How did you get those?" asks Mildred.

"David asked the judge for them. He said they were no longer needed as evidence and the case of Chester Cranberry is as dead as he is."

Mildred laughs.

"And who is our friend here?" asks Mildred reaching for the box of ashes. The butterfly lifts off and lands on one of Sylvie's roses.

"When Mom died, I used to come out here and sit to talk to her," says Maggie. "I did it when you weren't around. Aunt Sylvie would come out and sit with me. A butterfly like this one would come and land on my shoulder. Aunt Sylvie would laugh and say Tilly would know. I liked to think it was Mom."

Mildred presses her lips against the top of the box. As she places the box in the hole on top of the keys, Maggie says, "This will be your home for all time."

"I'm sure she heard you," says Mildred.

"I was talking to you, Grandma. I don't want you to give this property to me. Not now. It is your home, and it always will be."

"We can talk about that later," says Mildred. Mildred approaches the rose bush and picks off all the drooping heads. She harvests the petals and fills both of their palms. Together, they let them rain onto the box before taking handfuls of freshly mined soil and sprinkling it in the hole. Maggie looks at their hands and starts to giggle. "You've got dirt under your nails."

Mildred looks up and waves her fist at the heavens, "Damn you, Aunt Sylvie!"

Maggie rubs the dirt from her hands and grabs Mildred by the arm. "Coffee?"

"How about tea?"

"Tea it is."

As they walk back to the patio and into the house, a flock of birds take flight from the surrounding trees and bushes.

"What was that?" asks Maggie.

"It's the birds. They are saying goodbye to their old friend, Aunt Sylvie." Mildred looks back at the garden bench and claps her hands together to remove the dirt.

Maggie looks back at the garden bench where the butterfly has spread its wings and is soaking up the last of the sun's rays.

Sylvie

MONDAY

You got your strength back," says Sylvie, watching the birds circle overhead before scattering across the sky.

"I knew I would," Elcira says.

"You did not. You thought you'd be stuck here forever, or worse, whither away and-"

"What? Die?" Elcira laughs. "I went through that once. Never again."

"Ooh!" Sylvie is suddenly bathed in a warm glow.

"It's almost time to go, Sylvie." Elcira holds out her hand, and Sylvie takes it. "We just have one stop to make before we do."

"Where are we going? Will I be able to come back? I will miss them."

"You won't miss them for long."

"What do you mean?"

Elcira whisks her off, and in no time, they are in a conference room with a large, white model made of foam board and transparent Plexiglas.

"This is where Sam works?" asks Sylvie. "Oh, yeah, here he comes."

Sam enters the room and pulls out his phone. He starts at one end of the table and takes pictures from above and down at the level of the tabletop as he makes his way around the room.

"What's he doing?" asks Sylvie.

"I'm afraid he plans to scrap this model. Don't let him do that."

"What?" Sylvie panics. "How am I going to-?"

Elcira disappears.

"Where did you go?"

Sylvie puts her forefinger to her cheek and thinks as hard as possible. Nothing comes to her.

Sam takes the roof off the model and takes pictures of the top floor.

Sylvie finds herself fascinated. This will be a lovely cancer center. He can't destroy it. If only Maggie could see it. Maggie. That's where Elcira went. She's going to get Maggie.

Sam finishes taking pictures of this layer and removes the next and the next.

The bottom floor is even more elaborate than the middle one.

He steps away and Sylvie sighs with relief. She didn't need to do anything. But then he comes back with a large, black plastic bag.

"No!" Sylvie shouts to the room, not expecting Sam to be able to hear her, but he freezes.

"Who's there?" he asks, looking around. "Dad?" After shaking it off, he resumes.

This time, Sylvie gets so excited she farts.

"Good God!" he yells. He starts waving his hands and runs out of the room.

"I did it!" Sylvie is pleased with herself.

Suddenly, Maggie shows up with Elcira floating behind her. "Sam? Are you here? I got your text."

"What did you do?" Elcira asks Sylvie.

"I used my special powers," she says and giggles.

Maggie lifts the black plastic bag from the table and sees the separate floors of the model all laid out on the table. Room by room, she looks at the details, and tears start streaming down her face.

"I think we can go now," says Elcira.

"Now?" Sylvie cries. "You can walk away now? What are you some sort of demon? Who walks away from the movie before the couple gets back together."

"You know that's going to happen, Sylvie," says Elcira. "You made it happen."

"No, you brought her here."

"Mags?" Sam enters with a can of Lysol, spraying the air.

Maggie chokes. "What are you doing?"

"I'm sorry. It just smelled so bad in here a minute ago." He steps back and looks at his disassembled model.

"This is amazing," she says.

"I'm sorry I didn't ask you first," he says, "but I asked my mom what the rooms should look like, and she-"

Maggie runs up to him and kisses him on the lips. "Shut up," she says.

"You farted, didn't you?" asks Elcira.

"It was an accident," says Sylvie.

As they float down the hall, Sylvie suddenly stops. "You never told me if you did it or not."

"Did what?" Elcira tugs at Sylvie's arm, and they continue entering the light.

"Don't start that with me. You know what I'm talking about. You've been evading the question all along, saying you don't remember, and coming back like this makes you lose track of things. You don't just forget if you killed someone."

Elcira holds Sylvie's arm in hers and says, "I think maybe I would like to come back someday and see how all this plays out."

"You're still not going to tell me. I'm going to ask Deborah. That's what I'll do."

Elcira's laugh trails off as the light slips away.

About the Author

BILL CUSANO is an author, a retired deacon in the Episcopal Church and a believer that it is the process rather than the outcomes that matter most in our lives. Retired from the corporate world and an eight-year stint running a non-profit feeding program, Bill attacks every project as a ministry, giving it his full commitment. Needing to readjust to life after losing the love of his life to leukemia in April of 2024, Bill returned to writing full-time, resulting in The Old Cranberry Ladies Garden Club series, the motivation and inspiration for which came from his wife's voracious appetite for reading historical fiction. While this is Bill's debut novel, he has always been a writer, publishing short stories and poems early on, and then beginning a daily spiritual blog in 2008. You can follow Bill's Reflections From The Garden Bench along with other writings on his Substack account.

https://www.billcusano.com
https://x.com/cusanobill
https://www.facebook.com/bill.cusano
https://billcusano.substack.com

Also by Bill Cusano

Coming soon, The Widow Murderess, taking us back to the start of the ladies' garden club in 1833, with Elcira Cranberry and Deborah Townsend facing the challenge of running a farm, raising eight young children, and fighting prejudice in the New England town that bears the name of her murdered husband. Here is a preview.

Elcira

THE CRANBERRY FARM, CRANBERRY, CT 1833

Elcira closes the potting shed door and locks it with the key from the hook on the main house door. She taps on the door twice and then once. She waits for the response. One tap, a pause, and then two. Good. Now, they need to keep quiet. At least it won't be too hot in there, with the late spring breezes from the North carrying the sweet aroma of fresh-cut hay from the stables and surrounding fields.

The birds know.

They are witnesses. From a distance, they call to one another to spread the word so that all know to stay away. She can see them circling the fields, respectfully keeping their distance from the barn, even now, months after the incident. The field mice were safe for a while, but no longer. The birds have mustered up the courage to return. Now that the hawks and vultures make their way homeward or off to their next meals, everything is returning to normal, or almost everything. Some secrets need to stay locked away, hopefully for good.

The sparrows come first. They like having no competition. Like the mice, they did not have to worry about what might be hanging around in rafters or on rooftops.

Elcira steps into the lilacs, letting the pillows of fragrance slip over her face like a veil. She closes her eyes for a quick respite to reflect on the day Chester planted this yellow variety, one of the seven hues along this border, protecting the shed from the prying eyes of neighboring farmers and others who chance to come by to transact business or lodge a complaint. More of the latter these days than the former since the incident. But those visitors are not the ones she is concerned about today. She takes a deep breath, inhaling the refreshing aroma of life for her and the bees rushing to carry the first buckets of nectar back to their hives near the pond.

The snort of Colonel Townsend's Morgan startles her. The riderless horse, still bearing its bridle but no saddle, nestles up to her.

"What are you doing here, Charlie?" she asks, rubbing her hand on his snout. She grabs the reins of the chestnut-colored beauty and walks him to the well. "Want some water?"

She lets the bucket down with a splash and pulls it up using the crank. She places it before him. While the horse drinks, she pulls on the reins to position him closer to the well, lifts her skirt, and places her boot on the stone wall to boost her onto Charlie's back.

"Good boy," she says, patting his neck. "Let's take you home now."

When Daniel Townsend returned to Connecticut after the war with Britain, known as the Second War for Independence, in 1815, he was a lieutenant, already married and with a child, Penelope. Elcira remembers her mother talking about these eligible militiamen in his charge.

Go with your father, Ellie. You are the one who can ride like the wind. Your sisters cannot impress a young militiaman like you can. Besides, you are like me. You need to feel the breeze in your hair.

Pauline Engels, her mom, was especially fond of the looks of this dashing young man who would come to the horse farm to do business with her husband, Lincoln. She was always dressed to attract the eyes of men and women alike. Elcira remembers the way men looked at her, even married men, like Townsend. Elcira's father provided the U.S. Army and the Connecticut Militia with Morgan horses, one of which was Theodore, Charlie's father. Elcira learned to ride at an early age, but Mother taught her to ride bareback, like a man, not like a lady. *It's all about keeping your skirt between you and him.* Good advice for more than horses.

The ride to the cottage at the edge of the property is not long, nor is it difficult to negotiate, so long as the ground is hard and not awash in mud like it is today. A gallop would not be advised if one wants to keep from looking like a pig in its pen.

At the house, Elcira dismounts and ties Charlie to the post near the back door. She can hear men talking inside. Sneaking around to the screen and peering in, she sees Deborah, nanny to her children and daughter of the colonel's freed slave, standing with her hands folded in front of her.

"Can you present evidence of birth, Colonel?" asks a husky-voiced male, out of sight.

"Of course, I can," says Townsend, his voice polite but with a hint of authority only the colonel could convey. "I find this visit most disturbing, gentlemen and lady."

"The likes of her need to follow the rules, or they'd be subjected to a fine whipping, and a fine, that's right, isn't it, Constable?"

One doesn't need to get too close, nor would one want to, to recognize the lisp and slurred speech of the country store owner,

Mabel Crossan. What is she up to now? Deborah has been working here since Felix was born, and she has lived with the colonel since birth. Why would they be questioning her legitimacy now, when she is about to give birth to her child, Chester's child? Maybe that's it. Mabel wants to know who the father is.

It's more than that, though. Mabel has tried to keep her away from her store for years since Deborah was able to take her first steps. But Deborah's mom, Grace, was one to be reckoned with, even though she was born a slave. Those who didn't love her feared her, and she was good friends with the colonel's wife, Jenna. That was the kind of friendship Mabel despised.

"Perhaps if you just show us what proof of age you have, Colonel, we can get on our way. A birth certificate, perhaps?" A second male voice, higher in pitch than the first, sounds like Pastor Thompson.

"You all have known Deborah all her life. Why question this now? You must realize how odd this is, given the Gradual Emancipation Act grants freedom to women who turn twenty-one after March first of 1784. God grant you wisdom. Forgive me, Pastor. But this is 1833. As you can easily see, Deborah is pregnant with her first child. If she was forty-eight years old, would she be in that state?"

"I see your point, Colonel, but there have been reports of slaves coming North without having been freed, and we do have to abide by the law, which requires a pass when traveling." The Pastor steps into the light. A halo of red hair makes the top of his head glow like the moon in the slightest light. He's at his Sunday best.

"So, that's what this is about? A pass is required when traveling from town to town, not for transport within one's own jurisdiction. Have you forgotten what my role is, Pastor? Admit it. You're conducting a witch hunt."

"Can't you do something, Constable?" asks Mabel of Tucker. "You're the law here, not the colonel. Maybe we should come back when he's not here."

Elcira opens the door and enters. "Deborah, I need you to mind the children. Their lessons are just about completed."

"Oh, lookie here," says Mabel, standing at the front door with her arms folded and her black, ankle-length dress looking like death personified, "The Widow Murderess herself."

Elcira holds the door open for Deborah. "I believe you can accept the sworn testimony of two respectable individuals who can attest to her age. Isn't that correct, Constable Tucker? I'm one, and Colonel Townsend is the other. Now, if you don't mind, we have work to do. This is a big farm that we manage here."

"We?" asks Mabel, "Listen to her. I will not rest until this town is rid of the likes of you."

"And just who do you mean, Mabel?" asks Townsend. "Surely you don't mean the negroes. Once they all have their freedom, they will no longer be restricted to where they can go."

Mabel looks at Elcira and Deborah. "Stay out of my store."

"Come on, Mabel," says the constable. "There is nothing we can do here."

As they leave, Colonel Townsend nods, pulling on his beard. "They are going to be trouble."

"Yes," says Deborah, her right hand on her extended belly. "What got her started?"

Townsend places his hand on Deborah's belly. "They are convinced this little one is mine. They would love to have me relocated elsewhere in the state."

"We're not going to let that happen," says Deborah.

"Thanks for letting Charlie come and get me," says Elcira.

"He loves you. He always has," says the colonel.

"I had better let our guests out of the shed before it gets too hot in there."

As Elcira walks to the potting shed, she clutches the brass key in her hand, wishing she had the second one they found on Chester's body. She could have another key made or have the lock changed, but that would raise eyebrows and create suspicion. It is bad enough that witch Mabel has given her the moniker Widow Murderess. The fact that this key was found on the hook in the house should have eliminated all doubt of her innocence, but some just won't let sleeping dogs lie.

Maggie McAvoy-Evers is a therapist .. Nicky Toto is her patient.

DANCING WITH THE LOST

A NOVEL

Two decades ago, many of Maggie's friends and family
were murdered... Nicky Toto's gang did it.

WILLIAM JOHN ROSTRON

CARPATHIA PUBLISHING